# *THE DROWNING SCHOOL*

Mirador Publishing
Mirador
Wearne Lane
Langport
Somerset
TA10 9HB

# The Drowning School

## by

### Dawn Rowe

*FOR MAISIE*

After death begins a new journey
One for which you wrote the script.

Do you believe in Karma ?

# CHAPTER 1

## ANDALUCIA

Evan clasped his hands tightly to his ears, desperate to shut out the wild roaring, eyes rolling beneath closed lids; he imagined standing at the foot of a powerful waterfall, where the torrent water threatened to devour him and panic flooded his body, swirling deep inside until he found himself unable to breathe.

*'Deep breaths, relax,'* he thought, struggling to exhale through lungs that threatened to collapse. Looking for a way out he searched the dark corners of his mind, encountering old emotions that begged escape. Through the turbulent corridors of pain, he recognised hope and miraculously in an instant, the anxiety subsided and a strange stillness that resembled calm settled upon him.

"Concentrate on your breathing, slow and deep," Dr Wilson, the family doctor, had advised when Evan had plucked up enough courage to visit the surgery some years earlier. Of course, this was hidden from his mother for she would only have stressed, worsening her own health further.

"Anxiety," Dr Wilson stated matter of factly, looking him up and down with what Evan suspected to be an air of amusement. Evan hadn't found the doctor's advice to be helpful at the time but with practice, of which he had had plenty, it seemed to be working now.

Finally feeling better, he relaxed, even daring to open his eyes. Within a few minutes, he was able to take a sip of the frothy coffee that sat on the table before him in an undersized cup. Much to his surprise, it was good. It was only then, with his nose screwed up in distaste, did he turn to look fully at his surroundings for the first time since entering the bar.

Cigarette ends littered the tiled floor. Blank mustard walls offered the only element of colour. The brilliant sunlight was unable to cast its cheery rays into the oppressive room, barred by the tired canopy that hung heavily at the front window. Several large hams hung above the counter, bathed in dense fog from a cigarette that burned aimlessly in the ashtray below them. The place felt dirty and unwelcoming, yet despite the bar's dismal appearance, it was the best cup of coffee he had ever tasted in all of his drab sixteen years. A sturdy woman, with bands of heavy gold looped through her ears, glanced across at him from her place behind the bar. Her eyes, sharp as a rodent's, followed the shaky movement of his hand as he lifted the cup to his lips.

Life must have been hard for her too, Evan thought, noticing the weary lines at her brow. She stared at him for several seconds before conferring in Spanish tongue with the decrepit old man perched somewhat precariously on the barstool opposite her. He, in turn, shuffled round to look across at Evan. With a toothy grin and a rasping cough, he spat what surfaced from the depth of his lungs on to the floor. Repulsed, Evan turned away, horrified to think that this was to be his life for the coming weeks. Hardly amusing for a young lad, but then he had his mother to thank for that. She had, somewhat selfishly, packed herself off to a spiritual retreat in the West Country, with no means of contact for the next couple of months. Meanwhile he had been sent here to the mountains of southern Spain to stay with his father, whom, he reminded himself with a sickening dread, he hardly knew, and truth be known, whom he had no desire to.

Evan finished his coffee. Standing up, he fished a few pesetas from the pocket of his creased shorts before paying. This was the moment he had been dreading. He didn't know a word of Spanish, and it was, he considered, most unlikely that either of these two would speak a word of English.

The lady gave a patient smile, as blankly he shook his head. She merely chuckled to herself before leaning over to tousle his hair, raking her ludicrously long nails across his sensitive scalp. Raising a highly pencilled eyebrow, she signalled to his hand. He held the coins out towards her. After pushing the coins around in his palm she took one and much to his amazement gave him change; not only was the coffee good but a fraction of the price it would have cost back at home. Suddenly he became aware of the tightness of her blouse, how it strained to contain her large breasts. How odd he should notice but he could not help himself. There was an odd stirring in his lower regions, the bulge in his pants ever tightening. She was old enough to be his mother for God's sake but as she ran her tongue across vibrant plump lips he couldn't ignore the rush of excitement that shimmied through his body. With an awkward smile, he pulled on his cap and hurried out into the street.

The blast of a car horn sent him leaping back onto the pavement, heart pounding inside his ribcage; he figured that if he wanted to remain in one piece for the duration of his stay, and make it back to England safely, then he really should remember that they drove on the opposite side of the road here. He took a quick intake of breath, his brow collapsing in a fit of worry before straightening himself up to embark on the long walk back.

Evan found his father sitting in a wicker chair on the terrace. From there he looked absently across the peaceful valley below him. He looked up at the sound of Evan approaching. "Hey, kid, where you been?"

Evan sat down opposite his father, elbows pushed into his knees, feeling awkward, a pinkish glow rising in his cheeks.

"Oh, I just wandered down to the village for a look around." Turning, he avoided his father's questioning gaze. Instead, he looked out across the almond groves, up towards the mountain range which stood majestically in the distance, its craggy peaks lost in marshmallow cloud.

His father, feeling equally awkward, gave a deep sigh. "Evan, I know this is difficult, it's been a long time since we've seen each other. This has come as much as a surprise to me as it has to you, but you're here now and we must make a go of it." He stood up and, placing his hat on his head, tugged sharply on its peak. "Do you fancy going into the village for a drink, we can take some time to get acquainted?"

Evan nodded, feeling a fragment of hope, as he followed his father out to the car, but there was childish apprehension too. Climbing inside the car the unbearable heat overcame him; he hastily wound down the window, gasping for air, shocked by its intensity.

His father frowned. "I know. By this time of day, it gets like an oven. Don't worry, son, a nice cold beer will cool you down."

Evan felt his cheeks grow pinker, a beer; he had never had a beer before. His mother would go berserk if she knew what his father was suggesting.

There was an awkward silence during the short journey to the village, his father keeping his eyes fixed on the road ahead, the steering wheel clutched tightly between sweaty palms. Parking the car at an awkward angle on the pavement at the far end of the village, his father signalled for him to get out. Evan followed behind his father as he led the way through a side street which rose gently uphill between the faded terrace houses where women sat outside their front doors expressionless, their eyes following them to the entrance of a small bar. It was much like the bar Evan had visited earlier and with an inward groan, he thought, just as gloomy.

"It is alright in here. I know it doesn't look much but these little village bars are all the same. Except at this one the beer is always cold." His father turned with a reassuring smile.

Evan sat himself down at a table while his father went to fetch the drinks. He returned and Evan gazed at the beer with childish hesitation as it was placed in front of him.

"So, Evan," his father paused to take a thirsty gulp, which, Evan noted, emptied half the glass. "How has life been for you and your mother?"

Evan stiffened, surprised his father had the nerve to ask. Jack had walked out on them over seven years ago without a care in the world and only recently had bothered to get in touch. Now he dared to ask, as if he was interested. However, Evan knew better, deciding to humour him, shrugging off the wave of anger that gripped him like a second skin.

"Not too bad. You know it has been difficult with mother not being well most of the time, but we manage." His father nodded, waiting for him to go on. Evan shrugged. There was nothing else to say, nothing he wanted to share with the man who had abandoned them.

"How's school then?"

"I finished school last month," Evan replied, careful to hide his emotion.

His father rubbed his chin restlessly between thumb and forefinger. "Course you did, my how the years fly. So what plans do you have for the future? Do you have work lined up for when you return?"

Evan shifted uneasily on the rickety chair. "Nope, I don't know what I am going to do. Mother said we will worry about that when I get back."

"Well, what do you fancy doing?"

Thrown by the question, Evan paused. He hadn't thought about it until now and was stuck as to what he should say.

A couple of women entered the bar and his father turned to survey them, a smile crossing his lips. Evan was glad of the distraction, brightening at the sound of their voices. They both spoke perfect English and looked over to where they sat, smiling in recognition of his father.

"Stay here, lad." Jack leapt up from the chair, pausing only to grab his drink. "Just give me a minute, Evan."

However, he wasn't a minute. For what seemed like hours Evan sat alone, motionless at the table, watching his father flirt shamelessly with the women who were young enough to be his daughters. Not once in this time did Evan touch his beer, for if he had, he would have been tempted to stride across to where his father sat and empty it over him.

He did, however, manage to divert his thoughts, in an odd sort of way to the woman he had encountered earlier in the bar. Voluptuous, strangely sexy but what did he know of such things?

Finally, when the women rose to leave, Jack re-joined him. There was no apology. He hadn't even the courage to introduce him to the women. This really didn't surprise Evan, why would he, there was no way his father was ever going to confess to having a son and even more so one of Evan's age.

Evan left Jack sat in his chair on the terrace when they

returned to the house; from there his father observed the starry night through bleary, drunken eyes. Evan went inside to bed, not bothering the courtesy of a goodnight. Alone in the darkness, he stared up at the ceiling, hardly daring to move a muscle, as a small gecko scuttled overhead. He feared that it would drop down onto the bed and then he would be likely to scream, a most unmanly thing to do and something that would no doubt amuse his father greatly. Much to his relief the small lizard headed to the window where it darted outside in search of the cool night air.

Oh, how he despised his father and wished he didn't have to be here. What had his mother been thinking of, she must have known it would be unbearable for him. Oh, she had whittled on about how good it would be for him to spend some time with his father after all these years, and how she worried that he didn't have enough male influence in his life. The real truth was that she hated his father and would never have dreamt of sending him, if she hadn't been so hell bent on finding her inner self and in desperate need of a babysitter. There was no hope for her.

His mother had been a manic-depressive for as long as Evan could remember; that's why his father had left. She was perfectly crazy half the time, lying in bed with the curtains drawn and a damp flannel at her brow. Evan had to get on with life the best way he knew how. There was no choice, for there was no other family to take care of him, apart from his father of course.

He felt the familiar cold shiver creep up his spine. There was only one memory he had of his father, but he could not let it be, he held it trapped beneath a barricade of hate, never allowing it to surface, afraid that if it did he would be unable to control the wash of emotion that would tumble forth. It was these memories that caused the terrible headaches, he was sure of it.

Wide awake, he listened to the dull drone of his father's voice. He was speaking on the telephone. He was laughing, being suggestive, it was obviously a woman. Evan gave an unhappy groan, pulling the sheet tighter over his head. How on earth could he be expected to survive this to the end of the holidays? He wished his mother would see sense and request his return but somehow he knew that wasn't going to happen.

All he had in this moment was fantasy to keep him sane; that was all he had ever. Right now he was trying out his sexual prowess with her, the woman of Spanish tongue and weary brow, older yes but then experienced; that counted for a lot didn't it?

"Come on, it's a fantastic day. You don't want to spend it moping about in bed, do you?" His father breezed in, throwing back the shutters, letting in a blinding ray of sunlight. "I have left orange juice and bread in the kitchen. I have to work but I will be home about two." He paused at the doorway. "Don't get into mischief. See you later, kid."

Evan peered over the worn cotton sheet at his disappearing father. How old did he think he was, for God's sake? He waited until he heard his father's car pull away before creeping outside, dressed only in flimsy cotton pants. Sitting down at the edge of the pool, he dipped his feet into the water. It was freezing but he persevered and after a while, found his feet became accustomed to the not so unpleasant tingling sensation.

It was peaceful here, only the chorus of birdsong and the hum of bees. Looking across the valley he yawned, stretching his arms out before him, wondering how he might fill the day, aside from swimming or walking. He wasn't too keen on the sun, it made his skin go blotchy and there was only so much swimming one could do. Instead, he headed indoors where he found his wallet, peering cautiously inside. His mother had given him some money; where it had come from he had no idea. It wasn't much but if he was careful, he could afford a menial lunch out in the village for the rest of his stay. It was better than doing nothing and in this strange land, the bar and the woman with the kindly smile already felt familiar of sorts. He had to find something to fill his days and there was more chance of finding somebody there to talk to, he reckoned. Walking into the house to dress, he was briefly blessed with a sense of intrigue.

Evan passed a few desolate bars as he walked downhill

into the village, a green cross overhead one of the very few shops, a chemist he had sussed was oddly reassuring. Still he found he kept walking, eventually ending up in the same bar he had visited the day before. It was, he realised, exactly where he had been heading all along, the thought of a return visit making him feel somehow more secure. To his delight the woman recognised him the moment he entered, a broad smile, full crimson lips curling back in recognition. Today he had arrived armed with a Spanish dictionary, borrowed from the shelf in his father's study. He was, he decided, going to learn some Spanish. He had looked at it last night and studied a few simple words, and fallen asleep repeating them over and over like a mantra in his head. Now, with a hesitant croak, he spoke to her; she stood poised to receive those first faltering words.

"Café con leche, por favor?"

To his pleasure she smiled, going to fetch his coffee, handing it to him with a friendly nod. Bursting with pride, he carried it across to the table in the corner.

He had actually spoken a little Spanish! Suddenly the possibilities seemed endless, and mastering the Spanish language over the coming weeks was definitely one of them, he thought with a smug smile.

Evan concentrated on the pages before him, silently reciting the words, struggling endlessly with the pronunciation. After having been absorbed in the book in front of him for over an hour, he looked around, taking a break for a few moments, his brain overloaded and threatening meltdown. Evan gazed through the window; he noticed a white jeep enter the village. It swung around the bend and pulled up on the kerb outside the bar. Glad of the distraction, he put down the book. An attractive woman sauntered into the bar. Oozing confidence as she strode in, she ordered fluently in Spanish, and then went over to a seat near the window. There she lit a cigarette, drawing heavily and letting out a billowing cloud of smoke. Evan watched her with great interest.

She was a most elegant creature. The first thing which had struck him about her was her height. She wore a khaki skirt

8

of crumpled silk and a pale pink shirt tied at the waist, showing inches of toned, coffee coloured flesh. Her strawberry blonde hair was tied back with a tortoiseshell clip, wisps of escaping locks falling across her chiselled features. Rather glamorous, he thought, for a small mountain inhabited village. It was hard to put an age to her, the sunglasses lodged on her head looked expensive, as did the cigarettes that she smoked, which were elegantly long and as white as snow to the tip. There was an unnerving air of confidence about the woman, who seemed oblivious of anyone else in the tiny bar and so full of her own importance. Evan envied her at once.

He watched as the woman who ran the joint hurried across from the bar with her order. She brought with her a small glass of steaming black liquid, also another bigger glass containing a warm amber coloured liquid. There was also a small bowl, the contents of which Evan could not see. She left the attractive woman in peace. Evan watched keenly as the woman tipped the contents of the smaller glass into the bigger, taking a long thirsty gulp. Then, plunging her fingers into the bowl, she pulled out a big plump olive. Sticking her nails into its fleshy sides she sucked its juices, as Evan imagined one would enjoy an exotic fruit. She nibbled at its flesh until all that was left was a small stone, which she tossed into the ashtray alongside her smoking cigarette. Evan's mouth began to water. He was hungry, as his rumbling stomach reminded him, but there was something else as well, another feeling he didn't quite understand. A feeling that made his flesh tingle and prickle. He felt an appreciative warmth in the groin area yet combined they still seemed to result in the same feeling, a feeling of insatiable hunger.

As if reading his mind, the plump woman hurried over to where he sat clutching a small plate, which she placed triumphantly in front of him. Smiling and nodding, her eyes indicated for him to try it. Wildly embarrassed, Evan shook his head. He took a deep breath.

"Sorry, I haven't ordered any food."

She laughed, taking a step back from him; her hands

pressed firmly on her hips and spoke hurriedly, the words leaving her mouth in a spray of saliva. Evan felt his cheeks flush. "I don't understand. I am English Sorry." He frowned, trying to recall the words in Spanish and failing, even though he had looked them up not ten minutes earlier.

At that moment, the woman over by the window turned in amusement to face them. She spoke to the bar owner. Evan had no idea what words were exchanged yet listened helplessly to their heated conversation. Then they both stopped short, each set of eyes in turn settling upon him. He looked back and forth between the two women nervously.

The elegant lady spoke first. "What is your name, child?"

"Evan."

"Evan, that's nice. Well Esmeralda here would like you to try some of her tapas. She is offering them to you for free; would you like to try them?"

He peered down at the dish before him; it appeared to be potato salad and a few meatballs. It smelt pleasing and if it was free, he would be silly to turn it down. He looked back at the woman and nodded. "Yes please, I would love to try it. Would you say thank you and it is very kind of her?"

She gave him a quizzical look. "You don't speak any Spanish?"

"Not at all, I'm on holiday staying with my father but he has gone to work," he replied sheepishly.

"Oh I see." She looked to the other woman to explain, then turned to look back at Evan. "Esmeralda says you are most welcome, and insists that you visit her every day, especially as you remind her so much of her son, who is now grown up and lives in Madrid."

Esmeralda beamed down at him. He gave a shy awkward smile, averting his eyes from her breasts; instead he nodded his head in acknowledgement, as Esmeralda patted his shoulder, a signal for him to start eating. Esmeralda watched as he gingerly took the fork between his fingers and tried a mouthful of the food. He gave another smile and nodded to indicate it was good. She burst into laughter and hurried back to the bar, looking extremely happy.

"I think Esmeralda has taken quite a shine to you, young

man. You are fortunate, as she can be quite fierce when she wants to be. I am Alexis by the way." She extended a slender hand toward him.

"Pleased to meet you, Alexis, thank you for helping me out there."

"It's a pleasure. Now finish your Albondigas before they get cold." She nodded towards his plate then strode from the bar to return to her jeep. Evan watched, surprised by the dark mass which seemed to hug her body like a tight fitting shadow. As she hit the sunlight, it disappeared. Shaking his head he went back to the food, which was extremely tasty.

Evan went to the bar every day for the rest of that week but he didn't see Alexis again. Every day, Esmeralda brought out a plate of food for him to try. Always she would stand with her hands on her hips watching him eat, only to clap in delight when he had finished, before offering hunks of bread for him to mop his plate clean. At first, he found it unnerving, the food lodging painfully in his throat, but he was getting used to it now. Secretly, he was feeling rather special to be the recipient of such kindness. He had taken money along with him but she would never accept it, frowning at him, seemingly most offended at the offer. Evan felt her satisfaction came from watching him enjoy the food she had prepared. He felt quite sorry for her; she obviously missed her son very much. Slowly he found he could manage more and more words in Spanish, if only the basics, but it was getting him by.

That evening, as his father sat out on the terrace with a cold beer, Evan summoned up the courage to ask him for some help.

"So you want to learn some Spanish eh? Have you found yourself a pretty senorita then that you want to impress, chip off the old block eh?" Jack gave a deep throaty growl.

Evans cheeks flushed as he wiggled nervously in his skin. "No, nothing like that. It would just be nice to be able to order for myself in the village."

His father eyed him suspiciously. "Tell you what, son. Go and fetch me another beer from the fridge and I will talk you through some basics."

Later, Evan lay awake in bed unable to sleep, thoughts wandering to Alexis. He wondered where she came from, she was glamorous, unusual and, he sensed, sexy, something he had not thought of a woman before. His father was bound to know her, but he didn't want to let on where he had been going and where he had seen her. Besides, if it turned out that she was one of his father's girlfriends, it would be shattering. No, it couldn't be so, surely Alexis was better than that. A strong independent woman, one he should imagine that looked for similar qualities in her men, definitely not a man like his father, he thought acidly.

She was intriguing and definitely intoxicating; he had thought of little else. Still he smelt her musky scent which had wafted pleasingly into his nostrils when she had stood to leave. He recalled the image of her feet, encased in trendy open sandals. The glittering diamond toe ring had winked at him from one of her long brown toes. He gave an excited shiver. The warm, raw emotion trickled through his body. Not sure what it meant but liking it and the happy mood it brought to him. Snuggling further beneath the sheets he grinned, perhaps this wouldn't be so bad after all.

# CHAPTER 2

Evan braved the icy depths of the pool, surfacing at the far end, gasping, his chest tight and his muscles fatigued; he took a few moments. He had never been a strong swimmer. Jack Bailey stood watching his son, noting his unease as he handed him a towel.

Dripping wet, teeth chattering, Evan hauled himself out of the water and sat motionless, draped in the warmth of the towel, at the pool's edge.

"Listen lad, I have to go away for the night, do you think you can manage here alone?" Jack asked.

Evan began drying his mottled skin roughly, his eyes revealing nothing. He had only been here three weeks and already his father was trying to escape him. Unperturbed, Jack waited expectantly for an answer.

"I'm sure I can manage," Evan replied, tight-lipped. "Why, where are you going?" he asked, dropping his guard, curious as to what his father had planned that could be more important than spending time with his son. Innocently he looked up into his father's eyes. It had better be good, he reckoned.

Jack looked away, to hide the guilt. Then after taking a long deep breath, he spoke. "The job we are working on at the moment, we have a hitch. I have to go along with one of the other guys and collect some tiles from Portugal. Some fancy stuff that the governor's wife has got her eye on. Apparently, there is a six-week wait for delivery, which would considerably hold up the job. Seeing that money is no object for these guys, they have instructed us to go ahead and collect them ourselves." He shifted uneasily from one foot to the other.

Evan pulled his shirt over his head, his father's discomfort obvious. "You go ahead, don't worry. I will be all right," he said, somewhat unconvincingly.

His father smiled. "I knew you wouldn't mind. You're a good lad, Evan Bailey." He fished in his pocket and pulled out his wallet. "Here, take hold of this. You can get yourself a few drinks and something to eat while I am away; I don't suppose you can cook can you?" Evan took the crumpled notes from his father; it would be foolish not to take them, he considered.

He waited for his father to leave, only then did he look down at the money that had been pressed into his hand. Unfolding the faded notes, he was surprised to find just short of ten thousand pesetas Gasping in astonishment he stuffed them deeply inside his pocket and grinned. The job his father was working on must be paying extremely well. He wasn't going to complain, it was a lot of money, even if he was somewhat overwhelmed by his father's generosity; maybe it wasn't such a drama after all.

Evan went inside to change, transferring the money safely to his wallet and then hiding it beneath the mattress.

Now, with his father out of the way, things seemed more interesting. It was certainly less stressful, he thought, as he set about exploring the house. There was little of interest to a young lad; it appeared his father lived quite simply. The only treasure he found was a set of ancient-looking binoculars. Taking them outside, he looked through them. All he could see was the blue of the cloudless sky overhead. Fiddling with the set, he managed to bring them into focus. Pulling up a chair he looked through the glasses, down at the valley below him. It descended in sweeping layers, sprinkled with groves of almond and olive. Whitewashed properties nestled before him, some with aquamarine pools that glinted in the sun like exquisite jewels amongst the arid terrain. Despite the fact that the binoculars were quite ancient, they were surprisingly powerful and with a sudden surge of excitement, intrigued, he panned across the landscape, drawing in breath as he focused on one of the neighbouring properties, surprised, as very clearly he could see its occupants going about their daily chores.

"Wow!" he mouthed as it dawned on him that, he could see what people were doing, and even better that they were blissfully unaware of his prying eyes.

Sitting very still, trying not to blink, with hands held as steady as he could muster despite his obvious excitement, He zoomed in on each house in the valley, amazed by the clarity with which these dilapidated things allowed him to see. Scanning the olive groves back and forth, he spotted a white jeep bouncing along on the farming track below; he followed it with interest as it bumped and ground across the country track, leaving a cloud of dust in its wake. The jeep pulled up at the front of a pretty house on the western side of the valley he had been admiring just minutes before. As the driver alighted, Evan gave an appreciative murmur. Following the slender brown legs that swung effortlessly from the vehicle, with a start he recognised the unmistakeable strawberry mane, it was flowing loose today. It was her! The woman from the bar, it was Alexis.

Evan's hands began to tremble, his view momentarily distorted; scolding himself, he gripped the binoculars more tightly, the whites of his knuckles clearly visible beneath the skin. Every inch of him was poised expectantly. Not even aware that he was holding his breath, he watched as she strode through a stone archway dripping with vibrant Bougainvillea. For a few seconds she was out of his view. He waited breathlessly until she reappeared on the other side, emerging from the shadows to walk across the large terracotta terrace towards the front door. He watched her fish in the straw bag that hung lazily from her shoulder and pull out a set of keys, then opening the door she went inside and to his complete horror, shut the door smack in his face.

Disillusioned, he put the binoculars down on the tiled floor next to him. Licking his dry salty lips, he was thoughtful for a while, contemplating what this meant. Suddenly he was extremely grateful that his father wasn't around and that he had been left to his own devices for a while. There was a stab of guilt, technically he was spying, invading others' privacy and if someone saw him, he would be in a lot of trouble. Hesitantly he decided to take a break, going inside to fetch a cold drink. Thirstily he gulped it back then belched from the gassy bubbles. Thoughtful, he took stock of this situation; it took one calming breath before he ventured back out into the sunshine.

Evan looked sheepishly at the abandoned binoculars lying on the floor. The temptation was unbearable. If he was a respectable boy as his mother thought him to be, then he would put them straight back where he had unearthed them and leave them there. He contemplated this. All the while the binoculars seemed to beckon to him, inviting him to take another look. Turning to go back inside he stopped. Damn it, he was only here another few weeks, what would it matter? Besides, his father would be back tomorrow and then he would be putting them safely back inside the drawer in the study, exactly as he found them. Evan didn't take another second to think about it. Picking them up he studied the valley below for the little white jeep. "Bingo!" he breathed, as he shifted them up slightly to focus in on the house. Sweeping his insatiable gaze across everything that he encountered there, he felt a surge of excitement as beads of perspiration settled on the back of his neck.

It wasn't a large house, a whitewashed building with a sloping tiled roof, several small shuttered windows at the front not big enough to see inside or to let in too much sun. A gated archway to the left of the building led to a wide expanse of terrace with two steps leading down to a lower level that bordered a rectangular swimming pool, its waters sparkling invitingly. Two sun beds stood positioned a short distance apart, on one lay an open book and a towel. Just across from the beds stood a built in barbecue and across from that, a freestanding shower. Away from the pool to the right was a large carob tree beneath which stood a chunky wooden table with four blue chairs, the paint tarnished and flaking. Beyond the pool and its terrace, the ground went steeply downhill, wildly overgrown with prickly pear plants embedded amid rocky boulders. There were no immediate neighbours to the property. Clinging to the side of the hill, it appeared the only access was by an uneven dirt track that joined on from the only service road. Secluded, mysterious and set amid the rocky landscape, out of reach of prying eyes, other than his own of course, he thought, ashamed.

Evan paused for a moment, his eyes hurting from focusing; he could feel the indents in the skin around his eyes. He took a breather before resuming watch, ignoring the voice in his head that pleaded with him to quit. When he could refrain no longer, his eyes met with Alexis swimming in the pool. Alexis! Breathe, he thought, his pulse quickening. Her hair fanned the water as she swam effortlessly back and forth. It was almost a familiar sight if he didn't know better. He hardly dared to believe it, but it appeared she wasn't wearing a swimsuit, she really wasn't! She was indeed quite naked. Transfixed, he watched her swim the length of the pool once, twice, at least several more. Excitement hugged his groin as she pulled herself out from the water to stand naked at the pool's edge. He struggled to hold the binoculars steady as he followed her across to one of the sun beds, where, picking up the towel, she dried herself. Fascinated, he studied each stroking motion of the towel across her lithe body, in turn a ripple of excitement coursing through his own. She lay back on the sun bed, stretching her body like a cat in the sun. She held a hand across her face, shielding her eyes from the sun's glare. Evan felt his body quiver as he scanned her toned body from head to toe and back again, settling on her breasts, brown as a cocoa bean, round and ripe, rising slightly with each breath she took. He moved downwards, stopping at the mound of hair between her thighs, dark and damp, shimmering in the sun. She lifted one leg, bending it at the knee, whilst running her fingertips along her inner thigh, pausing to satisfy an itch, and then running them through the silky pubic hair, smoothing it down protectively.

This was more than Evan could bear. Snatching the binoculars away from his eyes, he felt the unmistakable tightening bulge in his pants. He needed to relieve himself and now! God, this was so much better than the smutty magazines he had dared to look at, alone in his bedroom. This was, he thought pleasurably, at last the real thing.

Lack of experience and heady excitement couldn't enable

him to do two things at once; as much as he would have loved to watch and masturbate at the same time, his hands were too shaky, much too shaky. Dropping the binoculars with a clatter, he plunged both hands into the front of his pants and in moments he gave a deep appreciative sigh.

It was not until he had recovered his breath and the excruciatingly good feeling deserted his body, that he finally managed to reclaim the binoculars, saddened to discover that Alexis had left her bed on the terrace and disappeared. Disappointed, he went indoors, placing the binoculars carefully on the table, shocked and sickened by what he had just done. *It won't happen again,* he told himself sternly. He felt weak, unusually tired, and ashamed. He headed toward the bathroom. He needed to take a shower and recover, let his mind stop racing before he could even think of going to the village for lunch.


As Evan entered the bar, he stopped short, surprised by the volume of people occupying the limited space. An attack of butterflies caused him for a brief moment to think of turning tail, but it was too late, all heads turned to look in his direction and the chortle of excited chatter ceased. It seemed like an age before they turned back to each other and the hub of chatter resumed.

Esmeralda looked smart today, he thought, as she passed him a cup of coffee. Her hair was different; her ruby lipstick exchanged for a vibrant shade of pink. She nodded towards the crowd, seated around the front table. "Ingles," she said, jerking her head in their direction.

Evan had no choice but to pass their table, as he manoeuvred himself to reach his usual spot. One by one, they turned to watch him pass, an older woman with a northern accent breaking the momentarily silence.

"You're most welcome to join us, lad." There were several agreeable murmurs amongst the group. The woman stood up. "We heard there was a young English boy in the village." She winked, noticing Evan's look of surprise. "Not much escapes our notice; word travels quickly around these parts."

Reluctantly Evan found himself pulling up a chair at the end of the table, where eight people sat, all of them eyeing him with curiosity. The woman appeared to be in charge of the gang and introduced herself. "Hi, I am Kathy Simpson and who might you be?"

"Evan Bailey," he answered, blushing and wishing he had stayed at home.

"Well, Evan, it's nice to meet you. We don't see too many English people in the village. Only us old lot," she joked, looking around at the group with a twinkle in her eye.

"In case you're wondering, you have stumbled upon our monthly meeting. We all reside here in the village, escapees from England and the rain." Looking across at Evan, she smiled, sensing the young man's unease, asking, "Do you live here too?"

Evan looked down into his coffee. "No, I am just here visiting my father."

"Oh and who is your father? English I am presuming."

"Yeah, Jack Bailey, he lives just outside the village in the hills." There was an excited murmur among the others. Kathy raised a brow. "Yes, the name rings a bell but I don't believe we have ever met." Evan didn't find that surprising; Kathy was the wrong side of fifty, too homely and too plump, not his father's type of woman at all. No. Jack definitely wouldn't give her any of his precious time - she was too vulgar.

He looked around at the others, as Kathy, obviously bored with him by now, launched into a description of the proposed new road that would link the main highway to the airport. The man to her right, whom Evan presumed to be her husband, held the mouth of a river trout. Most similar to the one Evan had caught in the stream at the end of the lane back home. He giggled at the thought. His attention then turned to the two younger men, both pale with translucent skin, dressed rather scruffily in sweatshirts with the arms cut off and faded denims. They were sitting close, as a couple may do, Evan wondered, then repulsed at the thought. An ancient couple sat to Kathy's left, in their eighties at least and maybe that was being kind. The kindly woman looked across to smile at him and Evan nodded politely in return. An insipid looking woman with a mass of brown curly hair, so much hair that it overpowered her acne scarred face, chose to ignore Evan, so he looked across to the guy sat at the end of the table. He was really the only one of any interest. Fresh from a hippy rock band no doubt, hair swept back from a broad friendly face with a stars and stripes hair band. He wore a faded denim jacket and cut-off jeans, and there was a faraway look to his shadowed eyes. He looked the most normal of the bunch. Evan couldn't imagine how he had managed to be a part of this, and as Kathy droned on in the background, he noticed the guy stifling a yawn.

Evan looked wistfully out of the window at the powder blue sky; he wondered what Alexis was doing in her little house. He was looking forward to getting back and taking up watch. Perhaps he would stop off and buy some chocolate and cans of cola on the return journey; he would have a stake out on the terrace this evening.

Mother wouldn't approve of his new diet, or the fact that he had to fend for himself. Giving a sudden shiver, he thought of the night ahead, for he hadn't much thought about it until now, and the sudden realisation that he would be alone in the house, just him and the geckos; it was a scary prospect.

Kathy stood up, scraping the legs of her chair across the tiled floor with a high-pitched screech. "Well that just about covers everything, does anyone have any questions?"

Everyone looked blank, so with a triumphant shake of the papers in her hand she announced their meeting closed.

"I think it must be time for a glass of vino. Who would like to join me?"

Evan, hoping to slip off unnoticed, found himself collared by the guy in the denim jacket.

"So what do you think of it out here, Evan?" He gave a casual smile. "Bet you're finding it a bit boring, aren't you mate?"

As Evan smiled, he gave an inward sigh. "Yeah I am a bit, everyone seems to be so…"

"Old?" He offered. "Know what you mean but you get

used to it. Foggy Williams." He grinned, extending a solid hand to Evan. "Do you fancy a drink, son?"

Evan nodded. "A coke would be good."

Foggy returned with the drinks. "So you're out here staying with your old man. I didn't know Jack Bailey had a son, the sly old goat." He shook his head in disbelief.

Evan took a swig of coke. "No, I don't think many people know. I think he would rather that I remained a secret. He left mother and I a long time ago. When I arrived here three weeks ago, it was the first time I had seen him since he left."

"Hey that's a bit rough." Foggy smiled sympathetically. "So where is he today?"

"Portugal, he will be back tomorrow."

Foggy rubbed his temples, he felt sorry for the kid. He knew of Jack Bailey, heard a bit about him, mainly what an arse hole he was. He finished off his beer.

"So what have you got planned for the rest of the day?"

Evan shifted uncomfortably. "Not a lot. Pick up something for tea and then head home. There isn't really that much to do here is there?"

Foggy grinned. "You can say that again. Look why don't you come back to mine? I don't profess to be much of a cook but I can fry a couple of sausages and knock up a bit of scrambled egg."

Evan decided in that moment he liked Foggy. Sitting alongside him in the rusted Renault car, they chugged along the dusty track at little more than snail's pace. Finally Foggy pulled up at a grassy clearing and switched off the engine. He turned to look at Evan. "Afraid we have to walk from here, son, across those fields to get to my humble abode." He pointed in the direction. "It's not too far," he added.

They walked the short incline along a well-trodden path of straw-coloured grass. At the top Foggy turned to smile, pointing down the hillside about three hundred yards to an ancient caravan. "That's home I'm afraid, nothing fancy but it's a roof over my head."

The caravan was decidedly cramped inside. A small unmade bed was at one end with a table littered with books and records alongside it. At the far end stood a small stove crowded with dirty plates and pans. Foggy cleared a stack of books from one of the chairs. "Here, park yourself there, while I nip out and wash this lot up. The only tap is outside and if you need the loo there is a toilet of sorts out there." He pointed to a dilapidated corrugated building, its doorway draped with a heavy Hessian material, torn and ragged at the edges. "I would have tidied up a bit if I knew I was going to have some company."

Evan had never witnessed such poverty. He was suddenly filled with admiration for Foggy and the cramped living quarters he inhabited.

The sausage and scrambled egg was good, washed down with a tin cup full of sweet tea. They took their chairs outside into the early evening sun.

"You know I have big plans for this place someday." Foggy looked around at his surroundings, his eyes filled with hope. "It's hard for a struggling musician to make a living, but I have been working on some songs. Around December time, I'm going to England to see what the rest of the band thinks."

"Is that what you do then?" Evan asked with genuine interest, secretly pleased that he had been right.

Foggy picked up his battered guitar and softly he began to strum. "Yeah pretty much, I do a few odd jobs for people here and there, make a bit of cash to live on. I sunk all my cash into buying this piece of land." He gave a wistful sigh. "I have been out here a couple of years now. Split up with the girlfriend, couldn't find a job I liked and so ended up here. I enjoy the solitude, it helps me to write."

Evan looked around; it was a beautiful spot, the land stretched for miles before meeting the horizon. He could imagine a house with a large sweeping terrace that admired the view, a place where Foggy could sit and play his guitar, inspired by the wild countryside and the explosion of blossom on the surrounding almond trees in the springtime.

The deep blue sky framed this breathing canvas as Evan sat back to listen to Foggy's haunting tune. Closing his eyes, he imagined himself lying beneath one of the almond trees and looking up between its branches at a perfect night sky adorned with stars.

# CHAPTER 3

Evan sat by the pool, awaiting the arrival of his father, the air uncomfortable and sticky, yet pleasantly fragrant with the scent of jasmine that grew wildly over the back porch. The light was beginning to fade, the crickets chorused in the undergrowth around him. The terrace lights reflected in the pool, lighting the still waters. Patiently he waited alone as the night sky grew ever darker, until stars appeared in its velvet depths. The only light was cast from a sliver of the August moon overhead, which reflected on the slender trunks of the almond trees across the valley. A gentle breeze brought a welcome cool to the oppressive night and he shivered. Nipping back inside to fetch a blanket, which he wrapped tightly around his shoulders as he went back outside to keep watch, pulling his knees tightly to his chest, he nestled in the wicker chair.

Sitting very still he looked across the valley. He would be able to see the lights of his father's car the moment they rounded the bend and turned onto the track which led up to the house. It grew much later and now he felt a sudden panic, he no longer felt comfortable out here alone. The nocturnal wildlife had awakened, offering strange haunting calls from their camouflage. Hesitantly, he made his way to bed, only marginally calmer. Once tucked between the comforting sheets, he tried to fight the overpowering urge to close his eyes, afraid to go to sleep, but he was powerless to resist.

When Evan opened his eyes, dawn's light spilt in beneath the shutters. Leaping from bed he went in search of his father, but found the house empty. He rushed around to the front, in the hope of seeing his father's car parked at some obscure angle, but the driveway was bare and there were no tracks in the dust to show it had ever returned.

Shoulders stooped he made his way back to the kitchen as hot tears pricked at his eyes; he struggled momentarily to hold them back. He gave a hard sniff but it was no good. Bitterly disappointed, for he had secretly been looking forward to his father's return, exchanging conversation, telling him about his dinner with Foggy and impressing Jack with the Spanish words he had learnt. Foolishly he had fantasised that Jack would be eager to return too, having missed his son.

Evan, disarmed by the strength of his emotion, let the disappointment flood out. Once it started, he couldn't control the angry torrent that released from his body. All the past pain and hatred that he felt for his father emerged, submerging him in the painful memories of the past that were so clear it was as if it were only yesterday.

-------------------

Mother had gone to bed at lunchtime, suffering the terrible headache, the one she always had, except this time it was worse. He had sat observing her, watching sadly as she had swallowed the handful of tablets that would marginally ease her throbbing temples and enable her to sleep, if only for a short while. He had watched her sleep, her face pale; she lay motionless against the dark cotton pillow. The faint rise and fall off her chest was his only security that she was still breathing.

After a time he had left her and returned to his own room, where, taking a book from the shelf, he tried to read, looking for some comfort in the words on the page. Yet they had only danced before his eyes, distorted by the tears.

His father had arrived home just before dark. The house was unlit and unwelcoming. Jack had staggered in and before he had even made it down the hall Evan smelt the alcohol on his breath, the strong putrid scent, rising from every pore of his father's body, as he came closer to his room.

He had looked in on him. Evan lay curled in a ball on the top of the bed. His father had grunted, jerking his head, eyes rolling wildly, the whites of them showed menacingly in the darkness.

"Get to sleep now, Evan." His tone was gruff and demanding. He didn't care that Evan had lain there since lunchtime, that his stomach growled with hunger and that his chest ached from sobbing.

His father had closed the door with a sharp thud, making sure that the catch closed firmly, that Evan was safely out of his way.

Evan had lain very still, what little energy he had now fading. His body felt cold and, sensing trouble, he felt numb with fear.

The sharp cry brought him to, his eyes immediately open wide. Alert and afraid he waited in the dark, not daring to breathe until it sounded again. Leaping from his bed, Evan fumbled with the door handle in the darkness then headed toward his parents' room.

He heard muffled sobs from his mother, the fear inside him ever rising and heightened by the foul scent of his father, which hung heavily in the air.

Flinging open the door, he shouted out to his mother, voice trembling, and then he surveyed the scene before him. The bedside lamp cast a soft glow across the room. His mother lay on her stomach on the floor, her long fleecy nightdress hoisted to her waist, her head at an uncomfortable angle against the marked wood. Her whole body jerked with sobs. His father knelt astride her, his manhood forced between his mother's thighs; he thrust back and forth with a callous smile on his face, only bothering to look up as Evan cried out, and then ran to comfort his mother.

"Leave her alone! Get off her, you bully." He pulled savagely at his father's arm.

His father grunted and unwillingly lifted himself off his mother's crumpled body, but a fire blazed in his eyes. Pulling up his trousers, he cursed aloud. His mother dragged herself up on to her elbows, her face red and swollen.

"Evan, it's ok, I'm ok, go back to bed now please." The desperation in her voice scared him and he began to cry. She cradled his head against her chest, stroking his hair and wiping the tears that coursed down his cheeks with the tips of her thumbs. "There, there," she soothed.

He looked up to see his father leaving, their eyes met, and the steely glare he encountered caused Evan to whimper aloud. Never had he seen father this angry. He turned away filled with dread, afraid of what might happen next.

-------------------

Looking up, Evan shielded his eyes from the bright sun. He wiped fiercely at his damp cheeks, pulling himself up off the cold, tiled floor to look around the empty kitchen. When his father returned he would have this out with him. No longer a defenceless child, it was about time he confronted Jack. He wanted to know why his father had treated his mother that way, no better than a dog. His mother was very sick, nobody had ever helped them, and it appeared nobody cared. That bastard had a lot to answer for. When he got home, he would speak to his mother too, she had her part in this. How could she allow it to happen? She should have sought help.

For the rest of the day Evan seethed inside. Not even Esmeralda's offering of bubbling pork stew could melt the hatred that had lodged in his being. When he returned back to the house there was still no sign of his father.

Evan had picked up some provisions on his way home. He put them away, his jaw set firmly as he slammed the cupboard doors shut. Then he stopped and reopened the cupboard door. His eyes alighted on the full bottle of brandy. He shrugged, what was the harm? Unscrewing the lid, he gingerly took a swig, grimacing at the strong taste which burnt his throat. He wiped his mouth with the back of his hand and let the fiery liquid filter down his gullet where it settled with comforting warmth, deep inside his belly. It felt nice, and after a couple more swigs he found a little of his anger dispersed, it had succeeded in dulling his foul mood. Grabbing the bottle by its neck and only pausing to pick up the binoculars from the table, he headed outside. Evan took a cushion from the chair and set himself down. Taking another swig of brandy and sluicing it around his mouth, he felt invincible. Picking up the binoculars, he looked in the direction of Alexis' house. Zooming beneath her front archway, he brought the glasses to focus on the terrace and gave a sigh of satisfaction as he found her sat at the table beneath the carob tree. Oh he knew he could rely on her to be there. Then he drew in breath; there were two glasses set out on the table and a bottle of wine, the chair opposite her was empty but left at an awkward angle. So, she had company. Incensed, he paced the length of the terrace. That wasn't supposed to happen; it was just supposed to be the two of them. Snatching up the binoculars, he looked back at her house with a sense of longing. Then he saw the offender, a stocky man with spiky, sun-bleached hair, and bronzed upper torso. His stomach streamlined to his red silk swimming trunks as he sauntered across to Alexis, a towel draped across his shoulders, shiny as conkers. He was clutching another bottle of wine that he set down on the table. Evan watched as Alexis threw back her head to gaze appreciatively up at her companion. Her toe ring shimmered and her skin glistened, still wet from the pool. She was laughing, her face vibrant as she looked agreeably over the man's body.

A stab of jealously ran through Evan's own body as he grabbed the bottle next to him and took a quick succession of swigs. Then he turned his attention back to Alexis. He watched the graceful movement of her body as, eyelids fluttering, she leant across the table to stroke the strong upper arm before her, where her fingers lingered on his skin just a moment too long. Evan saw the hunger in her mate's eyes as they wandered appreciatively across her body. Alexis appeared vulnerable, dressed in a skimpy bikini, her breasts barely concealed by the slash of material. Evan wanted to cover her up. They talked and laughed, drinking the wine and never taking their eyes from each other for a moment. Evan paused for another drink. The earlier comforting warmness had subsided, giving way to a strong, reckless need. His heart hammered in his ribcage, his lower region throbbed. He felt powerful. Different to usual and he intended to have what he desired.

Focusing the binoculars, he switched from one to the other, conscious of the longing that swam between them, a pulse of magnetic energy suspended in the air. He watched the man move behind Alexis; he placed his hands firmly on her shoulders, rubbing them in strong circular motion. Alexis writhed in delight beneath this sensual touch. Evan held his breath as the man gently pulled her hair to one side and leant to kiss the nape of her neck, for Evan could feel the softness and inhale the sweet scent he encountered there. She turned to face him, her arms going around his neck, where they entwined. In a moment their lips met, their tongues searching each other's mouths with great intimacy. Effortlessly the guy slid Alexis from her chair onto the flaking wooden table. He placed the wine and glasses down on the floor out of their way. Kissing her neck, he undid the clasp of her top, letting her breasts tumble free to jut enticingly toward him.

Evan watched Alexis wriggle free of her panties, her eyes wild and careless. He gave an inferior groan as he watched the now naked man who, extremely well endowed, cavorted in front of Alexis like a wild stallion. Inexplicable jealousy exploded deep inside Evan. Resentful, he watched their faces, saw the pleasure contort this man's otherwise good looks.

It was coming now and Evan couldn't stop it, he hadn't as much as touched himself, but suddenly his loins gathered beneath him. Watching the man enter Alexis, foraging into her warmness had done it. It burst forth from Evan, a tidal wave of desire, flooding his crotch, seeping from the side of his pants; he let his head loll back, taking a deep gasping breath, his eyes closed in utter ecstasy.

"What on earth are you doing?" A voice shrieked from behind him.

Evan opened his eyes in alarm, sitting bolt upright and sending the bottle of brandy crashing across the terrace, where it smashed, sending amber liquid seeping across the tiles into a large stain. He looked up in utter shock at the young girl stood behind him, a protective hand covering the wet stain which saturated the front of his pants.

"Who the hell are you?" he stammered breathlessly, jumping to his feet and hurrying towards the house.

She followed quickly behind him, into the kitchen. "Were you spying on someone?" she asked casually.

Evan moved behind the table that was thankfully high enough to hide the embarrassing stain. Taking a moment to recover himself he shouted, "What the hell do you think you are doing sneaking up on me?" He looked at the young girl properly for the first time, she was certainly pretty.

She gave a nonchalant shrug. Her raven hair was tied back in bunches, held with pretty pink rags, her tanned face made even more appealing by a generous shower of freckles just across the bridge of her nose. Her eyes were a muted shade of amber with a mischievous glint. She was about his height and at a guess, she was around his age. Naturally slim, the baggy denims she wore did nothing to show off her lithe figure. Her t-shirt, torn at the shoulder, revealed a small tattoo of a butterfly.

She eyed him suspiciously from where she stood. "Did you just come in your pants?" she demanded, looking him haughtily up and down, her tone mocking.

Evan, shocked by her directness, felt his cheeks colour. Unperturbed, she went on. "What were you watching that made you do that? I am not stupid you know."

Evan managed an awkward smile. "You don't know what you saw Miss, besides you never answered my question." He surprised himself, with his clever response.

She grinned back at him. *What beautiful even teeth she has*, he thought, quite smitten.

"No I didn't, and I can assure you I wasn't sneaking around. Foggy sent me over. He is a friend of my mum's. He said you were here for a few weeks and you might like some company. He said you were lonely." She raised a quizzical brow, giving Evan another, haughty once over. "Seems Foggy was wrong, seems you have plenty to keep you busy here." She sniggered.

Evan ignored her. "As a matter of fact Foggy is right, I am bored, bored out of my mind to tell you the truth."

She gave an exaggerated yawn. "Welcome to Spain, Evan, this is about as good as it gets." She held out her hand. "I am Benita, nice to meet you." She stifled another giggle. "Oh and don't worry I won't tell anyone what I caught you doing. Your little secret is safe with me."

Evan smiled; he supposed it was intended to make him feel awkward. "That's an odd name, Benita; I have never heard that before," he remarked casually, keen to appear cool about the whole subject.

Benita grimaced as she opened the fridge door, helping herself to a drink. "It's Spanish; I was born here, my father is Spanish." She opened the can of coke and drank it all back, thirstily. "You do know that this stuff rots your teeth?" She looked across at him.

Evan sat down, signalling for her to do the same. She shook her head, tossing the empty can in the bin. "Sorry I have to get back. Maybe we could meet up in the village mañana, which in case you don't know means 'tomorrow'. I could show you around," she offered.

Evan smiled. "I would like that very much. What time?"

Benita tilted her head to one side, thoughtful for a moment. "Let's say ten, or is that too early?" She made her way towards the door.

Evan nodded. "No ten is fine, where will I find you?"

She looked back across her shoulder with a devilish grin. "Don't worry Evan, I will find you. I suggest you go and take a cold shower, I think you must need one, see you tomorrow."

As Evan lay in bed that night, his mind raced ahead to the morning. He was looking forward to tomorrow, there was something quite arousing about Benita, and she was different to the girls back home, very forward and outspoken, much more mature, and strikingly pretty too. For once, he didn't fret over his absent father. The brandy had left him feeling relaxed and had certainly enabled him to deal with that embarrassing episode earlier. He fell into a deep sleep, mulling over the possibilities of mañana. He liked that word, mañana.

Evan woke at seven, his head thumping, with an

excruciating tightness around his forehead. He couldn't even swallow; his mouth was too dry to produce any saliva. Supporting his throbbing head in his hands, he made his way to the kitchen for a glass of water. He felt ghastly, and then he remembered he was supposed to be meeting Benita. He gave an inward groan, scouring the cupboards for some painkillers, annoyed that everything was in Spanish. Wearily he grabbed the dictionary trying to decipher which tablets were for a bad headache. The nearest he could get was the word, 'head' on the back of one packet and thoroughly worn out with it all, he decided to take a gamble, swallowing two of the torpedo shaped tablets.

By ten o'clock, he was feeling remarkably brighter, as sitting on the steps of the town hall in the scorching sun, he waited. Benita appeared ten minutes later, although he didn't recognize her at first. She wore her hair down today, it fell sleekly to her shoulders and she was dressed in a simple cotton dress.

She sauntered over. "Sore head?" she questioned, looking Evan up and down pitifully.

"That's what you get for drinking your father's brandy." She sat down beside him.

"Yeah I know, it's not pleasant, it felt good at the time though."

Benita gave a pained expression. " I tried it a couple of times, couldn't really see what all the fuss was about, it made my head swim and I felt really sick the next day."

Evan turned to smile at her. "It's mad isn't it."

She leapt up as if suddenly bored with his conversation. "So what do you want to do?"

He shrugged. "What is there to do?"

"Mm. Good question." Placing her hands on her hips she looked around. "I am rather hungry. What about you?" she asked, looking down at him.

"I could eat a horse."

"Well that's decided then, let's gets some food. Got any money on you?"

"A bit." He pulled a note from his pocket. "Will this do?" he asked waving it in the air.

"You bet." She snatched the note from him and set off at a brisk walk. "Come on, we haven't got all day." He picked up his rucksack and hurried behind. She was very bossy but he wasn't complaining.

Benita tore around the shop, snatching things from the shelves. Evan followed silently behind, bemused by his new friend. Benita paid and put the change straight into her own pocket. He didn't bother to comment. She glanced over her shoulder to see if he was keeping up, as without a word, she headed up the lane and out of the village. She strode confidently ahead, and he found himself jogging to match her long stride. Benita turned off the lane into a field and picked her way carefully across the rocky terrain until coming to a riverbed which had dried up in the heat of the summer sun. Large boulders of ragged rock threaded along the sides of the riverbed. Benita followed along the edge until she came to a large smooth rock which protruded into the river, almost forming a bridge to the other side. Its surface was flat and she clambered up on to it. Sitting down, she turned to see what was keeping Evan, who lagged a short distance behind.

"Come on, hurry up, join me on this rock," she beckoned.

Promptly, she emptied the contents of the shopping bag onto the rock. As he sat down beside her, she handed him a bottle of water, only after she had had a quick guzzle herself. Then, taking the packet of doughnut rings, which she tore open with her teeth, she offered one to Evan. Biting hungrily into her doughnut, "Yummy, these are good," she declared, through a mouthful of chewy dough.

Evan nibbled gingerly at his, looking around at his surroundings. This was an amazing place. "I never realised Spain was so wild," he said.

Benita took another large gulp of water, and then helped herself to another doughnut.

"It's better in the winter when the river is flowing. You can catch terrapins with your bare hands."

"No kidding, that sounds great. It is a shame I won't be here to try."

"Me neither." She shook her head, noting the look of

surprise on his face. "I am going to college in Scotland, Glasgow to be exact. I will be studying hard and staying with my Aunt Alice." She swallowed the last of her food. "How about you, Evan, will you be going to college after the holidays?"

Evan shook his head. "Nope, in fact I have no idea what I will be doing, probably getting a job of some description."

She gave him an odd, sideways look. "You must have some idea what you want to do."

He threw a pebble across the dusty riverbed and watched as it smashed against the jaded rock on the other side. "That's what my father said. I guess I will take whatever I can get."

"Talking of your father, how was his trip to Portugal?" Benita lay back on the rock clasping her hands behind her head.

"I dunno, he isn't back yet." He shrugged, tearing his eyes away from Benita's body stretched invitingly before him.

They sat in silence for a short while until Benita sat up to face him. "Do you fancy a swim?" she asked, smiling.

"Sure." he nodded, watching her as she stood up and smoothed the creases from her dress.

"I know this fantastic place. It's only a ten minute walk from here, if you're up for it?" There was an air of mystery to her voice. She made it seem exciting, he thought. Damn it, she made everything exciting and just being with her enlivened him no end.

Nodding, he began to pack up the bag. "Sure, it sounds fun."

The day had grown hotter, or was it him? They meandered along the dusty track, still following the curve of the river.

"Where are we heading?" Evan asked, looking ahead at the wild expanse of fauna, not sure if he could manage much further without some more refreshment.

"There is this fabulous house and it is just around the next bend, the owner only comes up at weekends." She stopped, turning to look at him. "You wait until you see the pool, it's incredible, simply huge." She stretched her arms out wide. "It's the most glorious house I have ever seen and...." her eyes lit up. "I know exactly where the spare key is kept. I will show you round, you're going to be amazed Evan Bailey."

As they took the next bend she pointed up to the top of the craggy rocks. "Hope you are good at climbing?"

Evan gulped; he had never been good at heights. He shivered despite the heat. The river had carved its way between the rocks, leaving a gulley, and Benita expected him to climb up one side. The shiny surface of steely stone looked inaccessible; he felt a rush of adrenalin-induced fear.

Benita noted his cautious expression. "Hey, it's not as bad as it looks," she assured him, taking the cumbersome rucksack from him. "Let me take that. Now you follow me closely and I suggest you don't look down," she added.

Not even daring to look down for one second, he followed Benita as she clung to the rock face, as sure footed as a mountain goat, inserting her feet into the tiny crevices and small ledges. He took a deep breath, he needed to remain calm. He looked up ahead; it didn't appear much further now.

Benita pulled herself up onto the top of the rock and looked back down at him.

"Come on, keep going." She held out a welcome hand, he grabbed hold of it, afraid he would lose control and slip back. Benita gave him a sharp tug, pulling him up to safety. He fell, gasping for breath, on the granulated earth, taking a moment to recover; the air compressed in his lungs took a while to surface.

The large house sat just ahead of them. "Wow that's incredible!"

"Told you that didn't I." She swung the rucksack over her shoulders. "Come on, I can't wait to get in to the water."

As they neared the house, Evan couldn't help smiling to himself. This was more than he had expected, he had no idea that a place like this existed out here in the middle of nowhere, concealed by mountains on all sides.

The elegant building was set over two floors; it stood looking down at him. The roof rose to a turret that housed a dovecote, the walls were awash with the cerise bells of bougainvillea. A large cobbled terrace protruded from the back of the house straight toward the mountain tips and at its heart was a large, shimmering pool with an island of tropical plants at the centre. He took the steps that led up on to the terrace two at a time, eager to take a closer look at the house.

Benita had dropped the rucksack on the cobbles and was frantically pulling her dress over her head. He looked at her in surprise.

"Well you don't think I am going to swim in that." She threw it over the back of a nearby chair. He turned away, embarrassed, as she stood staring at him in her cotton underwear. "I suggest you do the same."

Evan stripped to his boxers, looking at the inviting pool, keen to plunge himself into the cooling waters. Benita, naked apart from a small pair of briefs, leapt from the pool's edge, diving headlong in with a large splash, Evan following quickly behind.

He swam a length of the pool then stopped, clinging to the edge. From his position down in the water it felt as if he were half way up the mountain heading towards the clouds. He took a deep pleasurable breath; this had to be the most incredible place he had ever visited and the most memorable experience he had ever encountered.

Tired from their walk and the nerve-wracking climb, he slipped from the water and dragged a sun bed to face the midday sun, lying back and letting the warm Mediterranean rays dry his wet skin, which they did within seconds.

"Tired already?" Benita asked, looking down at him. Dripping wet herself, she stood naked. He looked up at her, then quickly away again. Her small pert breasts, erect nipples, like pink liquorice comfits pointing directly toward him. He took a deep breath, she was trying to shock him and he wouldn't bite.

She giggled. "It's alright Evan, I know you're embarrassed." She leant across, blocking out the warming sun, and jiggled her boobs in his face, then skipped across to the other sun bed with a wicked laugh. He managed to smile. Benita was all mouth, he was sure of it; he had no doubt she was as good a virgin as he was himself.

He found it easy to snooze, the long walk having zapped all his energy.

"Come on sleepy head, we better leave." Benita restlessly shook his shoulder. "It's a long walk back to the village. Besides," she turned to look at the house, "I think we have spent long enough here."

Evan gave a thankful sigh when Benita revealed that they would be leaving by a different route. He hadn't relished the climb back down what he could only liken to a cliff.

The village was quiet when they returned; the locals were taking their siesta.

"Thanks for today, Benita. I have really enjoyed it." He felt a lump in his throat and realised he wasn't comfortable with their parting.

"Me too!" She nodded, and for the first time she looked sincere, there was none of her fun and games, but in a flicker the sincerity was gone.

"Perhaps we could go there again some time?" Evan asked, tentatively.

"Sure." She nodded. "Take care, Evan." She half smiled. "I will call for you at the weekend?" She raised her hand and ran off down the street without a backward glance.

He watched her disappear, thinking how odd she could be. Despite that, there was something alluring and boy did she know it.

He supposed he should be heading home himself and set off up the hill, his legs heavy from their earlier escapades. Just as he was reaching the edge of the village, Foggy drove alongside; he beeped the horn and pulled the car in just ahead.

"Hi Evan, how are you doing mate?" He stuck his head out the window grinning.

"Hi, Foggy." He smiled back, pleased to see him, hopeful of a lift. "I have been doing well. I went for a walk with Benita today and she took me to an awesome place."

Foggy raised a brow. "You want to watch yourself with

that one, Evan!" He winked. "Pretty little thing is Benita. Get you into trouble, if you're not careful."

Evan laughed. "Yeah, I have got her sussed, Foggy. She is all mouth." He gave a knowing grin. Foggy smiled, a glint in his eye, but then in a moment his expression changed. It was decidedly pained as if something was troubling him. "I am glad I ran into you kid, there is something I feel you should know. I just got back from doing some gardening for an English couple that live in the next village. They flew back from England a couple of days ago."

Evan waited, hands pressed in his pockets. He had no idea what Foggy was going to say but the look of concern on his face had him worried. Foggy tapped the steering wheel looking straight ahead as if deciding whether he should continue. "See, the thing is, Evan, well you know your father's in Portugal?" Evan nodded and his heart began to hammer. Had something terrible happened to his father, is that why he had not returned? Is that why Foggy seemed so troubled? He took a deep breath, steeling himself for whatever Foggy would say next.

"Thing is, Evan, it appears that your father is actually in England. The couple I worked for, they saw him at the airport. They just happened to mention it to me in passing." Evan felt his body begin to tremble.

"England," he repeated slowly.

"Are you ok, Evan?" Foggy leapt out and hurried round to him just as Evan reached out toward the car for support, but failed; his nails merely raked across the tarnished paintwork as he slithered to the floor a mix of shock and the heat. Foggy knelt down next to the lad, who lay in a crumpled heap on the dusty tarmac. Instantly Foggy regretted saying a word.

He watched the lad's eyelids flutter and tapped the side of his face.

"Come on Evan, lad," he soothed, whilst silently vowing to take Jack's head the very next time he ran into him, the selfish prick.

# CHAPTER 4

Foggy emerged from the caravan clutching two bottles of beer. Placing them down on the table he raked his fingers through the knots in his hair. "Jesus, lad, you gave me quite a fright back there. I never had anyone pass out in front of me like that before." He handed Evan a beer. "Get this beer down your neck. Put some life back into your bones. I don't mind admitting that you freaked me out a bit there."

Evan accepted the beer with a vacant gaze, took a large swig and blurted, "I can't believe he never told me the truth." He looked over toward the ripe, melon sun setting in the west. Hurt and numb he pondered why his father should dislike him so. "Why do you suppose he never told me the truth?" He looked questioningly across at Foggy.

"No idea, lad. Bang out of order though. I mean you have come out here to stay with him, build a relationship with the old bugger and he clears off on a little jaunt. I hate to say it Evan, but your pa has always been a selfish git. Try not to take it too personally, some people are just plain old selfish and those sort never change."

Evan nodded. What did he expect? His father was an utter bastard. He knew that already, he had the emotional scars to prove it. Sadly, Jack didn't care about him. He was going to have to face up to the truth, but it was so hard. Fathers and sons should be able to bond no matter what. They should look out for each other, at the very least want to spend occasional time together, he thought bleakly.

"You can stay here until your father gets back," Foggy said helpfully.

"No, thanks for the offer but I want to go home." He shrugged. "Not that it really is home."

"I understand." Foggy nodded. He felt for the poor kid. It

38

wouldn't do for him to cross Jack Bailey over the coming weeks. Right at this moment there was nothing he would like more than to wipe that smug little grin off Jack's face, something he would no doubt live to regret. He was already in enough trouble back in England, he was supposed to be keeping his nose clean out here, but as he gazed across at Evan and saw the utter misery in the young lad's eyes he knew he wouldn't mind taking the risk.

Foggy dropped Evan home. Evan watched the Renault chug away from him down the track in a cloud of dust. Turning back towards the house, he shivered.

So, he was in Andalucia and his father was in England, funny that! He had enough money to see him through to the end of his stay and he was sure Foggy would take him to the airport to catch his flight home, if his father didn't show before then. He went into the kitchen pulling off his dusty trainers. Why was it that whenever anything good happened to him in quick succession it was followed by something utterly crap?

Fixing himself a sandwich he made his way out to the terrace. The bread was dry, past its best, unappetising, so with little enthusiasm he ate the centre, leaving the hardened edges for the birds. Pushing the plate to one side, he stretched out his tired legs to rest on the chair opposite and found his thoughts drawn to Benita. She wasn't intending to call until the weekend; that was two whole days away, what would he do until then? Suddenly he wanted to be with her. He wanted her here now, in control and bossing him around. Benita would decide what they would do next. What he wanted more than anything, he realised, was to fit in, be a normal sixteen year old and put the past behind him. He had his whole life ahead of him; it would just be easier if he could make peace with his father.

The following morning he wallowed in bed, failing to see any good reason to want to get up. Bed felt safe, a haven from the harsh reality of life. A life he was no longer sure he could tolerate. Staring into space, he lay daydreaming. Benita was beside him in his mind. He could feel her skin against his own, silky and warm with the scent of cocoa butter. He turned to look at her, to study the curve of her full lips and marvel at her fine features.

The sound of a motor vehicle out front forced him to sit up. With heart hammering, he waited anxiously for the sound of footsteps to follow, partially relieved, the other part of him snarling. He sat still, straining to hear, surprised when he heard the sound of two doors close. Hardly daring to breathe he listened to the approaching fall of steps; there were definitely two and one set unmistakeably belonging to a woman. Therefore, his father intended to fuel Evan's raging fire further still, by inviting one of his floozies back. It went quiet; he waited to hear the key in the lock, sliding from bed and pulling on his clothes, cautious, even a little afraid.

Evan was startled by the loud knock on the door. Why on earth would his father knock? Slowly he crept down the hallway toward the kitchen.

"Evan, you up mate?" a cheerful voice called out from the other side.

He hurried to the door, blinking profusely against the intense light which poured in; it was a few moments before he could focus on the two smiling faces before him.

Foggy stepped inside. "Did we wake you up?" He patted Evan's shoulder then turned to smile at his female companion. A short, boyish-looking girl, dressed in jeans and t-shirt with faded pink winkle picker shoes. "Meet Jenny. A good friend of mine, she is over from England."

Jenny bounded over to Evan, planting a big kiss on each cheek.

"Nice to meet you, Evan. Foggy has told me all about you on the drive over. How your old man has buggered off and left you all alone. Bloody disgusting I say. Anyway, we have come to take you out for the day, cheer you up a bit, if we can. We are heading down to the coast. Do you fancy it?" she asked, tilting her head to one side, a deep pleading in her eyes.

"How about a cuppa while you decide Evan? I guess you haven't really woken up yet and here we are barging in organising your day for you."

"Oh, no I would love to come, if I won't be in the way." Evan could not contain the excitement in his voice.

Jenny sat down next to him, patting his knee. "In the way, our way! Not a chance, boy. It's nothing like that!" She looked over to Foggy, spooning sugar into three cups. "We're not like intimate or anything." She shook with laughter. "Were just mates, isn't that right, Foggy?"

Foggy brought over the tea. "Sure, we go way back, eons. Jenny's a good mate, popped over to see me while she is travelling Europe, a slight detour from the campsite in Malaga." He watched Evan gulp back the tea. "So do you fancy it?"

"You bet." Evan grinned, jumping up from his seat. "Let me grab a few things and I'm ready."

Jenny sought out a table at the front of the restaurant, overlooking the crowded beach, littered with holidaymakers stretched out on a colourful array of beach towels. Foggy ordered the drinks. He passed Evan the menu. "Whatever you fancy, it is my treat."

Jenny started gassing and never stopped. This and that, it didn't matter. Foggy sat staring out to sea. Evan wasn't entirely sure if Foggy was even listening to her, but he certainly was, every single word. She was fascinating; he languished in her endless stream of chatter.

Evan delighted in her random, high-pitched fits of laughter. He wasn't certain if what she had said was actually funny but he laughed just the same, her enthusiasm was infectious. It was all so new, he never realised someone could be this happy all of the time, she never stopped smiling; it was beyond odd. Slowly the sadness of the previous evening seemed to evaporate into thin air. For once, there was somebody who was witty and entertaining. He didn't have to say a word, just sit and listen to her riotous tales of the last five weeks. Five weeks with three equally madcap friends in an ancient tent. She even managed to negotiate a nine-inch pizza at the same time as himself and Foggy, without breaking from her story once. When dessert finally arrived, Evan realised that Foggy had actually fallen asleep.

Following lunch, Jenny suggested a walk along the beach. Foggy groaned about his aching legs, so they left him stretched out on the sand, his head resting on Evan's rucksack.

Evan followed Jenny along the footpath leading up along the top of the cliffs. "It is beautiful out here isn't it?" She turned to look at him. "Foggy is so lucky, I wouldn't mind living out here all the time."

Evan shrugged. "Think I prefer England really."

She paused, looking out to sea. "Yeah, guess you're right, suppose you can have too much of a good thing, mind you the weather is better; at least it is warm and not raining nonstop." Smiling, she leant back on her elbows, lifting her face toward the sun. "So, Evan, what brought you out here? Foggy told me that you and your old man don't get on that well."

Evan sat down beside her on the warm earth, shielding his eyes protectively from the sun. "I never really wanted to come here. It was my mother, she kind of made me. She has gone to stay at a spiritual retreat in Cornwall. Apparently it wasn't suitable for me to join her."

Jenny sat up, hugging her knees into her chest. "Oh, how interesting, I love that sort of thing, is she into spirituality then?"

Evan shrugged. "Suppose she must be, to be honest I don't really know what it's all about. My mother's been ill, she gets very depressed," he explained, surprised that he had even admitted such a thing to a stranger, but Jenny seemed nice, he felt as though he could trust her.

Jenny saw the sudden sadness wash over the boy. She felt compelled to hug him. He was a funny little thing. Scrawny with scared eyes and he didn't say an awful a lot, but she felt a warmness toward him. There was something very likeable about the lad.

"I knew someone that went to a similar sort of retreat once. It's all about finding your inner self. The spirit is the part of you that no one sees," she offered.

Evan looked up, keen to hear more. Knowledgeably she continued. "It's all a bit complicated and a bit of a mystery really, but there are some people who believe that when we die, it is not the end. That there is a part of us that lives on and that part is supposedly the bit that's really important. You should meet my friend Susie, she knows heaps about it, and she can even read the cards."

Evan looked confused. "What sort of cards?"

Jenny unearthed a bottle of water from her bag and took a large swig, then offered it to Evan. "The tarot cards, they're really neat. They have these really weird pictures on and she can tell you about your future, just by looking at them."

Evan cocked his head to one side. "That sounds wicked, has she ever read your future?" Jenny threw her head back, giggling. "Oh yeah, she has done mine. According to Susie I am going to marry an Irish man and have three kids."

"Do you believe her?" Evan asked with interest.

"Well, I guess I do, but I will have to wait and see. Anyway, I am not planning to marry for years yet. I want to see the world." She stood up. "We better go back and wake Foggy or he will be burnt to a crisp."

"I would really like to meet your friend, Susie."

She turned to tousle his hair. "Maybe one day you will, Evan."


Evan felt lonelier that night than he had done for the entire duration of his trip. He had taken the binoculars out earlier, but Alexis wasn't home and now the golden day had retracted, the sun had sunk behind the mountains hours ago and the velvet sky had appeared, lit by the pale moon which painted the hillside in a mystical sheen. The sounds of the night echoed in the stillness, as the valley below him slept.

Evan didn't feel safe tonight, he felt afraid. The sharp pinched cry of the owl made him shiver. He wished he had finished the last of the brandy, if only to make him sleep. He wasn't sure if his mother was safe; he had no idea where his father was. He had been stupid not to accept Foggy's invitation; at least he would have felt secure there, cramped inside the little caravan, comforted by the sound of Foggy breathing. He lay awake for hours, restlessly willing himself to sleep. Growing thirsty but too afraid to leave the warmth and safety of his bed, he didn't want to venture into the darkness of the empty house and worse still, now his mind was beginning to play tricks on him. He was sure he could hear someone moving about on the terrace, somebody trying not to be heard, but he had good ears and he was on to them. His heart pounded. What did they want? Perhaps they assumed the place was empty, knew that his father was away, and hadn't banked on Evan being there. But what were they looking for? There was nothing here of any value. In that instant he felt the goose bumps rise on his skin; he had left his wallet on the kitchen table. What an idiot. If they broke in they would be sure to lift it. He wasn't going to retrieve it, even if it was all he had to survive on - he would rather starve than come face to face with a knife-wielding maniac in the middle of the night.

He felt his chest tightening, he couldn't breathe now. The air sucked from the room made it difficult to inhale. The sound of rushing water as it pushed along the river, spilling over its banks and forcing everything from its path, overwhelmed him. He didn't know how to breathe; he may as well have been drowning in this river, as he floundered helplessly beneath the cotton sheet. He raked his fingernails along the side of the mattress as a second wave of panic consumed his thrashing body. The room was spinning; he felt faint as the foamy spray of water hit him in the face; he had no energy left, he couldn't fight it any longer. Then it passed as quickly as it had come, deserting his body, leaving it limp and lifeless in its wake. The only evidence that this terrible feeling had been real was the trickle of cold sweat running down his chest. His eyes felt heavy as he slumped back against the pillows. Exhausted by the sudden panic attack there was nothing to fight with, not even his own fear, he felt ridiculously empty; exhausted, he closed his eyes.

Esmeralda bounded toward the door; she threw her arms around Evan's shoulders, clutching him to her breast in a warm welcome. Then catapulted him into the nearest seat, where she left him dazed. She hurried to the kitchen and returned with a large milkshake and a bowl of stuffed olives.

"Where have you been, boy? Where have you been?" she boomed in Spanish tongue, noting the dark circles beneath his eyes and the paleness of his skin.

Evan's Spanish was limited but he knew what she meant, he just found it hard to answer her. As he struggled to reply, his brain tired, he spotted Benita, who sauntered into the bar. He didn't need to ask for her help, there was nothing she liked better than to take control as expertly she took charge of their conversation.

"Esmeralda says she has missed you. She is asking where you have been the last couple of days." Benita punched his arm playfully. "She has made you some special food today."

He nodded, smiling up at Esmeralda who smiled back, hands clenched to her chest like those of a proud parent. She turned and hurried off to fetch the food.

"Hear you went down to the coast yesterday."

Evan shook his head in disbelief. "Is nothing a secret around these parts?"

Benita giggled. "You're learning, you can't as much break wind around here without somebody knowing." She stole one of the olives, spearing it with her tongue, and then poking her tongue out at him. "That's the thing I can't stand about this place, you know the worst thing it's the English, they are the worst."

Esmeralda arrived with a large steaming earthenware pot. She set it down hissing and spitting before them. Benita raised an eyebrow. "Mmm Gambas Pil Pil, you must be in favour." Evan looked down at the steaming shrimps in hot garlic oil, it smelt divine.

Benita stole a hunk of bread from the side plate. "Don't mind if I do." She plunged it into the hot juices, mopping up the steaming liquid, then crammed it all into her mouth at once. "Oh, that is so good, sure is worth hanging out with you, Evan." Once she had helped herself to a shrimp, she sat back on her chair with arms folded to watch Evan eat. "Do you always eat that fast?" she asked.

Evan smiled before wrapping his lips around a large shrimp spiked with garlic.

It was damn good, thank God for Esmeralda. He finished

45

up and took a slurp of his drink. "Are we still on for tomorrow?"

Benita put her feet up on the table, picking a piece of shell from between her teeth. "Why, what's happening tomorrow?"

"It's Saturday, idiot, you said we would go out again at the weekend."

Successfully she pulled the offending shell from her mouth and deposited it with the olive stones. "So I did, ok same time?"

"Sure, same place, eh?"

She stood up. "Yeah same place, but don't look so cheesy about it. It's not a date you know."

"No shit, Benita. You'd figure I would want a date with you."

"Wouldn't you then?" she asked alarmed, momentarily caught off her guard.

"No, of course not, were mates, right?"

She gave a definite nod. "Most definitely."


Tonight felt better, Evan thought as he plonked himself down, binoculars at the ready.

It was calmer, less intense than the previous night. He raised the lens to look in on Alexis.

Dressed in a silk robe tied at the waist, her hair piled on the top of her head like a tightly coiled snake, she pottered around the terrace with a watering can, feeding the plants and dead heading as she went. As he watched her, he tried to decipher his own feelings. What made her so enticing to him, after all she was so much older? What one thing did it for him? It was becoming clearer. At first it had been a strange emotion, what he expected to be lust, but finally he was crossing the bridge of ignorance. He needed to be close with a woman, Goddamn it, he was sixteen years old and his hormones were running riot. He wanted to feel her skin close against his. He wanted to screw her, he needed to know what it felt like to be with a woman, yet what surprised him was why her? But then he guessed he was figuring that too. He couldn't imagine losing his virginity to someone like Benita;

she was too girlish, too innocent. He wanted someone stronger, he needed a teacher. Someone who would fulfil his insatiable urges, show him and guide him, draw on his strengths and improve on his weakness. Teach him to love like a master. Was he different, he wondered? Did all boys feel this way?

He watched Alexis shrug off the silk wrap and tiptoe across to the water's edge. Lightly she set herself down into the water with all the grace of a swan. She swam effortless lengths, sending the softest ripple across the surface of the water. As she dried, stretched before the fading sun, he studied her face as she watched the setting sun melt into the hillside in a liquid blaze of amber and peach. He could see the colours reflected in her eyes and as he looked harder, he saw sadness, too. He longed to comfort her, to relieve the pain that he felt lingered deep inside her somewhere and for a fleeting moment he felt he understood her inner torment.

As the light faded, he left her there, no longer able to see clearly as the sun dropped out of sight and coolness descended upon him.

# CHAPTER 5

Squinting at him through narrowed eyes, she waited until he was within a stone's throw of her tapping foot. Then, with hands on hips, she launched her verbal assault. "Evan, you utter imbecile, I said ten o'clock, it is now half past, can't you tell the time? Another five minutes and I was leaving. Let me tell you, you are lucky that I am still here!"

"Sorry, Benita, I really am. I came here as fast as I could. I overslept, I haven't been sleeping well," he said sheepishly.

She chewed impatiently on her lip. "Well, you're here now I suppose." Springing from the stone steps where she had been seated she barged past him. "We are going to Foggy's. Apparently he has a surprise for you," she said haughtily over her shoulder.

"Really, any idea what it is? I love surprises."

"Not a clue, come on, shift it." She tossed her bum bag at him. "You put that on, it is giving me jip." She pointed to the red chafing on the side of her waist. "I think the strap is rubbing."

He pulled a face. "Hardly surprising really, there is not very much of you covered today." He looked at her tiny cotton shirt, tied in a knot just above her navel.

"It's fashionable," she said, pulling an equally sarcastic face. "Something you obviously know nothing about," she muttered forging ahead, deeply impatient.

He watched her saunter along. Most of the boys back at home would fancy her like crazy. She was petite and nicely put together, as wild as a mountain cat and a definite tease. They would be jumping all over her, not him though. She was too young and far too immature. He smiled indulgently, watching her firm bottom wiggle from left to right in her skimpy pink shorts. He had set his sights much higher.

Foggy was gathering logs in the olive grove when they arrived. "Thought that maybe we could have a little party." He brushed the flaking bark from the front of his shirt and looked up at them, smiling.

"Oh fantastic, I love parties." Benita jumped up and down excitedly. "What can I do to help?"

Foggy gave a satisfied grin. "Thought you'd be pleased. For starters, Benita, you can wash up all the plates and then when you're done with that, you can wash some salad and boil some eggs for egg mayonnaise." He turned to look at Evan. "You can help me collect more wood and then I want to bang a few nails into that old table over there, it's getting a bit rickety and threatening to collapse."

Evan rolled up his sleeves, keen to get started. Foggy noticed his enthusiasm and smiled. There was a lot to like about this lad.

As they brought up the last of the wood, Evan spotted an old van coming up the track. "Who's that, Foggy? Looks as though they are coming to see you?" He signalled to the top of the hill. Foggy came over to stand by his side. "That's right, Evan, they are, its Jenny and her mates. It wouldn't be a party with only three of us, now would it," he said, chuckling and waving an arm in welcome to his guests.

Evan couldn't conceal the huge grin. He watched as the girls spilled out of the camper van and made their way down the hillside. The sound of Jenny's deep throaty laugh sent his spirits soaring.

Flames licked the darkness, illuminating the faces that gazed idly into the heart of the flickering fire. Evan sneaked a look across at Susie; she hadn't been what he was expecting. In fact, she appeared rather ordinary, not the hooked-nosed wise old bat that he had imagined. In truth, he mused, that wasn't fair; just because she saw the future didn't have to make her a witch. She was quiet and more relaxed than Jenny, who for the last hour had been unusually quiet herself. She wasn't the only one. Benita, now surrounded by older women, had buttoned her lip and sat listening to the gentle tune that Foggy played for them. When he had finished Jenny came round to throw an arm around Foggy's neck, planting a kiss at the centre of his forehead. "That was brilliant as always," she enthused. They all nodded in agreement.

Sara, Susie's friend, a tubby girl with two long dark plaits three quarters the way down her back, collected up the glasses, took them across to the table under the olive tree and refilled them with more of the delicious scrumpy cider that the girls had brought along. Several candles burned low in their glass jars on the table where the leftovers of dinner stood. Foggy had done them proud.

Sara handed them all a glass then sat cross-legged in front of the fire. Jenny danced across to Susie, where she whispered something in her ear and both women gave a secret knowing smile.

As Evan watched them closely, Jenny turned to look at him. "Susie says she will read your cards if you would like." He felt his cheeks flush as both girls looked across at him.

"Ughm, yes, if it's no trouble," he stammered.

"Well come on then, what are you waiting for?" Jenny signalled for him to join them at the table where she pulled up three chairs. Evan sat patiently as Susie shuffled the cards. The flickering candle cast a shadow across her face. Nobody spoke but they all watched. He observed the way she expertly mixed the cards before she turned with a reassuring smile to hand the deck to him. Nervously he took hold of the frayed cards. He looked up at Susie, his expression blank. "What should I do?" he asked shyly.

"Shuffle them, silly." She giggled. "Don't look so worried, Evan. They won't bite."

Awkwardly he attempted to shuffle the cards, which slipped through his fingers. He was painfully aware that both women looked on. He did the best he could then looked expectantly at Susie, who instructed him to split the cards into three piles with his left hand. When he had done this, she took over from him and, placing the pack back together, she paused to smile across at him. Her eyes held a reassuring gaze before she began to lay the cards across the table in a pattern.

"Mm, let's see what's going on around you." She placed

both elbows on the table, her head in her hands as she studied the cards with an experienced eye. Nervously Evan watched. He noticed one or two raised eyebrows, then he turned his attention to the pictures laid out before them. He hadn't a clue what any of the strange images meant, some looked pleasant depicting scenes of happiness and strong attractive people, but he noted with a sense of apprehension there were a few that appeared less pleasing and even worse, that these were the cards that seemed to be drawing Susie's attention.

After a lengthy silence she cleared her throat to look across the table at him with what he perceived to be a look of pity.

"The cards tell me that life has been hard for you. There is someone around you who has been ill for quite some time."

Evan nodded in agreement and a shiver coursed down his spine. How could these cards, mere pieces of illustrated paper, tell her this?

"Please don't worry, Evan. This person is going to get better, so much better, that they will be a different person. There is a man, a very selfish man and you have much anger towards him." She paused, taking a deep breath. "This man will not bother you soon, he is your past."

Jenny slipped her hand beneath the table and gave Evan's leg a reassuring squeeze. He looked over, glad of her encouragement, offering a quick smile before turning back to Susie, willing her to continue and tell him more.

"Evan, you will be working with your hands in the future, you will become very talented in the path you choose and there is great creativity at the base of this. Love, my friend, will be very straightforward and I see a marriage at a young age." Combing her fingers nervously through her hair, she took another breath. "I see no children from this marriage, but," her voice became quieter, her breathing shallower, "this will be by choice." Evan was not bothered at this revelation, he couldn't imagine fending for himself let alone a child, and at least she saw love for him. More importantly, his mother was going to get better.

"What about that card, Susie?" Jenny leant across the table to point but Susie scooped the cards back together.

"You didn't read…" Jenny shut off; Evan noticed the fierce sideways look that Susie shot her before she turned to smile at him.

"So, Evan, I hope that was ok, but please remember I am no expert and that the cards are always subject to change."

Evan nodded. "Thanks, Susie."

"You're welcome, now perhaps you wouldn't mind getting us a top up." She signalled to their empty glasses.

As soon as Evan left to fetch the drinks, Jenny turned to Susie. "What did you see? I know you didn't tell him everything, it was that card at the top wasn't it?"

Susie turned to her friend and lowered her voice. "I couldn't tell the poor kid, I daren't."

Jenny nudged her arm. "Understandably so, but you can darn well tell me. You know I won't breathe a word."

"Death, Jen. That's what I saw and it's the first Goddamn time I have ever seen it like that."

Jenny drew in a shaky breath, alarm in her eyes. "My God, it's his father isn't it? He's going to croak it, the selfish old bastard." She looked across at Evan returning with the drinks. "Well I can't say I am upset," she whispered.

Susie bent her head low, covering her mouth with her hand. "No Jen, it's more than that, I don't know exactly who it will be. But it is following him, I think we are talking multiple," she hissed through gritted teeth.

Evan handed them their drinks, which the women took over by the fire and huddled in a group. Evan spent the rest of the night mulling over what Susie had told him. Foggy played and the girls sang but he didn't hear them, his mind was somewhere else, racing far ahead into the future. Yet again, he shivered despite the warmth of the fire.

When Foggy was all out of tune and the girls all out of song, Jen and Susie went up to fetch sleeping bags from the van. They laid them down around the fire, on top of a plastic ground sheet. Evan was grateful to climb into its welcoming warmth, as the night had grown chilly. Gazing up at the sky, alive with twinkling stars that shone within a cloak of blackness, he gave a long contented sigh.

"Look!" Jenny pointed up at the sky, her voice echoing

with excitement in the stillness of the night. "I can see the Milky Way." Every head looked up, followed by a chorus of awestruck murmurs. Evan folded his jumper neatly beneath his head to suffice as a pillow; he looked up toward the vast space overhead. He knew he would never forget this night for the rest of his life. His body ached with pleasure as he gazed up into the sky and beyond. Like the cards, it was intriguing. Nobody really knew what the future held or what existed beyond the stars that looked down at him now. Past caring, he looked wondrously up at their beauty.

Foggy rounded the bend, starting to climb the track, the car idling as he changed gear. He glanced across at Evan, who sat tight-lipped with his hands resting on his knees.

"Good night wasn't it, bet poor Jenny has the hangover from hell this morning."

Evan didn't reply but nodded in agreement as he kept his eyes fixed on the potholed track ahead of them. As they neared the house he saw that his father's car was outside; finally he had returned. A surge of anger silenced him, he was unable to speak. Foggy felt the change in the boy as it filled the entire car.

"Looks like the old man's returned then?" There was a testing edge to his tone. "You know I can come in with you if you like." He smiled across at Evan who appeared emotionless. Evan opened the door before the vehicle had come to a standstill. "Thanks Foggy." He gave a quick nod. "I will be down to see you later in the week."

Foggy raised his hand but the lad was gone, hurrying through the gates to see his father. He sat for a moment, contemplating if he should go in and support the lad, but thought better of it. Now was not the time to tell that bastard just what he thought of him.

Jack Bailey sat reading a newspaper. He looked up at his approaching son with a sheepish grin, closing the paper as Evan marched toward him, eyes narrowed in rage.

"I know, son." He stood up, holding both hands defensively in the air as Evan bore down on him. He went to open his mouth to explain but was knocked back several paces as Evan's fist hit him square in the jaw. In the following seconds it took to right himself Evan had disappeared inside and he heard a door slam. Running his hands through his hair he took a deep breath, considering what had just happened. He was a little shaken and greatly surprised, as he didn't think the boy had it in him. Then he turned to go indoors, surprise turning to fury as he went in search of his son.

Flopping down on the bed Evan's body began to tremble, he had shocked himself. The hate evaporated, giving way to a fear that threatened to saturate his body. Jack's footsteps echoed on the stone floor as he strode up the passageway. Evan waited anxiously for his father to knock. He was horrified when the door flew open with such ferocity that he felt the rush of air across his skin. Such was the rage in his father's eyes that it looked as if he may combust at any moment.

"You ungrateful little shit." Jack grabbed a handful of his son's t-shirt, wrenching him onto his feet, and thrust his face directly into Evan's and looked deeply into his son's terrified eyes.

"What fucking right do you have to do that? So I was longer than I anticipated. Mummy's boy had to get on with it." He thumped his hand backwards, flinging Evan back down on to the bed with considerable force. "I didn't want to have you here for Christ's sake. Got landed with you, that stupid cow of a mother. I should have told her to piss off and take her little bastard somewhere else." He saw a flicker of emotion in Evan's eyes. Smiling callously, he stepped back, crossing his arms to survey the lad. He took a deep breath. "Yeah, sorry, that's right kid. Don't know who he is, but sure as hell isn't me." He sniggered.

"You're lying." Evan pulled himself back up, whisking a hand across his face to mask the emotion.

"It's the truth, kid. Your mother never told you? Me and her, we never fucking did it, let alone make a child." He gave a smug laugh, enjoying the power.

Evan lifted his shoulders and squared up to his father.

"No, you only ever raped her, didn't you, you bastard. You were so disgusting you had to force yourself on her." He began to sob but he stood his ground, watching his father's face closely, waiting for a reaction. His father's fist shot through the air; there wasn't time to turn as the full force of it landed across the side of his head, knocking him off his feet. He landed on the bed, instinctively curling into a ball.

"So if that's true then Evan, what the fuck does that make you?"

Evan lay sobbing. Jack's heavy footsteps faded down the hall. He heard the crash of the front door, followed by the scrunch of tyres in gravel as his father's car made off at great speed down the track.

Some hours later Evan woke. He shuffled across the hall to the bathroom. There was a distinct chill in the air and the light had faded. Switching on the light he went across to the mirror to examine his swollen cheek, which now resembled an overripe damson. Shakily he touched it, wincing at the pain; he swallowed hard but was unable to stop the flood of tears. He sat down on the closed toilet seat, crying like a baby, his chest heaved and his lips trembled uncontrollably. Just as it seemed to subside, the emptiness circled him again and his eyes began to fill up. Grabbing handfuls of tissue he wiped pitifully at his face until he could no longer see clearly through swollen eyes. Stripping off his clothes, he climbed inside the shower, turning the water on full force; he stood shivering beneath a jet of cold water that made his teeth chatter and his skin sting, waiting for his body to go numb.

Jack Bailey returned home just after eleven, after several pints of lager and half a bottle of whisky. Stumbling in the front door he felt along the cold stone wall for the light switch. He opened the cupboard and fumbled around looking for the bottle of brandy, the thought of which had kept him somehow on the windy road home. He unscrewed the lid and took a large swig, surprised when that was all he got. Puzzled, he put the bottle down on the table. It was damn near full when he had left last week. There was only one explanation, he decided, making his way toward Evan's room, pausing at the bathroom to use the toilet; he had been busting the entire journey home. As he entered, swaying from side to side, he hit the soaking floor. The tiles resembled a sheet of ice and the only thing that softened the crashing fall was the fact that he was so intoxicated. Too slow to prevent what was happening, he felt his head smash against the wall, plunging him into a cloak of darkness.

# CHAPTER 6

Perched on the edge of the sun bed, she peered down at Evan with a look of concern. He looked back and a faint smile crossed his lips.

"Oh. Poor, Evan," she cooed, stroking his swollen cheek with her fingertips. "He should be locked up for doing this to you."

"Well he did do it and there is little I can do about it, accept get lots of sympathy from you." He couldn't help enjoying the attention despite the pain.

"Tell the police for a start," she yelled.

"No I don't want to get him in to trouble, he has sort of apologized and besides he got his just desserts when he split his head open. He had to have six stitches and I expect it will scar for life." He gave a lopsided grin.

Benita's eyes lit up at the thought.

"Well I hope it does, it's the very least he deserves."

Evan rolled onto his side, so he could look more deeply into her eyes, shielding his own from the sun's glare. "Don't forget I hit him first."

"So you bloody well should have." She stood up and went over to the adjacent sun bed to retrieve her bag, plonking it down by his head. Taking a deep breath she looked across the crystalline waters of the pool to the mountains. She lifted her arms toward the sun, stretching toward its warmth. "It is beautiful here isn't it?"

"Sure is, I am so glad you brought me here." He looked across at the house, just as spectacular today as the first time he had set eyes on it.

Benita rifled through her bag, then with a triumphant squeal pulled out a packet of cigarettes and a lighter in the shape of an angel fish. "Aha, knew they were in here somewhere." She pulled one from the packet, lit it, inhaled deeply and returned her gaze to Evan.

Evan watched in surprise. "Never knew you smoked."

Letting out a large smoky breath she smiled. "I have one now and again, don't tell me you have never tried one."

He shook his head. "Actually I haven't, it never really appealed."

"Then you must today." She thrust the packet under his nose. "In fact, seeing that you're only here another week, we must be really daring."

"Oh and apart from having a cig what would that entail?"

She was on her feet in a moment. "Come on, follow me. I told you I knew where the keys to this place were kept and I still haven't shown you around." She giggled. "Let's have our own little party. They have a drinks cabinet in there filled with the strangest stuff, they will never know." She took hold of his hand, dragging him to his feet. "Come on Evan, let's have some fun."

Evan marvelled at the interior of the house as he followed Benita obediently like a dog from room to room. She raced ahead in eager anticipation.

"Oh to be this wealthy." She clasped her hands to her breast. "Wouldn't you just love a place like this, Evan?"

Nodding, he followed her into the grand living area, where two cream leather sofas and a large oval glass coffee table with ornate brass legs looked lost in the vast space.

"Sit down," she signalled, going across to the highly polished corner cabinet and throwing open the doors to reveal a well-stocked bar. "So what do you fancy?"

Evan joined her, where together they peered inside. "Brandy would be good, at least I know I like it."

She turned, grinning at him. "And you know it gives you a thumping hangover the next day."

"Yeah there is that." He shrugged, letting his shoulders droop and flopping down on the sofa. "Surely all alcohol does that?"

Benita shrugged. "I guess you are right, well who cares? We are having fun today aren't we?" She raised a quizzical brow toward Evan.

The French doors opened out onto the upper terrace, which looked majestically down upon the pool. Benita threw back the doors, then she lit two cigarettes and handed one to Evan. Then, fetching their drinks, she placed them on the table and in a fit of giggles collapsed down beside Evan, who took his first ever draw on a cigarette. His face turned purple as he struggled to breathe through a coughing fit. She handed him the brandy. "Better have a swig of this."

He took a large gulp. "Wow that's better." He wiped his mouth with the back of his hand, looking across at Benita. "What have you got?"

She swirled the amber liquid around the large balloon-shaped glass then took a small sip. "It's apricot brandy, it's very strong." She grimaced as she swallowed the hot liquid. Hurriedly taking another puff of her cigarette, she looked surprised as she eyed Evan drain his glass.

"Steady up, Evan. don't forget we have to walk home yet."

"I thought you said this was a party." He winked, giving her a wicked grin before going over to help himself to another glass.

"So I did." She drained her glass, gave an uncomfortable splutter, then looked shyly across at him. "Wow that's like swallowing fire."

"Sounds good, maybe I should try some of that next." He slumped down beside her. "Are you looking forward to starting college? You only have another week."

Pulling her legs up beneath her she was thoughtful for a moment or two. "Yes I am but I am nervous as hell as well. It's been a long time since I went to England. It's going to seem hectic after the tranquil pace of life here and then it will be strange living with my aunt, I don't really know her well."

"Yes it's going to be very different to what you have been used to. What sort of place does your aunt live in?"

Benita ground her cigarette out in the ashtray. "In a small village, apparently it's a twenty minute bus ride to the college. There's only my aunt at the house as she is a widow, my uncle was killed in a car accident. Not that I remember him. I was only four at the time."

Evan got up and sauntered over to the open doors, his hand clasped tightly around the glass of brandy.

"I'm kind of jealous in a way; I have no idea what I will be doing. It seems terrible that I hadn't really much thought about it till now."

Benita, sensing the shift in his mood, went across to his side. "That could be a good thing. Perhaps destiny has something special planned for you."

Evan shrugged, a distant look in his eyes. "Destiny hasn't been very kind to me so far. My father is an utter shit and -" He broke off.

"Go on," she urged, placing an encouraging hand on his shoulder. Evan felt an instantaneous glow inside, it was the first time Benita had ever touched him in such a way and it felt so good. It took a few moments for him to find his voice.

"Well my mother truth be known isn't much better. I mean she tries but she is always so down." He finished the rest of his drink. "That's due to my father though, he made her life hell."

"Did he hit her too?" Benita asked, gently rubbing his shoulder. He felt the shiver slide across his neck and down his chest. He turned to face her.

"Yeah he did, the bastard." He lowered his voice, averting his eyes back to the pool where they searched its depths. "That as well as raping her too."

Benita gave a shocked gasp, digging her fingers inadvertently into his shoulder blade. Evan turned to her with a sheepish smile and met her lips which forged forward to meet his until they were locked in a kiss. Neither pulled away, the kiss seemed to last an eternity. Her mouth was warm and her breath sweet, her lips deliciously moist. Instinctively he put his arms around her, drawing her thin body toward him and holding onto it for support as the kiss strengthened and the feeling that he never wanted it to end swirled in his mind.

Abruptly she broke the kiss, stepping back with a coy smile.

"Evan Bailey, you are some kisser."

He felt a warm flush; reticent, he looked down at the floor. Benita placed a finger beneath his chin, pushing it upward so that he was forced to look back at her.

"I am as surprised as you." She gave an awkward smile.

"It felt nice, didn't it?" He raised a questioning brow. Benita nodded; the pink flush in her cheeks confirmed it. He noted how her face had softened; her eyes had widened and her jaw relaxed, she seemed different much softer.

"Do you want to..." He stopped and looked away, embarrassed.

"Have sex," she offered.

He gave a nervous cough.

"Evan, we are both sixteen, it would hardly be crime of the century." She flicked her head back defiantly. Oh how grateful he felt for her directness at that moment in time. If it was down to him they wouldn't have even kissed by now, but then maybe she was experienced at this sort of thing. He felt an acute attack of butterflies in his stomach, suddenly anxious at the thought. What if he was totally hopeless? What if she laughed at him?

As if reading his mind Benita took his hand gently in her own. "I'm not any good at this. I only tried it once and it wasn't very memorable." She raked her fingers nervously through her hair. "It was a Spanish lad at school." She bit her lip.

Evan stood motionless for a while, considering what she had said, and then gently led her across to the sofa where he pushed her back onto the cool leather.

"I have never done this." He gave a small whimper accompanied by a restless shrug. "Guess we will just have to take it slowly and see what happens." Slowly he took hold of her hand, guiding it down to his crotch. Benita felt the hard bulge beneath the denim with a mix of anticipation and fear. Moving up to his lips she pressed her own hard against his, her breath becoming shallower as her body trembled. Wrapping his arms protectively around her, Evan kissed her softly until he felt her fear subside. The last thing he ever wanted to do was hurt her and if it took all night this would turn out right. Poised on the threshold of this life-changing experience he gave a heady sigh. There were many things he had encountered while in Spain but this moment took his breath away and it was to be treasured for eternity.

Jack Bailey sat at the bar contemplating another whisky and then thought better of it.

The kid was only around another week; if he never saw him ever again the least he could do was give him this one week. Manuel appeared as if by magic with a bottle, ready to top up his glass. He waved it away brashly, climbing to his feet.

The house was empty when he arrived home. There was no sign of Evan. He wondered where the kid went to, he wasn't around very much. Up to that point it hadn't much bothered him but a sudden pang of guilt hit him in the chest like a steam train and he realised with a sickening dread that he cared very much. There again he never had been able to stop being a selfish bastard and countless woman over the last twenty years would happily verify that fact. It had been wrong of him to deny being the kid's father. There was no doubt he was, his mother was an insane bitch but she never slept around. In fact the woman had hardly left the house in those days and, as he thought back to how it was, he felt uncomfortably ashamed. It was amazing that the kid hadn't turned out the same as his mother. Jack hated to admit it but Evan was a good kid and he had fucked up big time not being around for him in those early years. Grabbing a few beers from the fridge, he went out to his usual spot to watch the sunset. He took a thirsty gulp and checked his watch, thinking if Evan wasn't back within the next hour he had better go look for him.

Few words were exchanged on the long walk home. Benita strode ahead as he had now become accustomed to, Evan watched her but this evening was strange. Things were different now they had been so intimate; he was dreading their parting when they reached the village.

It had gone well, he supposed, for a first time. Inexperienced he could not be sure. Benita had said it was much better than her first time and he wanted with all his heart to believe her.

Benita stormed on ahead, trying to blank her mind as she picked her way across the dusty grove. Emotion was a pain; she shied away from ever letting it get the better of her. Sex with Evan had been a surprise. Not the sloppy attempt she had experienced before, it had felt grown up. She figured that he must be lying when he said he hadn't done it before. The way he had cradled her body, slipping gently into her, and rocked her body toward him had been so good, but it had left her feeling very confused. The pain that writhed in her chest had arrived there the moment their bodies had separated. A voice in her head seemed to be screaming at her to turn around and kiss him now, before it was too late, before they rounded the next bend and the village was in sight. She had to ignore it. This was too complicated, Evan would be going home and she was off to her aunt's; they would probably never see each other again. As much as she would like to change that, it was a fact and as they neared the village she made her decision.

Taken aback by the pain their parting caused him, Evan trudged home. What was this ache that had gripped him? His spirits lowered further when he saw his father's car parked out front.

Jack rose to his feet to welcome his son. "I was getting worried about you, lad. Have you had a good day?"

Evan ignored him, heading straight to his room. Dropping down his rucksack he laid back on the bed without bothering to remove his dirty trainers. Running his fingers through his matted mop of hair he wondered what Benita was doing and if it was possible that she was feeling as weird as him. Taking a few deep breaths to centre a mind that was whirling to and fro, he replayed that afternoon's events in his mind. Excited shivers ran across his sweaty body as he saw her laid before him, her amber eyes wide with edgy anticipation. He didn't want to get up and shower, he didn't want to eat, all he wanted to do right now was continue to lie here and think about Benita.

At least she would not be far from him when they returned to England. He could catch a train and visit her. Maybe he could move up to Scotland to be near her, get a job and perhaps a flat where they could be together making love all night long. His mind raced years ahead with all the endless possibilities.

A loud knock at the door brought him back to the present, with a start. "Evan lad, are you coming out? I have fixed us some supper. I thought maybe we could share a bottle of wine." Jack listened for any sign of life within, poised at the bedroom door waiting for an answer. It remained silent; he waited a few seconds before going on. "Sorry, Evan, I have been a real arse hole. I would really like it if you could come out and eat with me."

Evan waited alone in the darkness, willing him to leave, but the sincerity in his father's voice plagued him and if he wasn't mistaken, there was a note of regret too. Hauling himself from the bed he went over to open the door. Jack straightened himself up as his son appeared then smiled down at him, his eyes almost pleading.

"What is it?" Evan asked sharply.

"Nothing much lad, Just a curry, happens to be my speciality, curry." He gave a self-conscious snort. "Tell the truth, it's the only thing I can make." He placed a guiding hand on Evan's shoulder. "Beef, is that alright?"

Evan sat down at the table which had been laid and at the centre stood a bottle of red wine and two glasses.

"Why don't you pour?" Jack signalled to the wine, "While I dish up the food for us both."

It smelt good; Evan felt his stomach groan in anticipation, the day's events had made him ravenous. Jack placed the steaming plate before him. "Dig in, lad, I hope it's not too spicy for you?"

With stomach crammed to bursting point, Evan followed his father out to the terrace where they finished off the last of the wine. It was a glorious night full of brilliant stars, full of possibilities, Evan thought cheerfully.

To his surprise Jack didn't say much, there were no lectures or underhand comments, he seemed relaxed and turned to smile at him every so often. Evan wondered if it had something to do with the fact that he would soon be on a plane back to England. It didn't matter, he didn't care.

The evening had been civilised, nothing more, nothing less, and that suited Evan as he bedded down for the night. If this last week could just be civilised then he would be willing to forget that his father abandoned him and that they had fought. Besides, he needed to concentrate on other things, the most important thing that was playing on his mind was of course Benita and there were so many things he needed to say to her.

# CHAPTER 7

Jack's behaviour grew ever stranger as the week progressed. If Evan didn't know better he would have said that Jack was going to miss having him around the place. There had been a dinner every night since the curry. Jack had even given him some money to get a present for his mother. "A little surprise for your mum," he had mumbled.

Evan bought a beautiful fan decorated with coloured beads that sparkled in the light. It was safely wrapped in pink tissue in his bedside drawer.

Evan woke early and rushed to look out at the clear sky. It was going to be another scorcher; there was not a cloud in sight. Dressing in shorts and vest, he sauntered through to the kitchen to make some coffee. There was a note propped against the toaster, left by his father. '*Gone to Marbella, be back at teatime.*' The note was brief, to the point. Evan tossed the note in the bin, wondering if last night was possibly the last time he would ever set eyes on his father. One never knew, he mused as he lavishly buttered a slice of toast, topping it with marmalade. He had not seen Benita for a couple of days; she was getting ready for her trip. He could understand that she needed time alone with her family right now; she had promised they could meet tomorrow.

Foggy had sent a message to meet him for lunch at the bar and after he cleared away his breakfast things he went to pack his rucksack.

He took the scenic route to the village at a gentle pace, killing time. It would be time to leave soon and in a funny sort of way he was going miss this place.

Foggy was sat at a table in the corner reading a letter. He looked up and smiled as Evan sat down. Hurriedly, he folded the letter and put it in his pocket.

"Not long now eh, are you looking forward to returning to the land of the living?" he asked.

Evan gave a wide grin. The teasing smile left Foggy's face and he lunged across the table to inspect Evan's cheek.

"Is that a bruise?" he asked savagely.

Evan touched his cheek protectively. "Yeah I walked into the cupboard door." He turned and signalled for Esmeralda to take their order, desperate to divert Foggy's attention.

"I don't believe you." Foggy sat back, arms folded, looking at Evan through narrowed eyes. "That bastard has done that, hasn't he?"

Evan began to protest as Foggy slammed his fist down on the table, causing Esmeralda and the two elderly men at the bar to turn in alarm. Esmeralda hurried over concerned.

"It's ok," Evan smiled, "we would just like to order some food if we may."

Unconvinced, she shot Foggy a glare. He didn't seem to notice as he lit a cigarette, taking hurried puffs.

"I knew I should have gone in with you! I am a total fucking idiot, that's what I am." Agitated, he drummed his fingers on the table. Evan tried to ease the situation, firstly by ordering the food and getting rid of Esmeralda who stood rigid at the side of the table trying to fathom out what had got Foggy so upset.

"I hit him first, he has apologised and I would just rather forget it."

Foggy looked at him, disbelief furrowing his brow. "No man should ever hit a kid, not ever." He shook his head furiously. Stubbing out the cigarette; he promptly lit another and grabbed the pint of lager from the tray before Esmeralda had come to a halt with it, gulping it back with great thirst.

Evan sipped his coke, surprised, perhaps a little flattered by Foggy's reaction. "Please, Foggy leave it, for me, please. I go home in two days."

"Yeah you're right, kid." He gave a nod. "So what did you order?" He managed a smile at last.

"Serrano ham with Manchego cheese and a salad to share, did you want chips because I haven't ordered any."

"Na, that will be enough, besides I don't want to get

caught up here too long, I wondered if you fancy coming for a ride down to Malaga with me. I have arranged to meet a drummer."

"You're really going to do it then." Evans eyes lit up, until he remembered he would be going home and he would never get to see the band that Foggy was planning to put together.

Foggy laughed. "Course I am, though I dare say it will take a while to get up and running." He noticed the sparkle disappear from Evan's eyes. "Don't worry, kid. I will write and let you know how it is going and it goes without saying that you will be the first to get a demo tape."

"That's cool. I will be waiting to hear what a big success you are."

Foggy speared a piece of ham as Esmeralda put the plate down in front of him. "We'll see, but do you know what, kid?" He arched his brow. "You will be guest of honour at the first concert."

Evan grinned broadly through a mouthful of Manchego cheese.

Jack finished his boiled egg and snatched the last piece of toast from the rack as he got up.

"Got to dash, Evan. Be home about two if you fancy going for a drink."

Evan watched his father leave. It was a shame that they were finally getting along now, just as he was about to leave. He had returned last night from his trip to Marbella with a lobster for each of them, which he had boiled. The live lobsters cooking wasn't a pretty sight, causing Evan to leave the room, but once cooked Jack had served them with a tossed green salad and they were simply delicious. A couple of bottles of Rioja had complemented the meal and much to Evan's dismay his father had talked all night. He even managed sketchy details about his own childhood. It had been more than Evan had dared to hope for. Finally he knew just a little bit more about his roots. There was nothing much exciting about it. His father had been an only child and both his grandparents were dead.

Evan was not due to meet Benita until lunchtime. Clearing away the breakfast things he remembered Alexis. The last week had been so hectic he hadn't had chance to check in on her. He went to fetch the binoculars now.

Alexis had company. A guy sat at the table, a newspaper spread out before him. Alexis sat, legs crossed, a cup and saucer balanced on her knee. The guy looked a lot older than her. Evan could tell from their body language he was not a lover, possibly a friend. They were locked in conversation despite the fact he never seemed to look up from the paper before him. Evan soon tired of watching them and looked around the valley. Today it appeared to be deserted and there was nothing of interest. Maybe, he pondered, it was quite simply the fact that he had other things on his mind. Like going home tomorrow and leaving all of his new friends behind. Still, he consoled himself with the fact that at least Benita would be within his reach. He was going to dearly miss Foggy though. There was something about the lanky guy that he really liked. Foggy had shown him genuine kindness; he had never felt that before. It appeared Foggy really cared and Evan had already made up his mind that he would write every week. Foggy would like that and he in turn would look forward to receiving news from Foggy. If anyone deserved to be a success it was him and Evan hoped with all his heart that he would be one day.

Evan went inside to change, applying a liberal amount of his father's aftershave, hopeful that Benita would be intending for them to go up to the house together one last time. He couldn't wait to feel her close again, to seek comfort in her arms. He checked his appearance in the mirror one more time before setting off for the village.

Benita was waiting at the usual spot; he could not conceal the huge grin that spread across his face as he spotted her. Benita raised a hand in greeting. She looked tense, he thought, as he approached her.

"Hi, Evan." She rose to her feet and leant across to peck him on the cheek. There was a wave of disappointment; he had expected somewhat more.

"So, home tomorrow, bet you're excited." Her tone was brisk.

He shrugged. "A little," he said. Desperate not to appear disappointed, he managed an awkward smile.

"What! Don't tell me you have fallen in love with this place and you don't want to leave now."

"Not exactly but I am going to miss you and Foggy and our little trips out to the house." He winked suggestively at her.

"Well, me too I suppose. I can't lie; it has been good having you around these last few weeks." She looked around. "It has certainly made the last few weeks more bearable and taken my mind off college."

"Cheers, I love you too." He gave a nervous laugh, watching her face closely. She didn't smile, averting her eyes as she bent to pick up her bag.

"I thought we could go and get a coffee in the bar," she said, turning away. Scooping up his rucksack he jogged to catch up.

"I thought we might go up to the house for a swim," he asked hopefully.

"Impossible, the owners are there at the moment," she lied, pushing open the door to the bar, signalling for him to go in first.

As Evan sat watching Benita stir her coffee in an endless swirl, he wondered what he had done wrong. It was obvious she wasn't her normal self today.

"Have I upset you, Benita?" he asked, placing a hand over hers. She looked across at him in a daze.

"No! Not at all."

"Well you don't seem very happy at the moment. Was it the other day? Do you regret what happened up at the house? I mean I can understand if you're having regrets."

"Why, are you then?" Her eyes blazed. She shook her head, snatching her hand from beneath his.

"God, no." He felt his cheeks turn crimson. "Benita, it was beautiful. I have thought of nothing else since. I was kind of hoping that maybe you felt the same way." He took hold of her hand again, giving it a gentle squeeze. How did you tell somebody that you were painfully in love with them, that your whole being went into orbit every time you thought about them?

Leaving the bar, they strolled out onto the pavement, Benita shielding her eyes from the sun's rays. Painfully quiet for the last hour, she turned now to look at him. Her eyes were distant, her body language difficult to read, not Benita at all.

"So where shall we go now?" Evan asked brightly.

Pulling her sunglasses from her bag and sitting them on the top of her head she turned to Evan, her voice weary. "I have to get back, we have friends to dinner this evening and I promised mother that I would help her clean up."

"Oh, I see," Evan replied, bitterly disappointed. He thought that they would be spending the day together and the realisation that Benita had other plans was a terrible blow.

"I leave tomorrow," he said feebly. Just in case she had forgotten, sure that she could not be so cruel.

Benita pulled a scrap of paper from her bag; she held it out toward him. "I realise that. Here, this is my aunt's address if you feel like putting pen to paper." She shook it impatiently at Evan who stood forlornly staring at it. He reached out with shaky fingers to take it, slipping it in his back pocket, not sure what to do next.

Benita took a step toward him. Slipping her arms around his waist she stood on tiptoe to kiss his forehead. "Take care, Evan. I hope things turn out well for you."

Before he had time to reply she was off, striding towards the far end of the village, not looking back across her shoulder, not even once.

Evan, dumbfounded, watched her leave. As she rounded the bend out of view he felt the monstrous reality hit him. He would probably never see her again. That was it; she was gone. Benita was history and it hurt like hell. Total abandonment. He felt his eyes sting and he struggled to compose himself. The need for his mother had never been greater; in that instant he became painfully aware just how much he had missed her. He didn't want to get through another night. He needed to be boarding the plane for home now, falling into his mother's arms and letting her reassure him that everything would be ok.

He headed back. Every step required his full attention, it was an effort. He held tightly onto his tears, not allowing them to spill, afraid to let his feelings surface. It was easier to feel angry with Benita right now but he couldn't even muster the energy for anger as he plodded back in the crippling heat.

In the years to come Evan would marvel as to why he took a detour before returning to his father's house that day. Yet at that moment in time, it seemed a perfectly sensible thing to do, when his whole world was crashing around his ears and emotions stormed his body with such ferocity they churned his stomach and immobilised his limbs. The most obvious reaction seemed to be to run from the pain and to put as much distance between oneself and the cause of one's distress. Evan had faced pain on numerous occasions before today and in the past he had buried it, dug a hole so deep in his sub-conscious and left it there, where he had hoped it would rot and die. Something he had learnt was a fallacy. On this occasion, pretending it didn't hurt would not suffice and, whether acting out of misery or anger, he chose a new option. Something he had never anticipated before. Evan looked for a diversion, somewhere to channel all the negative energy that was bubbling up in his young troubled mind. A vent for the cruelty inflicted on him. He needed to halt this misery and in a way he acted out of instinct. What does one do when their whole world has just shattered into a million pieces?

# CHAPTER 8

The dust rising up from the rugged track lodged in Evan's throat. He stumbled along a little further, before stopping to catch his breath and ease the stitch that nagged at his side. Finally, as he reached the brow of the hill, his destination was in sight. With renewed vigour and the advantage of a downward slope he picked up pace.

Relieved to find that nobody appeared to be home he licked his salty lips in anticipation. He had guessed correctly she always went to market on a Saturday and wouldn't return much before five. That would mean over three hours of undisturbed indulgent snooping.

The door, as he had presumed, was locked. Eyeing the house much as a burglar would, he looked for a good point of entry. Dropping his rucksack from his back with a soft thud he deposited it beneath the candy pink geraniums and circled the quiet house.

Around to the left of the house a bathroom window had been left ajar. With minimum effort he rose up onto the sill and reached through to widen the gap. Squeezing through, Evan landed agile as a cat onto the stone floor the other side.

Cautiously he tiptoed along the hallway, peering sideways at the aged prints of barren landscapes that adorned the walls. At the far end he reached a heavy wooden door with an ornate cast iron handle. Pushing it gingerly, he was surprised at the ease with which the door swung open, and then he found himself looking in on the sitting room. Momentarily he found himself rooted to the spot as he took in the pale blue sofas draped with lamb's wool throws and the chunky wooden chest that doubled as a coffee table, on which stood a simple glass vase packed with vibrant sunflowers. On the mantle stood a heavy oak clock, above it a portrait.

The face that looked down at him caused him to gasp. The seductive lips drawn back into a smile, her eyes leapt from the canvas toward him. He recognised her instantly and moved closer to marvel at her beauty. Hypnotised by the magnetic eyes, so green they made him blink and then willed him to smile, to forget his immediate troubles. Running his fingers with a deep, aching sensitivity across the canvas, he traced her cheekbones, feeling their sharp angular rise as his fingertips skimmed across them and he experienced a warm rush to his genital region. Pressing a finger tenderly at her lips he felt the knot in his stomach tighten. He yearned to kiss them.

Slowly he turned to look around the room, well-kept and organised, filled with femininity and sexuality. The air was sweet and floral with the unusual aroma of toasted almond. It was soothing and exciting at the same time. His anger diminished as he began to mould to his surroundings, an air of welcome calm enveloping him.

When he could tear himself away from the moment he moved to the kitchen where it resembled organised chaos, the cupboards' contents visible through panes of frosted glass, some cracked. A gingham curtain with ruffled edges and snagged threads below the sink hid a collection of cleaning fluid and bleach; the sink, stained brown at the edges, was damaged to one side. Another vase of sunflowers sat above the magnificent fireplace, its opening so huge Evan could stand inside it at full height. Vegetables of every colour sat on the worktop, their plump flesh and vibrant colours awakening his senses, something vaguely erotic about their presence. A half-eaten loaf stood on the bread board, the ivory handled knife used to cut it left awkwardly by its side, a sharp reminder of his prying.

At the far end of the kitchen, draped across the arched doorway, daisy patterned voiles hung tantalisingly, separating him from more exploring. He went across to draw it aside. Intoxicated with anticipation, he looked in on the bedroom that lay beyond. A huge cast iron bed with a deep comfortable mattress, littered with dark mauve, red and gold velvet cushions stacked majestically high. The dark wooden furniture here looked ugly, too harsh in such a small room. It would be better suited to a castle, he thought, sitting down on the edge of the bed, trying his weight against the bed and impressed by the feel. Running his fingers along the heavy bedspread and then along the pillows, he drew breath and let them linger as he dared to imagine stroking her fine strawberry hair, in a moment of tenderness, combing his fingertips through to the ends.

Evan went across to the wardrobe, throwing open the doors, enabling him to touch her clothes. They were hung in meticulous order according to colour from chocolate brown to ivory white, each colour from vibrant to pastel in its correct place. He admired her organisation here, everything perfect, a reflection of Alexis herself. He moved across to the chest of drawers where he dived trembling fingers into yards of silk. Plucking a flimsy pair of buttermilk panties from the others, he stuffed them hurriedly into his pocket. A souvenir of his visit, he thought greedily. Standing back to survey the room, silently enticed by the undeniable tingle that rippled downward from his navel, he took a long languishing breath of her heady scent, which lingered heavily in the air. There was a cry from somewhere outside. He paused, cocking his head to one side. He could hear splashing, not gentle, more frantic. He felt a rising panic, Jesus he couldn't be caught snooping. Then there was silence. He waited a few moments. He spotted the glass on the dresser by the bed, which contained an inch of ruby liquid. Picking it up, he held it gingerly toward the light. The imprint of Alexis' lips was still visible on the rim of the glass, sending a shiver down his spine. Gently he took the glass to his own lips, placing them precisely where hers had once been. He tasted the remnants of wine, let it trickle between his lips and down his gullet like a meandering stream, held the warm sensation in his mouth. Allowing it to coat his tongue and roll across the roof of his mouth before effortlessly it slid down his throat, hot and sticky.

Stimulated, sexually aroused, he plunged onto the bed, collapsing amongst the cushions, their softness exciting every nerve ending in his body. Evan did not wish to rouse from this heightened state as he languished on her bed, his body pricked with fiery sensations. The intenseness he did not understand, but it felt so good and he wanted to relish every tremor that shook his body.

He left by the same window, pushing it partially closed just how he had found it. Sad to be leaving, he looked back several times, seeing only what he wanted to see, and it wasn't until he reached the brow of the hill he stood for a moment to take in the view, adamant that he would never forget this place and all he had witnessed, but there was an image he had seen, noticed it from the corner of his eye. He turned and headed back toward his father's house, the journey slow and unwilling. It came again, the cry, the splashing, the word it formed in his mind *help*. No, it was the guilt, he saw nothing and he heard nothing; that was it, just so, and he did the burying trick. It was, of course, the safest option.

Jack was home. Evan found him busy in the kitchen unpacking groceries.

"Hi there, lad. Hope you are feeling hungry; I have a mountain of food here."

Evan sat down at the table. He nodded as Jack passed him a glass of wine.

"Your last night eh, bet you're looking forward to leaving your miserable excuse of a father?" He went back to the unpacking, not daring to wait for Evan's reply.

Evan took a sip of the wine; it tasted strong and spicy.

"I will miss this place," he said finally as he looked around the kitchen. Jack turned to smile at him. "I sure have missed mother though," he added, careful to catch his father's eye.

"Yeah, well of course you have." Jack shrugged, as he started to peel the carrots. "Bet she has missed you too, lad."

She would have missed him too. More than Evan would ever know, he thought with a heavy sigh.

Evan went to his room to change. He packed up the rest of his things, leaving out a set of clothes for the next day. With a deep shuddering breath, he sat down on the bed and looked at his bulging case. How much he had grown as a person since he first packed it somewhat begrudgingly for the journey out here. Finally it seemed he was maturing, seeing the world from a different perspective. All the anger that had seethed inside his belly was beginning to leave. The familiar nagging had subsided. It felt strange, it had been with him for so long but it was pointless clinging on to it. He knew that now, even though there was an unusual emptiness settling in its place.

What he failed to realise, didn't or couldn't see, was that a new anger had invaded the old. It had stolen inside him and was lurking in the dark spaces of his mind. In addition, he was subconsciously doing everything in his power to keep it there. Anything but accept that Benita had awakened his sexual emotions, then unceremoniously dumped him and that it made him boil with rage every time he thought about her.

As he looked around the bedroom an envelope propped against the mirror caught his eye, which he hadn't noticed until now. He went over and reached across. His name was scrawled across the front and it was sealed. It looked like his father's writing. A letter, he wondered? A faint smile crept across his lips; it must be his father's way of making peace. Perhaps his father had decided to share his innermost feelings; obviously, he found it difficult to talk to Evan face to face so he had decided to write it all down in a letter. He thought about opening it there and then, keen to know what Jack was feeling right now. Slowly he took it over to his rucksack and slipped it inside. He would read it tomorrow when he was on the plane. Before he could change his mind, he zipped up the bag and went out to join his father in the kitchen.

Jack had put a lot of effort into their final meal together. They ate out on the terrace, where Jack had laid the table. A lantern stood in the centre of the table, casting a warm glow which fell across their faces as they ate.

"What do you think then?" Jack watched as Evan speared some of the steak and dipped it in the garlic sauce.

"Really good, I am impressed. Mum never told me you could cook."

"Ah well." Jack paused to take a sip of the wine, "Probably because I didn't cook much in those days, lad. I only started to dabble in the kitchen since I moved out here. I find it relaxing, to tell the truth. I don't do it enough though, but it always seems so pointless when it is just for one person."

Evan looked up, catching the shadow of remorse that crossed his father's face.

"Do you get lonely?" Evan asked, surprised.

Jack put down his fork; he looked through the darkness out across the valley.

"Yeah suppose I do." He shifted uneasily on his seat. "That sounds terribly selfish, doesn't it? Especially given recent events?" Jack took a deep breath. "I am sorry that I hurt you, laddie." He looked across to Evan, a tear in his eye. It was the story of his life, he never realised what he had until it was too late. If he wasn't such a selfish old git his life could have been a hell of a lot different. However, he reminded himself, he was Jack Bailey. He had never done anything thing the right way in his whole Goddamn life.

Evan felt sorry for his father; he saw the sadness in his eyes, felt the heavy ache in his heart. He wanted to tell him in that moment, that he forgave him and that he was glad that his mother had sent him here. That he had had the chance to get to know him and that one day he would return, but the words were lodged in his throat, so instead he took a sip of wine and followed his father's wistful gaze across the valley.

"Looks like someone is having a party tonight." Jack signalled to the stream of car headlights crossing the valley below them. They watched the small convoy of vehicles trickle along the track and rise up the side of the far hill, then drop down out of sight on the other side.

"Must be going to Alexis' house." Jack topped up their glasses. "Good old Alexis, she always was a bit of a party animal." He gave a gentle laugh.

"I thought you were friends with her. How come you didn't get an invite?" Evan asked with interest.

"Not friends, more of an acquaintance really, I should say." Jack stood up, bored with the conversation. "Come on, let's go inside, it's getting a bit nippy out here. Fancy a brandy, lad?"

Evan lay awake for hours listening to the soft hum of crickets below the window. This time tomorrow this would all be a distant memory. Jack, Benita and Foggy would be a picture in his mind that over time would fade. It would be back to the humdrum of everyday life. *God,* he thought with sudden fright. *It won't be normal, anything but.* He was going to have to get a job and start earning a living. The though hadn't really sunk in till now and for a moment he wasn't sure if he wouldn't rather stay here with Jack. Nice thought, but not really an option, he decided, rolling onto his side and it wasn't long before his thoughts wandered back to Benita.

Fittingly the sky overhead was cloudy the next morning as he wandered outside to find Jack pouring two glasses of orange juice.

"Morning, Evan, do you fancy some bacon and eggs to keep you going till you get back home?"

"No, to tell the truth I am still full up from last night," he said, pulling up a chair and plonking himself down.

Jack leant across to tousle Evans hair. Evan experienced his father's playful touch like an electric shock, he could never recall Jack touching him with a hint of affection ever before.

"Mmm, well how about a slice of toast then?" Jack called after him as he disappeared inside the house, desperate to compose himself as tears threatened to fall.

Evan returned in time to watch his father finish his breakfast, which was swimming in a plate of oil. He took a deep breath, swallowing the nausea which rose in his throat.

"Sounds like we have company, lad," Jack remarked at the sound of a car pulling up at the front of the house. A few moments later Foggy appeared with an awkward grin. Ignoring Jack who rose to his feet, offering a handshake, he sat down next to Evan.

"Just wanted to pop in and say goodbye, have a safe

journey and all that." He leant across the table and helped himself to a slice of buttered toast.

"Thanks, Foggy, I have got your address and I will write to you."

"Yeah you do that, lad. Let me know how things work out for you." He patted Evan's arm affectionately. "Well I better get off now. Watch how you go, lad." He winked at Evan then turned to leave. Evan got up and followed him to his car.

"Thanks, Foggy, for making me so welcome. If you ever come back to England you must promise you will come and see me."

"Yeah likewise, son, if you ever dare come back here." Foggy arched his brow and jerked his head in the direction of the house. "Oh and I wanted to say, don't let Benita get to you Evan. I know she is being kind of weird about you leaving."

Evan shrugged. "That's an understatement."

Foggy gave a wide grin. "That's women for you. Truth is I think she is kind of hung up about you leaving, though she would never admit it. Still her loss, eh Evan." He punched the air. "Chin up, lad. Plenty more fish in the sea, that's what I say. You take care now."

Evan watched him drive away. "Thanks Foggy," he said aloud. Jack joined him at the gate.

"Funny guy that one!" Jack shook his head. Evan ignored his comment, they were leaving for the airport shortly, and he didn't want to end on a bad note.

Jack loaded Evan's stuff into the back of the car. He turned to see a green Land Rover pulling up behind him, raising a hand when he recognised Alan Rose from down the valley.

"Morning, Alan. You are out and about early this morning, no problems I hope?"

"Yes early and yes big problems!" Alan came across to shake his hand, his swollen belly hanging over the waist of his cotton shorts. "Take it you haven't heard the latest news."

"Can't say I have, usual thing is it?" Jack asked with a playful wink. Then he noticed Alan's arched brow.

"Wish it was. No, something far more serious, Jack. Alexis has been found dead."

"What? Dead! I mean when, where…" Jack's knees weakened and he leaned against the car for support.

"Found at home, floating in her pool, last night. Be honest Jack, word is out that it's foul play."

"What, like murder you mean?" Jack hissed the words, taking a step back. Alan lunged forward, noticing how white Jack had become; he slipped a supporting arm around his waist.

"Yes, shocking isn't it, come on." He steered him toward the house. "I think a stiff drink is called for." Sitting Jack down he went in search of alcohol and ran into Evan coming out of the house.

"Oh sorry, I didn't realise Jack had company." He extended a hand. "Alan Rose, a neighbour from down the valley."

"Oh, nice to meet you, I'm Evan." He gave the older gentleman a polite nod before adding "Jack's son."

"Well, Evan, I don't suppose you would know where to locate a couple of glasses and some brandy would you?"

Evan brought the drinks out to the terrace. "Good man." Alan nodded. "I'm afraid poor Jack, your father," he corrected himself, "Has had a bit of a shock. Well, we all have, to tell the truth. Just found out a friend of ours has passed away."

"Oh that is terrible, sorry to hear that." Evan looked across at his father, whose face was ashen; he was visibly shaken. He didn't want to be unsupportive but suddenly it didn't look like Jack would be up to driving him to the airport. He checked his watch, there was still a bit of time. Mind you if he was going to have to make alternative plans it would be better sooner rather than later.

Jack silently clutched his glass of brandy. Alan finished his and poured himself another. He looked across at Jack.

"I was just the same when I found out, takes a while to get your head round it."

"I don't understand. I mean I only saw her the other day, she looked…" he shrugged. "She looked great."

Alan banged down his glass. "Yeah, couldn't agree more, but you're forgetting this could be a murder case."

Evan's ears pricked up. "Murder," he shivered. "That sounds creepy."

"Mmm, well we don't know for sure; let's not jump to conclusions eh?" Jack shot Alan a look and stood up. "Look, I hate to be rude Alan, but Evan has a plane to catch. I will call in on my way back, perhaps you will know more by then."

Jack didn't say a word to Evan until they reached the main road. "You can't believe everything Alan says, he gets a bit carried away sometimes. Pays too much attention to the local gossip, thrives on it in fact." He gave a knowing grin.

"Oh I see, well I hope he isn't right, it would be pretty scary having a murderer on the prowl." He settled back to enjoy his final views of the majestic mountains as they headed south, his thoughts constantly drifting back to Benita. He didn't care to ask who was dead, he felt half dead himself; it was just too complicated.

The airport was busy, with the summer season nearly at its end; droves of tourists hurried around departures in search of luggage trolleys, of which it appeared there was a dire shortage. Evan was glad he wouldn't need one, as he joined the seemingly endless queue at check in. Jack stood with him but he was distant, distracted no doubt by Alan's news.

Evan couldn't help feeling disappointed if Alan could have just left it a bit longer. Now it had overshadowed his departure. Jack was somewhere else.

At the desk, Evan handed over his ticket and passport. Suddenly he felt overwhelmed by sadness. He would love to stay here with his father but he knew he had been here long enough. He prayed his father would beg him to stay but he remained unusually quiet and Evan had no choice to accept he was really on his way home.

Jack directed Evan to a coffee bar and then took his son's hand. "This is where I say goodbye, son." He squeezed his son's hand between his own. "It's been an honour to get to know you, Evan, and if you ever want to visit again just let me know."

Evan felt a lump rise in his throat. He struggled to remain calm, his father's words echoing in his head. It seemed sincere even though Jack was not looking directly at him; instead, he stared down at his dusty shoes.

"Thanks for putting me up, father. I know we didn't get off to a good start but I am so glad we have had the chance to get to know one another. It means a lot to me and who knows, if mother was not so poorly all the time, maybe we would have had more of a chance. But you know how it is, I am all she has right now."

Jack did know, only too well; she had ruined Evan. He had wanted to tell him so for the last couple of weeks. To be able to put Evan straight about a few things, but the damage was done now and there really was no going back. Evan was on the brink of making his own way in the world and he had survived this long without Jack. No, he thought, shaking his head, it was best left.

Evan shifted uneasily, Jack sensed his discomfort. "Ok then, lad, safe journey." He leant forward, hesitant for a moment, before putting an arm around Evan's shoulders and risking an uneasy hug. Evan felt tears prick his eyes as his body began to shake.

"Bye, father," he said hurriedly, turning on his heel, not daring to look up as he made his way through the haze of tears to the departure gate.

Jack watched his son walk away as he chewed uneasily on his lip, keeping his emotion in check. "Bye, son," he called after the skinny young man with a battered rucksack on his back.

# CHAPTER 9

*Spring, 23 years later*

Caroline Bailey seated herself next to the window so that she would be able to catch her husband's eye the moment he entered the coffee bar where they had arranged to meet. Twisting her hands nervously in her lap she waited; he was late as usual and her confidence was beginning to fail her. Growing increasingly hesitant she gave a sigh of relief when she finally spotted him ambling through the doorway in an unhurried fashion. He saw her and smiled in recognition, coming across to kiss her cautiously on each cheek before sitting down.

"I am so sorry, Caroline. I was about to leave the gallery and I know I always manage to be late but…"

She held up her hand, indicating for him to be quiet. "It doesn't matter Evan, you are here now." She looked across at him with a weary smile, a nervous glow highlighting her angular cheek bones. Caroline noticed how painfully thin her husband had become, it showed in his face; he was looking gaunt and pale. She felt desperately sorry for him but there was no longer any love and she could prolong his agony no further.

"Evan, I cannot do this anymore. I agreed to this trial separation to ease your pain but I have had enough now, I know this is never going to work." She looked hopelessly across at him.

"I know," he replied, head bowed, avoiding her gaze. "I knew that was what you were going to say when you brought our meeting forward. You know I am heartbroken, it is destroying but I can't make you love me." He picked up a menu and studied the extensive list of coffees, the print becoming a blur in front of his eyes. There was an uncomfortable silence until the waiter appeared to take their order. Abruptly Evan stood up, brushed a hand through the air in a pointless gesture and looked down at his wife. "I'm off, no point in polite conversation; guess I will have to find myself a lawyer. I take it you intend to stay in the house?"

Caroline looked up at him. Once she had loved him but now she felt only pity, she didn't love him anymore but it didn't ease the pain. "No Evan, I moved out yesterday." She handed him her set of keys, "Move back whenever you want. I would like to keep the car if that is ok with you."

"Yes, yes," he replied, shocked at her decision and her clipped tone. "Where will you live?" he asked, suddenly concerned, totally bewildered.

"I am going to stay with my sister for a while, then – well, then I don't know but you love that house Evan, it was left to you by your mother. It is your house, it wouldn't seem right for anyone to be there except you."

He nodded. He was glad, there were so many memories there it would be easier to grieve for Caroline and their marriage in those familiar surroundings. He turned and left. He hated goodbyes and there really seemed very little he could say right now.

Evan headed back to the car. He needed to go home, work could wait; he wanted to go and lick his wounds in privacy. He stopped off at a shop for a bottle of wine and some cigarettes before heading west to the small cottage at the top of the cliff that he called home, but for how long? he wondered.

Letting himself in to the cramped hallway where the familiar smell of his life invaded his nostrils, the door closed on the outside world and then the enormity of it all hit him square in the chest, the wave of emotion, the overpowering sense of defeat. The place felt frightfully empty, cold and indifferent. Switching on the central heating as he passed he headed to the kitchen, grabbed a corkscrew and glass then headed to the study, a small cosy room with a large window which looked out across the rocky bay below.

The sea was angry and grey today like his mood, as it crashed against the worn rocks its violent hiss echoed around the still house. He took a large gulp of the wine then looked down at the glass in his hand. In it was his enemy, alcohol, the root of all evil, yet somehow it always made him feel better. Evan wondered if he would ever manage to curb this habit. He didn't blame Caroline; he had issues, he knew that. It was his childhood. He sometimes wondered how he had ever gone on to have a successful business. Not that it mattered anymore now that he was alone. It was all so fresh in his mind; the visit to his father's, the hope that things would be different in the future. He had not been back two weeks from Spain when his mother had announced she had found a new man. Harry, as it had turned out, had been quite a decent human being and if anything Evan had been glad for his mother. The trip to a spiritual retreat had been nothing short of miraculous for her. On Evan's return he had found a different woman in his mother's place. Finally she had found some faith in life and whatever they had filled her head with had worked. It was all beyond Evan at the time but he understood it more as time went by. It was apparent that Harry had had the most to do with her healing and that love had been the perfect cure. It should have been a good thing for Evan to have his mother in good shape but before he had the chance to digest the change in her being, the terrible news had arrived from Spain that his father had died and in a fleeting moment all of his hopes had been shattered. In turn he came to despise his mother and Harry, especially Harry, who, despite his efforts of compassion, could never take the place of his father.

Evan finished his glass of wine and looked out toward the sea where the choppy waters met the grey horizon in violent unison. He had survived, gone on to be a successful artist, his pain and hurt alighting in an emotional outpouring on the canvas before him. Caroline had brought normality back into his life but now she had deserted him too, unable to cope with his drinking and pain and the torturous nightmares from which he suffered.

Crossing to the mantel he looked at his reflection in the mirror. He looked, he realised, worn out. He ran his fingers through his hair. The once gawky sixteen-year-old had matured into a strong frame with a broad angular face. He was no movie star and he laughed at the thought but he could certainly paint, not as if that was of any importance now. But looking as he did today, he wouldn't get a second glance. He shook his head, he loved Caroline and he knew exactly why, what had attracted him to her. Quite simply she had reminded him of Benita, his first love. Caroline was as fair as Benita was dark and as timid as Benita was confident but they both had a waif-like vulnerability and now both had left a void in his heart.

Thinking of Caroline now just made him crave her more than ever. Tears threatened, he struggled to keep them at bay, that too familiar lump lodged in his throat. Evan fought the wave of emotion. He needed to escape, so pulling on his worn woollen jacket he headed down to the cove.

The wind grew spiteful against his cheeks as he picked his way along the narrow path, placing each foot with care through the upturned stones, clumps of jagged rock and tangled weed as the route ahead wound steeply down toward the shingle bedded shore line.

Evan stood at the water's edge, bracing against the foamy spray as it spat its salty breath toward him. He welcomed the ocean's assault, a sharp reminder of another failure. Alone, the roar of the sea drowned out all other sounds, even the feline shriek of the gulls gathering overhead. He scrabbled onto a flat rock. its surface worn smooth by the tide, and lay back to feel the ancient stone's coldness against his flesh despite the thickness of his jacket. It had been here longer than him and as one, at last he could lose himself to the sound of the ocean.

Then she was there, a clear vision in his mind invading his privacy. Alexis, with her strawberry mane blowing in the breeze, her coffee limbs flitting lithely before him, seemingly walking on air. He blinked furiously against the vision which had stolen into his mind so many times, fought her, tried to block her image to no avail.

"Leave me," he demanded silently, and in an instant she was gone.

Abruptly he stood up, looking desolately at the hard climb home and then regretting his decision to come down here in the first place. Plunging his hands deeper into his pockets he started back, his mind confused as he stumbled along kicking loose boulders, his feet raking through the carpet of weed. Why did she always appear uninvited? It was so long ago and yet she was still there haunting him. It was unsettling in moments of stillness but the nightmares were the worst. Evan could not sleep one night without her being there; she appeared so solid he could almost reach out and touch her.

Once he had painted her but the canvas had become so alive, each fleck of oil becoming a swarm of energy. She had stared into his eyes, delved into his mind; it had been too much to bear and it was the only piece of his work that he had ever burnt.

He reached the top of the cliff and looked back down at the incoming tide. Over the last twenty three years one thing had become apparent, something Evan had noticed quite by chance.

The apparitions of Alexis haunted him, he struggled to understand their meaning but for some reason he had come to realise they were stronger, more powerful on the eve of a new moon. It was an odd observation but nonetheless true and over time he had come to dread the arrival of each new lunar cycle. The woman wanted his soul, he was sure of it, but sometimes he wondered was there even a soul for the taking.


"You are a total ass, you know that don't you, Ed?" She rolled over onto her side, angrily pulling the sheet over her head.

Ed sat down on the edge of the bed rubbing his unshaven chin. "Oh my little wild cat, don't be so feisty, I'm not that late tonight." He chuckled softly, looking down at her.

"You are always late - always." Benita buried her head into the pillow and began to sob. She seemed to be making a habit of this. What was it about her, why did she always attract the wrong sort? Ed had to be the worst; he couldn't keep a promise to her if he tried.

"You don't mean it, darling." He slid his hand beneath the sheet, running his fingertips along her silky thigh, expertly prising her legs apart causing her to moan. It was no good, she couldn't fight him; she didn't want to. Benita turned to face him. She wanted to be angry, his behaviour was unacceptable but he would win this fight the way he always did. She gave in to him, curled her body against his, writhed beneath his touch.

Later, when he lay sleeping beside her, she drew a deep berating breath, hating herself for being so weak. Benita knew her life would be ruined if she didn't do something about the situation but her inner strength evaded her and always she forgave.

It was her fortieth birthday next month and what had she to show for her life? Having bummed from job to job she had settled as a secretary in a small accountancy firm in Glasgow, the money from which she earned barely paying her living expenses. Every relationship she had ever had, had failed miserably. Love had somehow eluded her. Instead of getting better it got definitely worse. She shifted restlessly with her thoughts for she knew she must end this relationship with Ed, soon; if not now it must be by the morning.

When Benita roused from her fitful sleep Ed had already left for work. She took a mug of coffee through to the living room, deciding to write Ed a letter. Then she leafed through her address book. She really should call Connie, she needed support.

Connie had been her best friend through college and although they often called or wrote, somehow they hadn't seen each other for years. Connie had got married two years ago, when she left Scotland to set up home with her new husband in Somerset. Somehow they had managed to lose contact. Benita always seemed to be caught up between work and her complicated love life. Connie was into antenatal classes and extra support tights. They were worlds apart now.

Connie's husband Ben answered the phone. "Benita darling, is that you? How absolutely fantastic to hear from you. I'm afraid that Connie isn't here right now but she will be very sorry she missed your call."

Benita took a deep breath. "Well actually Ben, I was

going to ask an enormous favour of you both. I wondered if there was the remotest chance that I could come and stay with you guys for a few days. I wouldn't get in the way - promise."

Ben was silent for a moment, then he started to laugh. "Of course you can honey. In fact I couldn't think of anything better right now. Connie could use some support, things haven't been going too well with the pregnancy. Be honest I think its stress so your visit could be the perfect distraction."

Benita gave a thankful inward sigh. If he had said no she would have been desolate. "Fantastic Ben, I will be with you by this evening."

"I take it you will be flying down?" Ben enquired.

"So long as I can get a flight. I will grab a taxi from the airport so see you soon, Ben."

The moment Evan opened his eyes he remembered the events of the day before. "It's actually over!" He said the words out loud in disbelief. What would he do without Caroline; suddenly life didn't seem worth living. He looked across at her side of the bed, so vacant and sad. She should have been waking, stretching her limbs like a cat in the sun and looking across at him with a gentle smile. He had never appreciated those simple things. Waking together, greeting a new day, sharing breakfast on the veranda as the sun crept from behind the hills. He sat up, rubbing fiercely at his eyes; he couldn't think about those things for if he did he was afraid he wouldn't get through the day. Instead he grabbed a towel and headed for the shower in the hope that the waters would somehow wash away all the hurt. When he emerged, towel tied at his waist, he saw a letter had been delivered; it lay on the front door mat. The air mail stamp caught his eye and he stooped down to pick it up. The post mark read Espana. Suddenly intrigued Evan tore it open and pulled out a very official-looking letter, the contents of which sent him reeling back on to the staircase where he plonked himself down and re-read the letter again and for good measure once more.

Benita caught the six thirty flight and landed on time at Bristol. As she settled back in her seat the cab driver made polite conversation but she didn't hear his words; she was thinking about Ed and her note. He would have found it by now and she could only imagine the stream of obscenities coming from his sexy crooked mouth. On cue her mobile rang. She looked down at the display flashing angrily that it was indeed Ed and promptly switched it off. Benita gave a deep sigh before settling back down to admire the countryside and then smiled as she saw the Tor rising majestically on the horizon and she knew they were getting close. Numerous times Connie had mentioned that they lived at the foot of the hill on which the Tor stood. Suddenly Benita was excited. She had always wanted to visit Glastonbury and she had missed her long girlie chats with Connie so much.

They pulled up at a shabby-looking cottage. Benita paid the driver and dragged her suitcase toward the front door, which flew open and a rather larger Connie than she remembered stood screeching in excitement.

"Benita, sweetheart! Oh I couldn't believe my eyes when I saw you climbing out of that taxi." She wrapped her arms enthusiastically around Benita. "Oh come inside, we have so much to talk about."

Benita smiled at Connie; she looked well despite what Ben had told her on the phone.

"Oh look at you!" Benita crooned, stroking her friend's swollen belly. "How long do you have left?"

"Six weeks and six weeks too long," Connie replied, looking down at herself, "I don't intend to repeat this in a hurry." she said lowering her voice as Ben appeared smiling.

"Benita darling!" He swept over to kiss Benita on each cheek. "You made it in one piece then? So come on, put me out of my misery. What is it, boyfriend trouble?"

"Ben," Connie gave her husband a disapproving glare, "don't be so rude, I am sure Benita will tell us in her own time."

"I wasn't being rude," Ben said sulkily, "I merely was stating the obvious."

Benita cut him short. "You're absolutely right Ben, spot on, it is boyfriend trouble but that isn't why I chose to come here and see you both." She grinned at Ben, who was standing with arms folded, smiling smugly to himself. "No I wanted to come and see Connie before the baby comes and you are all wrapped up in bottles and dirty nappies. It just happens that the boyfriend, or rather ex, gave me the perfect excuse."

"So I am right," Ben exclaimed in delight before poking out his tongue at his wife and heading back to the study.

"I think you have forgotten something," Connie screeched, looking down at Benita's suitcase. "Go on, be a love, that looks far too heavy for a wee girl like Benita to carry up a spiral staircase." With a sarcastic smile Ben headed off with the case leaving both girls sniggering, just like old times.

"So what would you like to drink? No, silly question, if it's man trouble it's got to be wine but I am afraid I won't be able to share it with you, even though I could murder a glass - along with that pathetic little husband of mine of course." Both women started to giggle. Benita was glad she had come. Connie always managed to put a smile on her face.

Ben kept a low profile during the evening, leaving the women to catch up on gossip, apart from being sent out to the village for some more wine, which led to him appearing every so often from the study for a sneaky top up.

Benita retired to bed, drunk but proud of her self-control. She had ignored all of Ed's frantic calls. She took a final look at her mobile. Ten missed calls, all of them from Ed. She couldn't resist a satisfied smirk as she leant across to switch off the bedside lamp. What a loser.

The sound grew louder until it became a high pitched whistle, not an earthly sound at all. Evan covered his ears, rocking back and forth in the darkness. He dared to open his eyes, he saw her. She surveyed him from the foot of the bed in a halo of brilliant light.

"Go away, leave me alone."

He prayed she would disappear. Panic gripped him; she had grown stronger. Then she spoke. This had never happened before. He held his breath; the sound was in his head.

"There is no excuse anymore, Evan. Evan, please." Her voice was muted and dark.

"What do you want?" he yelled to the still room.

Then she was gone. He blinked hard several times, looking across to the space where she had stood. Disbelief, perhaps shock, he didn't know but he cried softly, giving way to giant body wrenching sobs. What was happening to him, why was Alexis haunting him, why had Caroline left, why did everyone he cared about end up deserting him? And why had Foggy taken a drug overdose, dying alone in the middle of nowhere and left all his worldly possessions to Evan?

It was, Evan realised, his worst nightmare come true. Now he would have to go back to the mountains and face the past.

The time in Andalucia spent with his father had been life-changing in so many ways. By the time he learned of his fathe'rs death, sadly Jack had already been dead over three weeks and the funeral had been held. Worse still, the house had been cleared and Jack's possessions sold or taken to the rubbish tip. Evan had been devastated. There was nothing left of his father, only the memory of that eventful summer.

Ever since the day he returned from Spain he had fantasised of their reunion. Why had nobody contacted them sooner? Foggy would have done if he had been around but Foggy was interviewing band members in Madrid at the time. To this day Evan hadn't unravelled the mystery surrounding Jack's death. Apparently he had been fine; neighbours had seen him earlier in the day. At six that evening he had been found dead. That was the same time that Evan had learnt of Alexis' death also; he had never known that it was her. Local gossips had begun to link the two deaths and the similar circumstances, although neither case was thought suspicious.

Evan had never thought on that final day with his father it would be the last time they would ever see each other. He had left with hope in his heart.

Sitting up, folding the pillow behind his head, he reached across for his cigarettes, lit one and inhaled deeply, filling his lungs with the acrid smoke which he held until he started to choke. It billowed into the room in an eerie haze.

The letter from the solicitor, now folded in the kitchen drawer, played on his mind. He had done diddly squat about it, too shocked to make any sort of decision. Poor Foggy, why was life so terrible that he would end his life?

They had last connected at Christmas; Evan had met him for lunch in London. He seemed upbeat, happy, there was no need to feel concerned. As Evan ground out the cigarette he wondered if a trip to Spain would be as awful as he feared, perhaps a chance to lay some ghosts to rest, hopefully Alexis. Her words echoed in his head. What did she mean? It was as if she knew he was going to Spain, wanted him to go but why? The whole thing seemed absurd and perhaps his behaviour even more so. He laughed; that must be it, he was going mad. Caroline leaving had been the final straw and he had finally lost the plot. He crawled out of bed toward the shower. He was mad long before now, he figured he must be growing madder, yes that had to be it.

# CHAPTER 10

"Well I can't come back yet, I'm not ready!"

"What do you mean you're not ready, you can't dictate to me when you come back, I have a business to run Benita. Do you want to keep this job or not?" Tested, the voice on the other end of the line drew in anxious breath and waited.

Benita chewed nervously on her jagged thumbnail. "Well, in that case you can stick your job, yep, absolutely I have had enough. I bloody well hate it and as for you, well you're nothing but a moody hormonal old bag, you are so anal and you have never liked me." Sucking in breath she hesitated, finally chorusing, "Good riddance." Benita trembled all over. Had she just made an irreversible decision, a terrible mistake? Most definitely from a financial point of view but for the sake of her sanity, most definitely it was the best decision ever.

At that moment Connie arrived in the hallway carrying a wicker basket full of laundry.

"Did I hear that right? Hormonal old bag, did I really hear you say that Benita?"

"Yes Connie you did, my boss, Margaret!"

"Ughm, so do I take it that Margaret is now no longer your boss?" she asked, smiling.

"Correct," Benita replied sheepishly.

Connie set the basket down on the table next to her. "Looks like I better make coffee, I need to know all about this, it sounds kind of interesting."

Benita stood up. "No, you sit down and put your feet up for a moment, I'll make the coffee. Besides there is nothing to tell really," she said, spooning instant into two mugs. "I hate working in that dingy little office, I hate the job, God I hate that job and I have been brooding over just how much I hate it for weeks." She looked quizzically across at Connie for a moment. "Have I outstayed my welcome here? After all I did originally say a week and I have been here nearly a month now."

"Benita, you can stay as long as you like, you know that. I'm not surprised you lost your job honey, I don't suppose your boss feels quite as amicable as me."

"I didn't lose my job, I jacked my job, big difference!" Benita reminded her. "Anyhow, I was thinking of putting the flat on the market too and moving down here, nearer to you. This place has sort of grown on me."

Connie gave a shriek of delight. "You're kidding, that would be wicked! Oh Benita, I would love it if you came to live down here. I could help you find a house, oh it will be so much fun."

"Well I have to sell my place first and that might take a while. The baby will be a few months old by then and you will be to grips with this motherhood lark and we can go out house hunting together." Benita handed her a mug of coffee then sat down beside her, thoughtful. "I am forty next year, Connie, and what have I got to show for it?"

"I know love," Connie soothed, "but things can change so quickly. I agree you need a fresh start and more importantly you need to stay away from arses like Ed."

"Easier said than done!" Benita interjected with a wry smile.

Connie went on, "There is the right guy out there somewhere, and you just haven't met him yet."

"Well he best crawl out from that stone he has been hiding under, because I'm not getting any younger and if he takes much longer I will be positively past it." Benita took a sip of her coffee. "Biscuits, Connie? I need a sugar hit, the enormity of what I just did is sinking in now. Margaret must think I am a complete and utter bitch."

Connie passed the biscuit tin. "Poor Margaret." She gave Benita a sideways glance. "Guess that is just desserts for being a hormonal old bag. How dare she!" Both women exploded into fits of laughter.

Evan looked across at the easel and the half-finished painting upon it. There was no enthusiasm to pick up a brush and lose himself in his work today. Instead, he went upstairs to pack a bag. The urge to leave was totally overwhelming, and he needed to put some space between himself and this place. Where to, he had no idea, but the further the better because he really needed to put some space between himself and Caroline and this house and, if at all possible, Alexis too, who seemed to make damn sure she was getting all of his attention these days.

Every night she appeared to him as he lay alone in the dark, when his breathing calmed and his limbs unwound in that soft meditative state before sleep. She would be there at the foot of the bed, a look of urgency in her eyes. Demanding, she would hold his gaze until he could bear it no longer and be forced to look away, and when he looked back she would be gone.

Evan threw clothes into a case, shivering at the thought of her. Whatever it was that she wanted, he had a terrible feeling that she wouldn't leave him alone until she got it, but how was he to fathom out what this was? If he had refrained from snooping on her all those years ago, then this would never had happened, he reminded himself , snapping the case shut and heading out to the car.

An hour later he parked the car in Glastonbury High Street. He wondered how the hell he had managed to arrive here; he had just driven and this is where he arrived.

The sun peeped through wispy cloud, Evan welcomed the warmth on his face, a sense of peace prevailed. He locked the car, slipped the keys in his pocket and took a deep breath. He made his way down the hill, glancing down at a young girl on the corner of the street, her vacant gaze unnerving. A small dog tied by a piece of string to her belt sat beside her and wagged its tail enthusiastically at Evan, giving a soft low growl as he passed by.

Leaving the sunny street, he entered one of the shops. A heavy scent of incense caught in his throat, making him cough. He smiled at the woman with kindly eyes dressed in a flimsy summer dress who appeared from behind a pile of books. The small diamond nose piercing caught his eye and he tried not to stare at it.

"Can I help?" she asked, sensing he had absolutely no idea why he had come in here in the first place.

Shifting uneasily he gave an awkward smile, though she appeared friendly enough. "I don't know really." he paused, looking around the shop's cramped interior, across the brightly coloured selection of candles, focusing on a large crystal suspended at eye level in the far corner. "It may sound strange but I sort of ended up here. I had no intention of coming here and I'm not really sure why I did."

Her eyes twinkled in amusement as she came across to the counter, putting down the large crystal she had been threading onto a piece of ribbon.

"No that's right, nothing is ever by chance. It is good of you to be so honest. Now let us see what it could be that you need. Why fate has brought you to my shop. A crystal perhaps?" she asked, sweeping her hand across to the array of crystals positioned on a large stone, "or maybe a book." She pointed to an overcrowded bookshelf at the back of the shop.

"I have no idea!" Evan shrugged. "I very much doubt a crystal, I wouldn't know what to do with one and yes maybe a book, but like I said I have no idea what sort."

The woman circled Evan. "Are you sick?" she asked, pursing her lips, studying Evan quizzically.

"No! Well, not that I am aware of. I don't feel unwell if that's what you're asking."

"Unhappy then?" she pressed. Evan stood hesitant for a moment. "Ah, woman trouble, is that it?" Her eyes lit up when she saw the flicker in his eyes.

"That obvious, is it?" he asked, following her across the room. "Or was that just a lucky guess?"

Ignoring him she pressed something smooth in to the palm of his hand. "Here, this is what you need. Rose quartz, to help heal your heart. You must sleep with it under your pillow and," she hurried off to the book shelf, "we can find you something here as well, I am sure we can." She rifled through the books, leaving Evan turning the crystal over in the palm of his hand and wondering what on earth it could possibly do for him.

"Look, perhaps I will just take the crystal, I'm not much of a reader as it happens and I can't settle my mind to much at all at the moment."

"Oh well." She stood up to look at him, her disappointment apparent.

"Really, the crystal will be fine," he assured her.

Evan left with the crystal in his pocket, wrapped in silver tissue paper at her insistence. He crossed the street to the pub, and ordered a pint.

It was quiet inside. He sat next to the window, where he watched the comings and goings in the street. Two women with a child in a pushchair were the only other people in the bar. He smiled politely as he went to fetch another pint to satisfy his overwhelming thirst. The older smiled back, the younger simply frowned. He had just settled back down in his seat when the younger woman stood up, kissed the other woman on each cheek and prepared to leave. The sleeping child had now woken and begun wailing. Looking flustered the woman left. Evan struggled to hear their parting words over the din.

He was surprised five minutes later when the older woman came across to join him.

"May I?" She signalled to the seat opposite and proceeded to sit down.

"Of course, help yourself," he replied, smiling; she wasn't unattractive.

"I hope you don't mind me joining you?"

Evan shook his head, "No of course not."

"I am on my lunch break. My daughter could only stay for a while; it's the little one, she is teething, poor thing. Anyhow I figured you looked lonely, I thought you wouldn't mind some company."

"Can I get you something to drink?" Evan asked, suddenly remembering his manners.

"Oh, why not," her face brightened, "a glass of wine would be nice, white please."

Evan returned with her drink, "So are you a local?"

"Yes, I have lived here for ten years. I guess you could call this my spiritual home. I work in the shop at the top of the hill, have you been in there yet?"

"No, to be honest I have only just arrived. I just sort of ended up here and I went in the shop opposite and came out with this." He fished the crystal from his pocket and laid it on the table. "I'm sorry, I don't think I got your name?" he added.

"Fiona, and yours?" she asked, unwrapping the crystal and holding it up to the light.

"Evan, Evan Bailey." He offered his hand.

Fiona's hand was warm and firm there was something familiar about her touch. "Evan, that's a nice name, unusual. Well, Evan, you got yourself a nice rose quartz there." She handed it back to him.

"Oh, so you know your crystals then, Fiona. I don't have a clue myself. The lady in the shop suggested it."

Fiona began to chuckle. "Ah, Pat, yes she is very good at sorting people out. Actually she is a very clever lady. She practices healing with crystals so she knows her crystals so to speak. Why choose rose quartz? Are you looking for love?"

Evan felt himself flush. "No not exactly, I have just broken up with someone. I think she meant it for healing purposes." He shrugged. "Not that I expect it to heal my heart for one moment."

Fiona sensed his despair. "Crystals are powerful, never underestimate their power Evan! So where are you staying or are you just here for the day?"

"To be honest I don't have any firm plans but I may well hang around for a bit, it seems peaceful enough in these parts."

Fiona gave a deep throaty laugh. "Evan, this is Glastonbury, of course it's peaceful! You have come to Avalon and I am willing to guess it wasn't by chance." She drained the last of her wine. "Look, there is so much to see. Of course, you must go to the Abbey for starters and then up to the Tor, but I think that first you need a better understanding of exactly where you are. I feel a history lesson is in order. I would like to help make your stay here a pleasant and hopefully memorable one if you wouldn't mind."

Evan began to relax. "No not at all, fantastic. I would be most grateful, Fiona."

"Good, that's settled then." She stood up. "You will need a few days at least, three really to appreciate the beauty of this place so you will need somewhere to stay. I live alone and I have a spare room. If you have no objections you could stay with me, to be honest I would welcome the company."

"Well, if you're sure," Evan replied hesitantly.

"Of course I am sure or I wouldn't have asked you. So drink up and we can go up to the shop and arm you with some literature to get you started."


Benita came downstairs to find Connie bent over double in the kitchen, her face contorted with pain.

"What is it, Connie, are you ok?"

Connie looked up, beads of perspiration at her brow, her lips held tight. "No, I think it's the baby. Can you call Ben for me please?"

By the time Ben arrived Connie was sat uncomfortably on the chair, panting heavily, her face purple as another contraction consumed her body. Benita looked helplessly up at him. "Thank God you're here! I wanted to call an ambulance but she wanted to wait for you. I really think the baby is coming, I don't know what to do."

Ben leapt into action. "Right, Benita, upstairs under the bed is her case. Bring it down and grab a few towels in case, have the waters broken yet?"

Benita shook her head. "I haven't a clue, I presume not."

"Ok get those bits and meet me by the car."

Connie was sitting in the car. She smiled between sharp breaths and deep breaths. Benita threw the case on the back seat. "Good luck," she whispered, kissing her friend on the cheek.

"Call you later," Ben called, as they sped off down the lane.

Benita went back in to the house. Her legs had turned to

jelly and she had to sit down. "Thank God for Ben," she said aloud.

Searching through her bag for her cigarettes, she felt her hands trembling. When the panic subsided she headed out to the garden and sat on the bench under the apple tree, where she took several large drags on her cigarette and watched a group of people on the hillside opposite making their way up to the Tor. It was pleasantly warm. What a perfect day for Connie and Ben's baby to be born, she thought happily, looking up at the powder blue sky.

Ben called at four just as she was dozing off on the sofa in the conservatory.

"Panic over, they reckon it will be a while yet, she is only 1cm dilated. The baby is a bit early but they said it will be ok," he breathed.

"Oh good, I could have sworn she was going to have it this morning."

"Me too, anyway we are with the experts now. So make yourself at home and I will call you if there is any news."

"Please do, Ben. I mean whatever time. Let me know everything is ok won't you?"

Benita replaced the receiver. She didn't feel like sleeping now. She contemplated opening a bottle of wine but was interrupted by her mobile. Fishing it from her bag, she was horrified to see it was Ed. She hesitated for a moment before answering.

"Finally, where the hell are you, I have been worried sick." He was angry, his voice heavy with sarcasm.

"We are over," she said flatly. "So pack up and get out of my flat, post the keys through the letter box. And thanks for nothing Ed, you loser." Benita cut him off, turned off the phone and went in hunt of wine. Searching frantically through the drawer for the bottle opener, she was desperate; she needed it now to stop her body trembling.

Benita took her drink through to the conservatory; she stared up at the Tor. Before she left, she should go and see it up close. There was something quite magical up there, she could feel it. She had read about it in a magazine a few years back and now here she was sprawled on Connie's sofa gazing up at it. With a sigh Benita took a large sip of wine. If she was honest she was starting to get restless and now the baby was nearly here she would only be in the way. Taking her phone from her bag she looked down at it. Perhaps she should call Ed back and explain why she didn't want to be with him anymore. Suddenly Benita felt torn. Connie would be disappointed with her if she caved in, hell, she would be disappointed with herself, but there was a part, just the tiniest little part of her that was missing him. "No, Benita," she scolded herself, "Don't be so bloody weak." Hastily she stuffed the phone back in her bag.

Evan closed the book on his lap. He looked furtively around hoping that Pat wasn't lurking somewhere amongst the ruins as he had categorically stated that he didn't read. He had to admit that it was interesting. There was something hypnotic about being here, bathed in the warmth of the setting sun. He checked his watch, stretching his limbs from the cramped position he had been in sat on the grass. Fiona was going to meet him at the entrance of the Abbey and no doubt she would be armed with more books, determined for him to get the very best out of his stay. It was unlike him to be so indulgent; there were far more pressing matters for him to be dealing with, like the half-finished painting or going to Spain to claim his inheritance but he figured it could all wait a little longer. He needed to heal and if moping around some ancient ruins and sticking his head in an historical book was helping then he would bloody well carry on doing so.

Fiona was waiting anxiously for him and waved enthusiastically.

"I thought I might have scared you off," she said smiling as he joined her.

"No, quite the opposite, I have been swotting up on this place, soaking up the atmosphere and getting in the mood of this place."

"Come on." Fiona linked her arm through his. "I have sorted out some more bits for you to look through."

"Thought you might have," he said playfully, winking at her.

Fiona blushed, then dropping her gaze she tugged at his arm. "I got us a bottle of wine to whet our appetites for some history on the Tor and to accompany dinner, if you will join me of course?"

"I would be honoured." Evan nodded, smiling warmly across at Fiona, noticing for the first time that she had applied some make up and brushed her hair since the last time he had seen her earlier that day.

Fiona lived in a quaint cottage on the western fringes of town. Evan was pleasantly surprised by the large colourful gardens bordered by a meandering stream, a shingle path leading to the front door.

"It's a beautiful place." He admired his surroundings as she led him into the cosy living room.

"Yes, I like it. Now come through to the kitchen, I find it more comfortable there."

Fiona led him through to the airy kitchen where tied bunches of lavender hung from the ceiling and a mantel adorned with candles framed a rather antiquated Aga. She led him through the French doors, leading out to a small terrace area with a pond.

"Hey, this is really nice, Fiona. Did you decorate it?"

Fiona opened the wine and passed him a glass. "My daughter; she is an interior designer. I knew what I wanted and she helped me achieve the look. I am glad you like it." As if reading his mind she sat down opposite and explained, "I lost my husband 10 years ago. We lived in Bristol then. I hated being in the city, I have always been a country girl at heart. So when he died I sold up and moved out here. I knew the minute I saw this place I wanted it, it was like coming home."

Evan put a comforting hand over hers. "Sorry Fiona, that must have been rough."

"Oh, it's a long time ago now, but yes it was hard. So how about you Evan, you mentioned your relationship briefly, is the break up recent?"

Evan shifted uneasily, he wasn't keen to think of Caroline, he was too sore. "I am getting divorced. It's not what I want but hey, you know, these things happen."

Fiona, sensing his reluctance, decided not to push it any further. Evan was a dream. She couldn't help wondering to herself what sort of woman would give up a man like this. So instead she hauled a pile of papers from under the table and set them down before her.

"The Tor, as it happens, is my favourite place. Shrouded in myths and legends. You really have to go there to witness for yourself the extraordinary feeling. The views are magnificent; did you know that on a clear day you can see the cathedral at Wells?"

"Ah, Fiona, you know me, I am hopeless! I have only just learnt something of the Abbey here."

"How did you find it?" she asked, topping up his glass.

"Interesting, do you really believe that King Arthur was buried there?" He leant across the table to look closely at her and in turn every nerve ending in her body prickled. Alarmed by the inner stirring she looked back down at the papers on the table, avoiding his questioning gaze.

"Yes I do. The whole history of this place is fascinating and I could bore you with it for eons. Two thousand years ago the sea washed right up to the foot of the Tor, you know; in later years it receded leaving a vast lake. It was an island then and they called it Avalon, named after a demi-god who ruled the underworld. Once the meeting place of the dead, it is said. It went on to be a place for pre-Christian worship. It was there that they worshipped the goddess, as many still do here, to this day."

Evan looked suspiciously at her over the rim of his glass. "You believe all of this, do you?"

"I tell you this." Her eyes held a steady gaze with his. "One day when I was up there at the top of the Tor, sat alone lost in thought, not thinking about anything in particular I saw him, my late husband. Not six foot from where I was sitting. He smiled, he looked so serene and I knew it was really him." She paused to finish her drink. "It was quite magical and there is not a doubt in my mind about what I saw, Evan."

Evan smiled but inside his stomach began to knot. Alexis! she must have brought him here to this place; it wasn't chance after all. If it was as powerful as Fiona believed then it was perfect for Alexis. He swallowed hard and told himself to relax, she couldn't hurt him unless he let her.

# CHAPTER 11

It had grown dark; angry clouds assembled in the sky directly above him. Evan saw her amongst the ruins. She beckoned to him. Alarmed and afraid he held back beneath the shelter of the trees, hoping she would disappear. Then, closing his eyes, he counted silently to ten. He didn't dare move a muscle for some time until finally opening one eye he dared to look, but she remained there. There was something in the way she stood gazing across at him, her desperation filling the void between them. Slowly she started toward him. Shrinking back against the brittle bark of the oak tree he prayed for her to leave. The moon slid through a gap in the clouds, casting the ruins of the abbey in a ghostly glaze. In its silvery glow, she glided effortlessly toward him. He could bear it no longer, why did she haunt him like this? He wanted nothing of her. He opened his mouth to yell, he had to tell her that she must leave. There was no sound, the scream from his lips fell silent but as he lifted his hands to his face, in a sudden burst the eerie sound that left his throat in a tangled yelp made her stop; he clutched his hands to his head in desperation.

"Evan, its ok, try to breathe, there, take a big deep breath and another."

Evan felt soothing arms encircle his body, which was bathed in a damp sweat. He squinted in the semi-darkness, recognising Fiona.

"There," she soothed, stroking his hair whilst holding his heaving body against her own like a mother would hold their frightened child.

Evan rubbed fiercely at his eyes. "God, sorry Fiona," he stammered, "it was a nightmare." He looked sheepish as she switched on the bedside lamp, glad of the soft glow which lit the room.

Fiona looked at him quizzically, "Must have been a bad one, I reckon you must have woke the whole of Avalon. The scream that came from this room was blood curdling. Do you want to talk about it?"

Evan sat up, giving Fiona a lop sided grin. "I fear you would think me quite insane if I did."

"I am intrigued." She cocked her head to one side. "You must tell me, Evan. As they say, a problem shared." Her eyes pleaded with his. He gave a submissive sigh; it would feel better if he told her and somehow he knew Fiona would understand.

"It is always the same. Well, the same person at least." He swallowed hard. "She haunts me. A woman I hardly know, encountered just once, yet she haunts me. I dream of her often, it is as if she wants to share something." He twisted his fingers into the feather down duvet, painfully aware how bizarre it all sounded.

Fiona sat back on the bed, curling her feet up beneath her. "Does she speak to you then?"

"No, never. Well." He hesitated. "She did once but that wasn't a dream. I may as well tell you." He leant his head against the pine headboard and shrugged. "It sounds daft but she often appears to me. I don't know if it is just my imagination but I see her quite clearly. You see that's why I did not find it so surprising when you said you saw your late husband up at the Tor." He took a deep breath before he went on. "I met her once, a long time ago. Only for a few moments, she was interesting, perhaps more. In my weak adolescence, I was attracted to her. There was no doubt about it, she was a very sexy woman. That was all it was, just a brief encounter." He looked across at Fiona, who studied his face, her expression cautious. He smiled meekly.

"So you don't know if this woman is still alive?"

Evan looked away. "Oh yes, I know exactly what happened to her. It turned out she was a friend of my father's. She was found dead; therefore I think her ghost is haunting me. Why? I have absolutely no idea."

Fiona sat thoughtful for a moment before speaking. "It would appear to me that she has a message for you. Of course I am not experienced at this sort of thing but I certainly know of someone that can help you, Evan."

"Really, they wouldn't think me mad!"

Fiona laughed. "Quite the opposite in fact. I will try to arrange a meeting, I think if you are to ever be free of this woman you will need to find out what it is that she wants from you. Only then can her spirit rest."

Evan shivered. "It all sounds so creepy, who is this person that can help me?"

"Wait and see, there is nothing creepy about Barbara and I know she will be only too glad to help, she spends her life doing this sort of thing." Fiona leant forward, placing a light kiss on Evan's forehead. "Try not to worry."

In that moment Evan felt a rush of warmth, which swept through his body flamed by Fiona's touch and the hope of being free of Alexis once and for all. Fiona's kiss was warm and comforting. Relieved and suddenly overcome with emotion Evan leaned forward, pressing his face close toward hers, gently brushing his lips against hers. She didn't pull away but met his lips hungrily, unable to control the dizzy feeling that swam between them. They moved quickly, Fiona pulling her nightgown above her head and discarding it on the floor, their kisses firm, furious with the need to get naked urgent.

"I didn't intend this," Evan whispered through gritted teeth.

"Me neither," she hissed, sliding beneath him, breathless, deliciously awakened by the weight of his body upon hers; it had been such a long time. Suddenly her loins were alive again and ever so softly she began to weep.

Benita picked some flowers from the garden, arranging them in a glass vase she found under the sink. Connie and Ben would be home with their new baby son a little after lunch. She stood back to admire her handiwork than carried them through to place them on the mantel. The house was immaculate; she had been hard at it since six that morning.

The floors had been washed and polished and as much as Benita hated ironing, Connie's laundry basket had been emptied and everything was freshly laundered, pressed and neatly put away.

Benita looked at the clock; there was nothing left to do and it would be some while before their return so she was finally going to attempt the climb up the Tor.

It was a beautiful morning; the sun warmed her bare arms as she walked along the lane that led to the meadow at the foot of the Tor.

The climb was steep. As the sun strengthened high in the sky above her she slowed pace, pausing to look back down at the lands below her. It was beautiful; the further she climbed the more she became aware of an overwhelming sense of peace. The peak of the Tor beckoned and she pushed on, beads of perspiration gathering at her brow. The monument at the top towered above; she shielded her eyes from the sun's glare to appreciate its beauty. Sitting down on the soft grass to enjoy her inner peace, it felt good. She sat with her eyes closed with the sweet smell of freshly mown grass wafting into her nostrils from a well-tended garden somewhere below. The sun warmed the top of her head, adding to the aesthetic feeling. Benita felt at one with nature, protected from her worries, and she wondered why it had taken her so long to come.

It was only the sound of her name being called that jolted her from her hypnotic state.

Benita opened her eyes, squinting against the glare of the sun. A figure approached; she waited for her eyes to focus, surprised that Ben would walk all the way up here to find her, he must have guessed where she would be. As her eyes adjusted to the light she realised it wasn't Ben at all. A strange tingle rippled through her body as the stranger neared and recognition formed on her lips, "Evan." There was no mistaking him. Was she dreaming?

Benita felt the tingle in the depths of her belly, an inexplicable current which reverberated to her chest. He was almost upon her and this wasn't a dream.

He stood square before her now, looking into her eyes with disbelief, then he smiled. Benita stared back at the face from the past, matured with fine lines at the corner of his eyes, the skin no longer boyish and soft but unkempt with whiskers. There stood a man whose brow was etched with worry but who was undeniably handsome.

Evan spoke first. "Benita, it is really you, I can't believe it! I am shocked, how weird, you are the last person I would have expected to find here." The corners of his mouth eased into a smile. There was no hiding his delight at seeing her.

"Ditto, whatever are you doing in Glastonbury, Evan Bailey?" Benita leapt up, dusting off her jeans. Not waiting for a reply she went on, "It must be, let me see, well over twenty years at least. My God it is strange, I thought I would never ever see you again."

Evan laughed. This was so Benita, he could never get a word in. "One might ask you the same." He leant across to kiss her on each cheek. "It is certainly a welcome surprise. I don't live a million miles away from here but as it happens I am just visiting, and you?" He didn't dare to tell her in that moment that it had all suddenly become very clear to him, why he had ended up here. Fate had brought him to this moment, to Benita, and it seemed in that instant that one way or another all roads were leading him back to Spain.

"Much the same, visiting friends. I have been here a while and today I was determined to come up here and admire the view. So how are you Evan, has life been kind to you?" she asked, with genuine interest.

Surprising himself, Evan took a hold of her hand. "Let's go down to the village for a coffee. Perhaps then we can catch up on the last twenty three years." He winked at her. "Twenty three years! Wow, it's incredible." He gave a low whistle as he carefully picked his way down the hillside, gently guiding Benita along beside him.

Benita sat outside the café, watching Evan struggle with the door as he emerged with two large mochas. He sat down opposite her and smiled. "Well, this is unbelievable. I am ever so glad that I bumped into you. So let me guess, happily married, how many kids?"

Benita laughed. "No kids, no husbands come to that, just a string of failed relationships and nothing interesting to tell, so you see Evan it may not be that exciting."

"I'm really surprised." He couldn't conceal the smile of relief. It certainly made things simpler.

"Well, I have been married, no kids but soon to be divorced. So not a lot different from you really," he confessed, taking a slurp of coffee. She was stunning just as he remembered her, perhaps a little drawn. If only she knew how many sleepless nights she had caused him to have, even more than Alexis, he thought wryly. Now when he had resigned himself to the fact that he would never see Benita again she turned up in the most unlikely of places. Evan was reminded of Fiona's words of wisdom. Had she not warned him that the Tor was a magical place? Right now he couldn't agree more.

Evan surveyed Benita with interest. She exercised her usual self-control, her guard was never down and by the second mocha he was no closer to understanding the last years of her life. Benita seemed keener to talk about him while revealing very little about herself. He watched her fidget restlessly and draw heavily on her cigarette; she may appear confident but he could see past the façade, the depths of her eyes revealed a woman in crisis. In his mind things started to fall into place. Benita had never married because she wasn't stable enough. She didn't understand herself, in fact she didn't love herself and quite simply that made it virtually impossible for her to love another. How observant had he become? He marvelled at his intuition but was it really so clever? Benita may say very little but actually she was an open book and he wasn't done reading her yet.

"So when do you go home?" Evan asked casually, watching her awkward response with interest.

"I don't know, like I said I may never go back. Anyway for now I need to be around to help with the baby. I am sure Connie could use an extra pair of hands around the place."

"So I can't tempt you to come home with me? I mean it sounds like you need to get away and I have an empty cottage."

"You mean come and take care of you!" she retorted.

"Not at all, that's not what I mean Benita. I mean you can't palm yourself off on Connie and Ben, I bet they would like to be alone with their son. Look, I am off to Spain next week; you could have my place to yourself. I don't think you need to run the risk of bumping into Ed and from what you have just told me it seems the sensible option to steer clear for a while."

Benita stood up. "Thanks Evan but no thanks, I can sort my own life. I have managed it for this long."

Evan couldn't help but chuckle to himself, she was so stubborn. "Ok, please yourself. Look, take my address and number and please stay in touch; it has been too long."

She took the card from him, peering down at it. "Artist indeed, I would never had said you would become an artist. Con artist perhaps." She burst out laughing.

"Ah well there you go, there is a lot about me that would surprise you. One day I will show you my most treasured piece of art. I think you will love it as much as me."

"Maybe." She gave an awkward smile. "So bye Evan, good luck on your trip out to Spain." She offered her hand but he waved it away, instead rising to his feet and encircling her body with his arms.

"Don't be shy." He squeezed her tightly. "You look after yourself and we will speak soon, when I get back from Spain I will call you whether you like it or not."

He watched her head along the High Street, amazed that he managed to remain so calm, despite the niggling urge to chase after her. Twenty three years later and he was letting her walk away again.

Somehow it felt different this time, there was an inner faith that he would see her again and that this time she would be around for longer. He left a tip on the table and, pulling on his heavy rucksack laden with books, headed back towards Fiona's cottage.

Fiona had left a note propped on the kitchen table.

"Sorry to miss you Evan. Be back at five with a bottle of wine for us to enjoy while you tell me all about the Tor. Love Fiona." Evan felt a nauseous wave of guilt. Fiona had been in such high spirits when she had left this morning. He had misled her, which wasn't nice when she had been such a kind host. He placed the flowers he had brought her as a thank you down on the table and penned a note excusing his sudden departure. He explained how he needed to get to Spain, which wasn't really a lie, and that he would contact her the moment he returned. Now he wasn't telling the truth but it softened the blow and he hoped she wouldn't be too distraught.

As he drove away from Avalon out towards the neighbouring village of Street he felt a satisfying inner peace. It stayed with him for the entire drive home and for the first time in ages he began to hum, his spirits lifting at last. He didn't need to question why.

Depositing his bag at the foot of the stairs Evan rushed through the house let himself out of the back door and sauntered along the cobbled path up towards the studio, where the overgrown lavender brushed his legs, releasing a fragrant aroma and scenting the evening air. Turning the key in the lock it clicked open and as it did so he took a deep steeling breath.

It was the large canvas at the very back of the group covered by a dust sheet. He had to move several pictures to access it, pulling it out toward him, careful not to disturb the other oils that leant against it. The muslin sheet covering it slipped back revealing a corner of the canvas as he carried it outside and stood it on the wooden bench. Slowly he pulled back the sheet and, taking a few steps back, he stood to admire his work.

The clouds in the picture seemed to move across the sky, each wispy shape ready to float away in front of his eyes. The house stood just as he remembered it, bathed in a peachy glow from the setting sun, its amber tones reflected in the waters of the pool which shimmered so invitingly that he could almost feel the wetness against his flesh. There she was, he drew in breath. Benita lying naked against the stone terrace, her right hand raised, shielding her eyes from the light as she looked across at him. Her young body was stretched out before him. Small rounded breasts jutting forward, her skin bronzed, delicious. He had captured the moment perfectly, just as he had seen her all those years ago. He felt an intense stirring in his loins as he always did when he had dared to drag this picture from its hiding place and bring it out into the daylight so he could drink in the mood and the pleasurable memory of her. This time there were no regrets. Somehow fate had brought her back into his life and this time he would see to it that she remained. He had thought of her often and wondered many times if he would ever see her again. Now he had the chance to tell her how he felt, that he had never stopped loving her and that's why his marriage had been a total disaster if truth be known; well, apart from Alexis of course. He realised, begrudgingly replacing the painting to its resting place, that it would take some time. Benita would need to come to him this time, she wasn't a woman to be forced into anything, experience had taught him that and he wasn't going to make that mistake a second time round. With some gentle manipulation she would come and he had no idea how, just an inner sense that this time things would work in his favour.

Evan woke early the following morning. He made a pot of coffee which he took through to the living room, sitting down in his mother's old chair, its tired facade hidden beneath a chenille throw. Pulling the solicitor's letter from the pocket of his robe he picked up the phone, dialled the number, heard a click and then the unfamiliar international dialling tone.

He made an appointment for Monday at ten. If he arrived in Spain on Sunday it would give him enough time to find a place to stay and reacquaint himself. All he needed now was a flight and, suddenly feeling good about the prospect of a trip to the sun, he turned on the computer to see what was available.

Benita couldn't sleep; the constant whimpers of the baby made her decidedly edgy. In truth it wasn't just the baby that was keeping her awake, it was the thought of Evan.

He had changed so much; she had to admit it, he was really quite handsome and somewhat charming. "An artist,." she mused, wondering what it was that he painted. People, places, landscapes perhaps. How romantic, she thought, turning onto her side and wriggling further beneath the cosy quilt.

The high pitched cry of the baby in the next room snapped her out of her daydream and she realised with a heavy heart that Evan was right. Connie needed to be alone with her family and it was time she made a move and left the new family to bond. Dragging herself from the warm bed she hauled her suitcase up on to the ottoman and began slinging in her clothes. Question was, where would she go? There didn't appear to be many options. Reluctantly she realised she would have no choice but to go back to Scotland. Besides, she told herself, there were things she needed to attend to there, like the flat and finding a job. Benita gave an inner groan at the thought but it had to be done, she reminded herself as she zipped up her case.

Sitting back on the bed she found her thoughts returned to Evan and his kind offer. She was careful to divert them; listening to her heart had gotten her into trouble too many times, she thought wisely.

# CHAPTER 12

The flight to Malaga landed five minutes ahead of schedule. Evan had his clothes, passport and a pair of tatty trainers crammed in a small holdall. He was not planning to be in Spain long. Bypassing the baggage carousel he sauntered out of the arrivals hall, through the double doors and into the warm Mediterranean sunshine.

Climbing into a cab, he instructed the driver to take him to Fuengirola, to the office of the lawyer he was due to meet. He settled back against the worn leather to take in his surroundings, realising meeting Benita again had given him the strength to see this through.

It seemed busier than it had been the last time he was here some years ago, but hardly surprising now that so many Britons had brought property here, he thought, looking out on yet another new high rise development blocking out the bright sun.

It was an unpleasant sticky kind of warm; looking up at the clear blue sky he thought back to the heavy grey cloud he had left at Gatwick and decided it would be wise not to complain about the lack of air conditioning.

The cab pulled up at the offices of Rodriguez Castaneda ten minutes early. He knew from his phone call earlier in the week that the lawyer spoke perfect English, a great relief as his Spanish was at best awkward. He had learnt a lot when he had come to stay with his father, he had Esmeralda to thank for that, but his knowledge of their language was rusty. He smiled at the memory.

The manana syndrome took effect immediately, as he found himself waiting in the cool marbled hallway thirty minutes past the appointment time. Being kept waiting was definitely a favourite pastime of the Spanish, he thought as his stomach rumbled for the hundredth time, reminding him that he had not eaten for some considerable time.

Finally, a tall gentleman in open neck cotton shirt sauntered down the corridor. He introduced himself as one of the senior partners and led Evan through to a small side office.

He signalled for Evan to be seated then, closing the door behind them, he sat down opposite Evan and looked at the stack of papers before him on the desk, finally raising his head to look Evan square in the eye with a knowing smile that crinkled the corners of his mouth.

"Mr Bailey." He stopped to clear his throat. "You sit before me as sole beneficiary to the estate of the late Mr Michael 'Foggy' Williams and it is my duty to read the late Mr Williams' Will and explain to you your options." He paused to look up from his papers, checking that Evan understood and was keeping up. "For example, inheritance tax and the register of transfer et cetera."

Evan fidgeted nervously. What did this all mean? It would seem that Foggy had left something substantial, for the lawyer to talk of transfer fees?

He feigned a nervous cough, interrupting Rodriguez midflow, who in turn cocked his head giving Evan a quizzical sideways glance

"Is there a problem?"

Evan smiled cautiously. "Not a problem as such, I just think it would be a good idea if you could explain to me what it is that I have actually inherited."

Rodriguez smiled broadly. "Of course." He flipped through his papers and pulled out a file. "It is all here. First, of course, we should verify that you are Evan Bailey. I trust you have your passport here with you?"

Benita closed the door of the taxi and watched it drive out of view. She felt suddenly apprehensive as she stood at the bottom of the driveway alone. This had been a stupid idea, she thought, a sudden wave of panic threatening to send her sprinting back down the lane after the cab. How ridiculous of her to turn up at Evan's home unannounced. For all she knew his wife may have returned and decided to give it another try; after all, a lot could happen in a week.

On her return to Glasgow earlier in the week, she had been horrified to find her once pristine flat littered with rubbish and the stench of rotting vegetables a most unwelcoming aroma. Ed had certainly outstayed his welcome and there were nothing but stark reminders of his presence there. The flood of mail on the doormat was her only way of knowing how long the place had been empty; from the postage dates it looked as if Ed had moved on sometime at the beginning of the month. Benita had spent two days solid cleaning the place, as well as employing a locksmith to change the locks. She had packed a case and locked some of her treasured possessions in a trunk, which she had dragged into the cupboard under the stairs and then asked the locksmith to fix a big bolt to make it extra secure.

Then she had gone to a local letting agent, leaving with them a set of new keys and instructing them to find a tenant for the next six months.

Had she been a bit premature in these decisions? It didn't seem such a good idea now as she quivered in her three-inch heels at the end of Evan's driveway. Not sure if she should go on and knock at the door or head back down the lane, she hadn't even had the good sense to ask the driver to wait for her.

She was still undecided as a car pulled up alongside her making her jump and the driver, a robust woman with shiny red cheeks, leaned out of the window.

"You looking for Evan Bailey?" the woman asked cheerfully whilst eyeing Benita suspiciously. "Coz if you are, love, then you are out of luck. He is overseas and has asked me to look after the place until his return." Immediately she noticed the look of bewilderment in Benita's eyes, so she added, "Ah, guess you didn't realise love." She gave a sympathetic smile. "You don't have a car here either, by the look of it?" she crooned.

Benita shook her head. "My own stupid fault. Guess I will

have to go back to the station." She looked hopefully at the other woman. "I don't suppose that you would be able to give me a lift?"

Ami Rogers nodded. "Of course I can sweetheart; it's a fair trip, especially in those heels." She opened the passenger door. "Hop in, love. I hope you haven't come too far?"

Benita raised an exasperated brow. "Scotland," she replied, struggling with her seatbelt.

"Here, may I?" Ami leaned across and slotted the seatbelt in with no fuss at all. "There is a certain art to it." She chuckled, slipping the car into first gear. "So I take it that our Evan had no idea you were arriving here today?"

"Correct." Benita nodded. "Rather stupid of me really, it's just that we ran into each other last week and he invited me to come and stay with him for a while. He didn't mention that he would be going away so soon. Of course, if he had," she shrugged.

"No, not like Evan at all." Ami shook her glossy black hair, flicking it back over her shoulder. Everything about the woman was big, including her hair, Benita thought as she surveyed the other woman out of the corner of her eye. Ami turned to concentrate on the road ahead. "I believe he has gone to Spain, he will be back in a few days, perhaps you would be wise to stick around and wait until he returns."

"Perhaps," Benita mused, unsure exactly what she was going to do now. Thanking Ami for the lift, she got out at the station and headed to the café in desperate need of caffeine, scolding herself for her own stupidity. The café was deserted apart from an elderly lady sat perusing the crossword in the newspaper, her cup of tea untouched, a scum on its surface. Benita ordered a pot of tea and a scone and sat down by the window.

The sensible thing to do now would be to text Evan, to say she had been a right clot, had arrived and found the place deserted and when would he be back. No, she thought with an inner gasp. That would be so embarrassing. She couldn't admit to being so presumptuous and he would find it hilarious. So she sat and sipped her tea and nibbled at the buttered scone, waiting for a glimmer of inspiration, a magical solution to appear to ease her predicament, whilst staring out across the sleepy village rooftops to the rolling countryside beyond.

"It is so very nice at this time of year, don't you think?" Benita looked up at the guy with the gentle tone who was pulling a chair out from the table beside her.

"Would you mind?" He signalled to the vacant space.

"Not at all, help yourself." Benita smiled, moving her seat across a shade. "Yes you are right; it's very pleasing at this time of year. Autumn happens to be my favourite season."

"Mine too." He smiled pleasantly in her direction and Benita wondered why on earth, with all the available seats, he had had to squash himself up next to her. As if reading her mind he leaned across the table, his tone hushed. "Excuse me intruding on you but I noticed you alone and you looked kind of lost, perhaps in need of some help. You can tell me to mind my own business but you don't see a lot of folk at this time of year around these parts and my partner Craig is away so I came out for a stroll to relieve the boredom and ended up here."

Benita had felt there was something different and now it dawned on her that he was gay. She smiled warmly, all at once not at all threatened by his presence. "How very observant of you umm?"

"David Barrow." He offered a delicate hand with perfectly manicured nails.

"Nice to meet you David and you're spot on, I'm not from around here. I came to visit a friend actually. An artist, Evan Bailey. Do you know of him?"

David shook his head. "Name rings a bell but I don't believe we have ever met. So are you meeting him here?"

"Well, this is the thing," Benita explained as David signalled for more tea and scones.

"Oh dear, so you are in a dreadful pickle darling. I mean it seems a terrible shame to trudge back to Bonnie Scotland knowing in just a few days he will be back." David looked thoughtful for a moment. "I know it sounds a bit forward but you're ever so welcome to stay with me. I live in an enormous house, myself and Craig usually, who is away working in the city this week. I become a little agitated being there alone, it's such a pile. Far too big for little old me but of course there is Mrs Lamb," he looked across at Benita's puzzled expression, "the cleaner," he added with a giggle. "Bit of an old bossy boots but keeps the place ticking. I would be over the moon if you said yes. Truth is, it gets rather lonely when Craig is away." Popping a piece of buttered scone into his mouth he continued, "Simply delicious, come on Benita, dig in," he encouraged.

David had kind eyes and although he talked incessantly Benita surprised herself by accepting his offer. She reminded herself sensibly that David could turn out to be someone quite different but she had a hunch and he really did appear harmless.

Walking along the lane another hundred yards or so they turned off into the driveway of Pettington Place. Benita turned to David. "You're kidding, right?" She looked up at the sprawling pile of bricks with gargoyles peeping out from beneath lacy ivy bibs.

David gave a soft throaty chuckle. "Pretty impressive isn't it, darn draughty in the wintertime though."

Impressive it was, Benita had to agree as they drew up to the front of the rambling gothic manor with its sweeping stone staircase carpeted in fallen amber leaves that led up to the heavy wooden door.

"I'm showing off a bit, I must confess." David stifled a giggle. "We normally use the entrance round the back, but hey, you know." He slid a ludicrously large key, which reminded Benita of the key from 'Alice in Wonderland', into the lock. It creaked open, leaving Benita bewildered, peering inside at the grand entrance hall where a roaring fire burned in the grate. For a moment she felt as if she had been transported back in time.

A rich red carpet bordered with gold stretched before her and cautiously she stepped inside. Several small fox heads with beady eyes that watched her hung the length of the panelled wall. For a moment she hesitated. David, sensing her anxiety, began to laugh.

"Dear girl, come in and shut the door behind you before we lose what little heat there is and then we shall all be freezing. Now let me show you around Pettington and perhaps then we can rouse Mrs Lamb and let her know that there will be two for dinner this evening." He went ahead, a wiggle in his step. Benita followed closely behind. It was the sort of house in which one could easily get lost and it certainly wasn't the most welcoming.

Evan left the lawyer's office and headed down to the seafront where he found a small bar and ordered a cold beer, which he sipped looking out across to the marina and the constant hive of activity surrounding the small sailing boats that rubbed shoulders with ocean going yachts.

he was still in shock from the news that Foggy had left his land to him, the precious land where once, a long time ago, he had fallen asleep under the stars. It still hadn't quite sunk in.

Evan had never returned there. In fact he had never been back to the mountains. On more recent trips to Spain he had stayed in a hotel by the coast and Foggy had driven down to see him. He knew that Foggy had never built a house on the land. He had never had enough money to. Foggy's dream of making it big was all it had ever been; a pipe dream. Foggy had never married nor had children, in fact he never had had much of a life at all, apart from the land where he had his battered old caravan and of course his music.

The lawyer had said that the caravan had gone, that the town council had removed it, as it had been parked illegally for all those years anyway. Most of the contents had been scrapped along with it, apart from the few papers that Evan held on his lap now in a green plastic bag. He rifled through them, the sunshine warming the nape of his neck. There were a few old lists and some music. It didn't mean much to him but when he got back he would get somebody to take a look over them. It would be good to bring Foggy's music back to life.

What would he do with the land, he wondered? The lawyer had already had it valued at around a hundred and twenty thousand Euros. He saw no problem with the land being built on, it classified as the amount specified that was needed to construct a house. Evan didn't need a house, he already had one, one that he loved dearly which looked over the sea to the distant horizon. He supposed he could sell the land for someone else to build their dream home but that was like throwing away Foggy's dream and he felt obliged to keep it alive. He took a sip of beer; there was plenty of time yet. What was actually more pressing was that he rang the bank back home and increased his overdraft. In order to inherit the land, first he would have to pay the four thousand Euro taxes and sadly he was already in the red. Chris, his bank manager, would not be pleased. At least at the end of the day he owned the house outright. Paying Caroline off had taken all of his savings and made cash flow sticky to say the least.

Tomorrow he would hire a car and take a trip up to the mountains; he would take a look at the land and maybe even drive past his father's old place. Theoretically, he had a lot to smile about but as the sun slipped behind a solitary cloud he shivered and for a fleeting moment he felt an overwhelming sense of dread.

Benita knew she shouldn't but it was so relaxing here by the fire listening to David, who was witty and entertaining. Therefore, when he reached over to top up her glass of wine she didn't object. She couldn't believe her luck really, it was like staying at a five star hotel. Her room was divine, looking out across the beautiful gardens and lake. When she had last looked out she had seen the moon reflected in its waters, a passing swan illuminated in its pale glow sliding gracefully amongst the rushes.

Mrs Lamb had appeared at six and set about preparing them a meal. David, overjoyed at his unexpected company, had been down to the cellar and unearthed some of Craig's finest bottles of claret. Now, as they sat in front of the roaring fire, David turned to look across at her. "So Benita, are you going to tell Evan how you're feeling when he returns?" he asked cheekily.

"I'm not sure what you mean." She gave a hesitant smile.

"Oh you!" David said gleefully. "There is no hiding it from me Miss! You are so obviously in love with this man." He raised his hands in the air. "Evan this and Evan that. In fact I am rather looking forward to meeting him myself, he sounds rather cute." He eyed her suspiciously then gave an excited shriek. "That's exactly it, isn't it? You don't even realise that you're in love with this guy!" He gave an exasperated tut. "This won't do at all because you are, you know, quite lovely. Your eyes light up when you say his name."

Benita set her glass down on the table. "Did they really?" she asked.

David winked. "They most certainly did. Oh tell me again, go back to the first time you both went to the house, when you scrambled up the rocks. Oh how romantic!" he declared, hugging himself.

Evan parked at the bottom of the hill; he got out of the car, weak at the knees as the memories flooded back. He began to walk the path, it was overgrown from little use, and it seemed shorter than it had done before. As he reached the brow of the hill he drew in breath, looking down at the land below him. To his utter delight, it was just as he remembered it. Shivering with excitement and happiness as suddenly he was sixteen again and Foggy was there strumming his guitar. He could here that mellow tune and smell the aroma of sausages spitting hot fat in the pan, on the stove in the caravan. His tummy rumbled and he sat down under the tree to take in the beauty before him. He wasn't sure what he had expected, but he felt sure that something would be different. The only change was the caravan being absent but he could see it in his mind's eye and the makeshift loo with its tattered curtain. Evan leant back against the tree, watching the goats climbing the mountain to the west, and heard the gentle chime of their bells in the distance.

A cawing crow on a branch overhead made him jump. A cloud crossed the sun, bringing a chill to his bones. As the sun reappeared he waited for its warmth, yet it grew colder.

He felt his body stiffen and the tiny hairs on the back of his neck stood up. The gentle hunger pains turned to a knot which tightened and tightened in his tummy. He felt afraid. He could sense her now, she was close. Not wishing to turn he sensed her presence behind him; he didn't want to face her. He wanted to close his eyes but the muscles wouldn't work. He was afraid and she sensed it. Her presence grew stronger and he felt a rising panic inside. Why had she come, why now?

The sound of the goats' bells was long gone. There was nothing but a heavy silence, which swept over him and settled. He was numb, she was so close, too close, and then the silence was broken.

"Evan, speak with me," she asked. There was sadness in her voice, that scratchy high-pitched tone that wasn't human. Evan turned slightly toward the direction from which it had come, afraid of seeing her should their eyes meet; he wanted to avoid meeting those cold grey eyes.


"Mrs Lamb knows everything that goes on in this village," David announced, passing the toast rack with one hand and the marmalade with the other across to Benita. "So I have it on very good advice that your young man returns this afternoon."

"Is that so?" Benita smiled across the table at him. "Well let's hope he is pleased to see me."

David lavished a slice of wholemeal toast with honey. "Oh, from what I have heard he will be utterly delighted."

# CHAPTER 13

It was comforting to be home, Evan thought, switching off the car engine, He sat there for a moment or two, relieved. The horror of Alexis' last visitation weighed heavily on his mind; he had heard her quite clearly, but it was all such nonsense. She wasn't real, just a figment of his imagination. The woman was dead, he knew that. If he had secretly harboured any doubt he needn't have. A few calls made before he had left Malaga had confirmed that she had died in august 1983 - drowned in the swimming pool. On file as a terrible accident, there had been alcohol in her blood and she had drowned, no one there to save her. So she hadn't been murdered, as he had believed may be the case for so many years.

Surely now it would stop, now he knew the truth. It had been her own stupid fault, drinking too much wine and bathing was a recipe for disaster. He could stop blaming himself; at least he should, all he had ever done was to spy on her. Yes, he had sought a cheap sexual thrill, masturbating whilst watching her lying naked around the pool, but it was hardly the crime of the century.

As he slid the key into front door, he stopped. That was it, now he must shrug the whole Alexis thing off, put the whole episode behind him. She didn't exist, he would never think about her again, he vowed as he went inside, relieved that Ami had been in and switched the heating on; it felt decidedly chilly after the milder climate of Spain.

David pulled up at the bottom of the drive. "Looks like you're finally in luck, darling. There is a car parked up front, I am presuming that would be Evan's?"

Benita slipped on her jacket. "No idea, I haven't a clue

what car he drives but it isn't Ami's so there is a good chance it will be his. Now you are sure it is ok for me to stay a few more days with you?" She looked hopefully at David, who was busy peering up the driveway keen to get a glimpse of Evan.

"Of course it is, kitten. Now if I see you wave I know I can toddle off and you will call me if you need me to come and fetch you."

Benita straightened her collar. "Perfect, David! Well fingers crossed, wish me luck."

"Oddles of luck sweetie, now get in there and don't forget to tell him how you feel. I will be eagerly awaiting all the gossip later on over Mrs Lamb's steak pie."

Benita made it to the front door then she turned to look back at David and for a fleeting second her courage threatened to desert her but before she could change her mind she rang the bell.

Evan opened the door looking slightly dishevelled. He looked at her, momentarily speechless.

"I know, I know," she said. Not waiting for an invite, as she brushed past him into the hallway. "I thought I would take you up on your offer. You were right, it was too cramped there with the baby and then I went back to Scotland and you," she brushed her hand through the air, "Well, you don't want to know. It's a long story. So before I knew it I was on a train down here and then you weren't here and so well," she took a gulp of air, "well you're here now. Hello Evan."

Evan began to laugh. "Hi Benita, how are you? Why on earth didn't you call me?"

Benita shrugged off her jacket and handed it to him. "Don't be ridiculous, that would have been far too simple. Anyway I am here now so I hope you meant it when you invited me?"

"Of course I did. This really is the most wonderful surprise. Where are your things?" he asked, puzzled, whilst looking at her jacket as he put it on the peg. "Surely you didn't come all the way from Scotland with just this?"

"Of course not, silly! I am staying in the village, well just the other side to be precise. You know, it's a long story. Is there any chance of a drink?"

Evan led the way through to the study and signalled for her to take the chair by the window.

"Wow, great view. What a fantastic place."

"Yes it is," he agreed, appearing from the kitchen with a bottle of wine and two glasses. "So tell me from the beginning, I am intrigued." He sat down opposite her and for the first time noticed how simply stunning she looked. When he had run into her at Glastonbury she had seemed tired, shadows beneath her eyes. It wasn't a criticism; she was always stunning in his eyes.

Today her eyes sparkled like jewels. She was dressed simply in sweater and jeans, her mandarin sweater bringing out the colour of her eyes; she was the Benita he remembered from Spain, cocky, self-assured and talking nonstop.

She took a thirsty gulp of wine and viewed him quizzically across the rim of her glass.

"You are staring! Why are you staring at me?"

"Sorry." He shrugged, dragging his eyes away from her beautiful face. "Anyway, you were saying?"

Evan finished the last of the wine and before she answered, asked, "So you can't be persuaded to come and stay here with me?"

Benita stood up, pushed her thumbs into the front of her denim pockets and sauntered across to the window. "It's not that I don't want to, but David has been so kind and I would like to stay on a few more days with him. He loves having company and he really is the sweetest man. I can't believe you two have never met?"

Evan joined her by the window. "I seem to recall you said he was gay, so why should we have met?"

"So, what has that got to do with it? I will introduce you to him, I'm sure you will get along just fine and he is just dying to meet you."

Evan grimaced. "I expect he is," he replied, picking up the empty glasses, and carrying them through to the kitchen, Benita following closely behind.

"Oh don't be childish; he has a boyfriend whom, I must

admit, I've yet to meet and apparently they are both very much in love. So you're absolutely safe on that score." She sat on the worktop and watched him wash the glasses. He turned and smiled. "Do you fancy a coffee?"

"Sure, but let me make it." She hopped down and began filling the kettle. Evan leant against the worktop, arms folded, watching her with amusement as she searched for the mugs. She went into lavish detail about her new best friend, David, and his wonderful house. Interrupted by a deep longing he took a few deep breaths to calm the stirring in his heart. Why did she always have this effect on him? In a moment, it would be highly embarrassing if he didn't force himself to think about something else.

"So enough of me, how was Spain?" she asked, passing him a mug.

"It was ok. Foggy left his piece of land to me. I guess I was the only living person he had really."

Benita smiled, and led the way back to the study. "He always had a soft spot for you, didn't he?" She made herself at home on the worn chair, Evan's favourite as it happened. "Did you go up to the old place? Is it still the same?"

Evan shuddered at the memory of what happened there. "It's pretty much the same. The old van has gone but it's still as beautiful as ever." He smiled at the memory of the vista. "If a little overgrown," he added.

"So what will you do with it?" she asked with genuine interest.

He sat down opposite her. "I have no idea, nothing for now." Keen to change the subject he leapt back up, restless and afraid she would leave. "Do you fancy a walk down to the beach?" He couldn't think about Spain now.

"Yes that would be nice, and after that you really must show me some of your paintings."

Evan dropped her back to David's about nine. The house was every bit as impressive as she had said. David, on hearing the car, had sprinted down the steps to greet them.

Evan liked him almost at once, despite his sexual preference.

"You must come in, Evan, and have a brandy!" David enthused, linking arms with Benita and skipping back towards the stone steps.

David really was the most incorrigible host and one brandy led to several until Evan found he was in no fit state to drive home.

"I won't hear another word." David wagged his finger under Evan's nose. "We have heaps of room here. Just look at the size of the place, will you. No arguments, you are staying." He stood, hands on hips, surveying his guests. "Now who fancies crackers and cheese? I have some divine Shropshire Blue that Craig brought back from the deli in town."

Evan had a room in the west wing, the opposite side of the house to Benita. He was glad of the distance between them, so he could not be tempted to sneak into her room in the middle of the night. From here the chance of finding it would be a miracle in itself. Besides, he thought as he slid into the red silk sheets, there was no way after the amount of brandy he had consumed that he would be able to perform. Unable to sleep, his mind drifted restlessly.

The moon cast a silvery glow through the window, spilling into the room, highlighting the heavily carved posts of the oversized, somewhat grotesque bed. Eerie shadows danced across the ceiling and for a moment Evan felt unsure. He cleared his mind and took a deep breath, choosing to ignore the haunting screech of a fox somewhere in the depths of the forest. He wondered if Benita was sleeping or if she was lying awake restless, much the same as him. It was good to have her near him again. He would have to be careful though, she was painfully temperamental and if he said the wrong thing she would be off - and he didn't want to risk that happening. It was a nuisance that he had been away when she had arrived here. If he had been home then she wouldn't have been caught up with David. Oh, he was a great guy with a heart of gold but he was a danger. For he was unwittingly giving Benita a safe haven; by allowing her to stay she could keep some distance from Evan. He wanted her back at the house with him, Goddamn it. Given the choice, he wanted her in his bed, their bodies entwined, and the taste of her skin lingering on his tongue.

Benita did things her way and at her own pace. For a time, he would just have to be patient. She would come to him when she was ready, of that he was sure.

The room grew unexpectedly chilly. Evan, who had eventually succumbed to his heavy eyelids, slept on, unaware of the dramatic drop in temperature. The gentle rustle of her skirts along the oak floor woke him.

In the darkness, he opened his eyes. She was there with him but she wasn't smiling. It appeared she was drowning. He could see her arms and legs flailing in the air, hear her gasping for air, the muffled coughs. He could see the terror on her face, her eyes wide with fear. He could see the water above her head. She followed his gaze as she desperately tried to reach the surface, her body becoming still,

She floated upward; he could hear her sobbing, then it was silent again as she was dragged back beneath the water. Her eyes never left his as they pleaded for him to help, to save her. He felt along the bedclothes - was this a dream? Everything felt real, he was awake.

"Evan," she gasped before plunging back beneath the water. "Evan!"

What could he do? He had to save her, but how? She couldn't drown in the middle of the night, in the middle a room that didn't even have any water in it. Her eyes were wide with terror, a tiny bubble of air crept from the corner of her mouth. Everything was still.

Evan felt the tears rush to his eyes and an icy cold arm encircled him. He began to tremble, a little at first and then uncontrollably. He felt himself recoil back against the wooden headboard.

In that instant she blinked and her head swivelled round toward him. He gripped the bed sheets, grabbing fists full of silk and knotting them within his palms.

He saw her lips open, her mouth was moving. Terror was ripping at his heart, he couldn't breathe, and his lungs were paralysed.

"Why didn't you help me?" she whined through steel grey lips.

Evan opened his mouth. The scream which had been sitting in his chest rung out in the stillness, sending the ducks on the lake soaring into the dawn mist.

Benita and David were woken by the bloodcurdling sound that echoed from the west wing. They met bleary eyed on the landing.

"Good God," David said aloud. "Whatever is going on down there?" He peered along the dark passageway before flicking on the light.

"Sounds like a nightmare but perhaps we had better go and check on him," Benita said, looking hopefully at David. She didn't fancy going alone. The terrible scream hadn't even sounded human.

"Yes, perhaps we best," David said, leading the way.

Evan heard the knock at the door, one loud brisk knock at first and then, when there was no response, an urgent drumming. He couldn't move, his whole body was paralysed. Even the tears that filled his eyes could not fall onto the silk sheet that was clamped around his body.

The door burst open, Benita and David peered cautiously in. He couldn't respond to their questioning look of concern, he couldn't move or speak, he couldn't even blink.

Benita hurried across to the bed. "Evan, what's wrong? Whatever has happened in here?" She cradled her arms around his neck, alarmed by the icy feel of his skin.

"Quick, David, he is freezing, fetch a blanket if you would. I think he is in some kind of shock. Oh, David, I don't know what to do!"

David stood open-mouthed, at Benita's command he leapt into action. "Don't panic, let me see, Benita. You go to the wardrobe and fetch another blanket please." He had to agree as he took in Evan's face that the man was in extreme shock.

Gently he shook Evan's shoulder. "It's ok old fella, whatever has alarmed you has gone now." He signalled to Benita. "You take over here while I go and get a shot of

133

whisky. We need something to revive him. I don't know what happened in here but it has scared him witless, literally."

A couple of whiskies later Evan was back in the land of the living. They went down to the drawing room where David revived the fire, then brought in a pot of tea.

Evan sat sheepishly, watching the flames of the fire, feeling somewhat foolish. How was he ever going to explain this? Benita would think he was insane and head off back to Scotland post haste and who knew what David would make of it all.

Benita broke the uncomfortable silence. "Do you feel up to telling us what went on up there?" she asked, concerned.

"Yes," David chorused. "Did you see a ghost or something? I always thought Craigy was having me on when he said this place was haunted."

Evan took a sip of tea and eyed their anxious faces. He couldn't lie, what was the use. Whether they thought him mad or not he would have to tell the truth.

Evan sat forward in his chair. "I think you had better pour us all another whisky. Then I will tell you everything right from the very beginning."

Benita tiptoed from the drawing room into the kitchen, closing the door behind her.

"He is sleeping now, thank God." She sat down on one of the breakfast bar stools and looked across at David, who sat at the table nursing a large mug of coffee. "I don't know what to make of it all really," she said wearily.

David looked up at her. "It's a terrible business, you could tell how hard it was for him to talk about it. I know it all sounds so frightfully bizarre, but I do believe him." He rubbed his forehead. "Just one look at the state of the man when we found him said it all." He shivered, looking around the kitchen in the early morning light. "The question is what to do next."

Benita shook her head. "It could have just been a nightmare."

"What, a nightmare that goes on for twenty years? I very

much doubt it." He got up and rinsed his mug in the sink. "Evan mentioned about this Fiona woman, you know the one in Glastonbury. Perhaps we should go back and see her. At the very least if we understood more about what is actually going on here, then at least we could be of some assistance."

Benita had to agree. It did all seem too bizarre to be real but she had read enough magazines and seen enough TV to know that things like this did happen, however unbelievable, or at least people claimed they did.

She knew Evan well enough to know he wasn't a liar and she too had witnessed his face earlier, it had been far from normal.

"I think you're right, David. Whatever this is we need some specialist help. Let's get dressed and when he wakes up we will suggest a trip to Glastonbury."

David headed for the door. "Yes we should. We need to get on to this right away and it won't be a moment too soon in my opinion." He stopped, turning to face Benita. "I suggest we take this very seriously, a haunting or a delusional man? Whatever, he needs and deserves our help."

# CHAPTER 14

Fiona took an early lunch. Having drunk copious amounts of wine last night, she was in dire need of a rather unhealthy breakfast with lots of fat-laden bacon, eggs and toast

Gathering up her bag, she sought out Louise, who was busying herself at the rear of the shop, dusting shelves that didn't need dusting.

"I have to go out now, Louise. Can you take over please?" she asked smiling at the plump assistant.

Fiona stepped out into the High Street, thinking how unusually quite it was today, as she made her way down the hill towards the café, her stomach rumbling

Evan saw her striding along. "There she is. Look, the woman in the green jacket, heading our way." He pointed her out to the others.

"Fiona," he called tentatively, not sure what sort of welcome he should expect.

Fiona took a moment to focus. "Evan Bailey," she shrieked, a stirring of excitement catapulting through her belly, and then noticed he wasn't alone, the attractive woman in particular. "Evan, what are you doing back, I thought that maybe you had gone to Spain."

"Well I did, briefly." He hesitated for a moment. "Look, Fiona, there is something we need to discuss with you. Can you spare us five minutes?"

"Yes, no problem, I am just on my break." She looked over at the others, then expectantly back to Evan. "Friends of yours? How rude of you, Evan, you must introduce us?"

"Yes, sorry. This is David and Benita, both good friends of mine. In fact they both suggested we come and see you."

"Oh and I was kidding myself that you might have missed me." She winked.

Evan gave an inner groan; he didn't need Benita thinking there was any romantic history here.

"I didn't mean to appear rude just rushing off like that last time, but -" he paused, "To tell the truth something important came up."

"It's ok, Evan," she soothed, sensing his unease. "I didn't figure you would be staying for ever. So, what brings you to Avalon this time?"

Evan gave her a quick hug." I knew you would understand Fiona, why don't we all go and get a coffee and then we can explain."

Any nagging doubts that David or Benita had harboured about Evan's unwanted visitor were soon to be dismissed by Fiona.

"So you are saying that this woman is haunting Evan simply because she needs his help," David asked, fascinated by Fiona's wealth of knowledge on the subject. There was much more to all of this than he had dared to hope.

"Yes, David. What we need to find out is why exactly she needs his help. As I had suggested to Evan before, he must meet with Barbara. I have left a message on her answer phone and I know that as soon as she picks it up she will rush back to us."

"Good, well until then we must be patient." David sat back and smiled at the others.

Barbara Gates lived on a ramshackle farm situated in the middle of nowhere. Once inside her home, it was cosy and inviting, despite the derelict outer appearance. Barbara, in her mid–sixties, was a large woman with thinning grey hair, heavy bags beneath eyes that suggested countless sleepless nights and a chin lost in folds of flesh.

She walked with a limp, any exertion made her huff and puff. Just walking to the front door and fixing them all a cup of tea had caused to her flop in the chair where she remained, struggling to get her breath back. Evan exchanged worried glances with David, she didn't instil much confidence in him, but soon he was to be proved wrong.

Barbara had been given very little to go on over the

phone, other than that Evan had been having visions and would like to clarify why? What the visions consisted of and of who had not been divulged to her at all.

Once she had regained her breath, Barbara looked at them in turn. She smiled, and Benita supposed it was to relax them. "I do apologise, it's my age and years of smoking no doubt." She excused the silent moments of regaining her composure. "Now, if everyone could please be silent while I take a few deep breaths and connect with my guides."

David could not contain the giggle, which came out as a sort of high-pitched hiccup. Hurriedly he covered his mouth, as they all turned to focus on him. Barbara frowned in his direction, her distaste apparent.

"Sorry, I'm just a little nervous, that's all. Please ignore me," he excused himself.

After several minutes, Barbara turned to look at Evan. She studied his face for a considerable time and then spoke. There was a marked change in her tone, it was deeper, throatier and oddly with no trace of a wheeze.

"She is with you now Evan, this woman. Do you know her? Because she tells me you do." Barbara nodded as if someone was talking in her right ear and continued. "She doesn't want you to be afraid but she is not sure if you have made the connection yet. She is asking do you know who she is."

Evan nodded nervously. "What does she want, can you ask her?"

Barbara was quiet, concentrating on a space in the air, just behind where he sat. "She is with you now, standing right behind you. She wants you to know that she looks out for you. That it is in her interest to keep you safe. This lady tells me that you have a bond that goes far and beyond the life you are living now. You have unfinished business and she says that you must not be afraid." Barbara stopped for a moment as if to gather strength.

"She needs to explain this to you but you won't listen!" Barbara fidgeted restlessly; she was becoming agitated. "She is desperate, Evan, she asks about the water. Why is she so concerned about the water?" Barbara broke from the trance for a moment to look into Evan's eyes. Her face softened for a moment and then she smiled. "I'm so sorry, I think I have lost the connection. Could you give me a few moments please?" Barbara shuffled restlessly in her chair until finally announcing, "It is no good, her energies were too strong, she has drained me of my own!" She signalled for Fiona to make more tea. "The last thing she showed me was that you must travel overseas, she says that you know where you must go and that she will be waiting for you. It is at this place where you will find your answer." She looked helplessly across at Evan. "So sorry, love. I will give you a special stone to protect you.

"If it would ease your pain but I must confess that I fear this is something you need to see through to the end. That indeed you must do as she asks. Do you know this place overseas that she talks of?"

Evan nodded. "Yes I do. I just don't understand why. Why has she chosen me?"

Barbara gave Evan a placating smile. "I think the clue is in what she has said to you tonight. It isn't just about this lifetime. Maybe your lives have only touched briefly here, yet in another you could have been anything, perhaps even lovers. But, my dear you will need to go and seek the answers for yourself."

David cleared his throat and interrupted. "It's all rather mysterious isn't it? I mean suppose we go to this place, wherever it may be. What then?" He shrugged his shoulders and looked at Benita for support. "I mean there's no guarantee is there!"

Barbara looked back at him, her eyes shining with an inner knowing. "I can guarantee that if you seek you will find. I have been dealing with spirits for over forty years. Our good lady does not wish to frighten you or lead you on a merry goose chase, she merely desires to be set free. Who knows if I hadn't lost the connection then maybe I could be more specific."

"Perhaps we could return tomorrow?" Benita asked hopefully.

"Young lady," Barbara looked her square in the eye.

"Let me tell you that a trance like the one you have just witnessed takes every ounce of strength that I have and for such a persistent spirit. Why, I shall be lucky if I have the strength to pull that off again within the next month. Let alone a day."

"I'm sorry," Benita stammered. "I had no idea."

"And how could you have, sweetheart." David leant forward to brush her arm.

Fiona sensed Barbara would like them to leave. She signalled to the others. "Come now, let's call it a night. We can go to mine and have a night cap and discuss this further." Evan thanked Barbara, although he wasn't exactly sure what for, and followed the others out to the car, all hope fading. There was no way he would be returning to Spain, absolutely no way at all.


Benita stood at the door, face flushed with excitement. "Hurry up Evan, pack a case. David has sorted us out a camper van, a very plush one at that. We are booked on the nine o'clock ferry. There is only one condition to him organising all of this, and that is that he can join us too. Especially as Craig has had to fly to Germany for a few days. So what do you say?"

Evan, who had been taking a nap, rubbed fiercely at his eyes. "I am speechless."

"Well don't be, just get a move on and pack," she said, haughtily, barging past him in the hallway and heading through the house. "Come on, chop, chop!"

Despite Evan's staunch resistance to a trip to Spain, Benita had worn him down with lots of encouragement from David and finally he had caved in, but only if Benita promised to escort him on the journey. Readily she had agreed and he was sure David had intended to accompany them all along too.

'Camper van' was rather an understatement, as David pulled up and honked the horn of the all singing, all dancing American motor home.

Evan couldn't help thinking this was all a bit of a charade. One, it appeared, that David and Benita were enjoying immensely. In fact, this whole business had gone too far. For two people who had looked at him that terrible morning in utter disbelief, they had now turned into fully-fledged ghost hunters. Neither understood what he was going through and he hadn't even confided to them about recent developments. It was no longer just a vision that came scared him half to death and then vanished; no, sadly things seemed to have intensified further. Ever since their visit to Barbara, which he was now fiercely regretting, Alexis had gathered pace. She was here with him now, he could sense her and although he had dismissed it at first he could even smell her. The unmistakable scent that had drifted into his nostrils all those years ago, then so pleasant, had now settled all around him and it made him sick to the pit of his stomach.

Half way across France, Evan drifted off to sleep. Benita sat in the front next to David and looked back across her shoulder at him sprawled across the sofa.

"Finally he sleeps. Poor thing he looks washed out. I suppose it must be quite draining for him."

David eased his foot back off the accelerator. "I can't imagine what it must be like for him. Do you suppose we will ever find the underlying cause of this, sweetie?" He turned to smile at Benita, who chewed nervously on her bottom lip.

"I hope so, for Evan's sake!" She popped in a piece of gum, offering some to David. "I only met her a couple of times."

"Who?" David asked absently

"Alexis. I have to say there wasn't anything spooky about her back then."

"Darling! You never let on before, when exactly?" David couldn't hide the surprise in his voice. Benita had never given any indication she had actually met the woman in question.

"It didn't really seem that important. As I said, there wasn't anything unusual about her. I saw her a few times in the village and once at a neighbour's party.

"I suppose it's fair to say she was attractive for her age. Certainly all the older men used to flock around her. My guess is, she was a bit of a tease. My mother once referred to her as a loose woman but I suppose looking back that's a bit unfair really. I mean after all she was single and she hadn't met the right guy."

"Absolutely," David agreed, nodding his head "So, a single forty year old woman, attractive, likes a bit of cock then drowns in her swimming pool after consuming too much booze."

"David, do you have to!" Benita screeched. "There's no need to be so graphic."

"Well, it's the truth! So what's the fun in haunting a man you met once or twice who, let's face it , was then a gawky sixteen year old with his brain in his pants. Who, as Evan has admitted to us, jerked off over her a couple of times. I mean hardly cause to come back and scare the poor bloke half to death, don't you think?"

Benita looked ahead; the Alps were in sight. She shook her head. "No, of course not, but there is more to it than that. Perhaps " She took a deep breath. "Perhaps Evan slept with her. I mean, you don't know do you?"

"It's a possibility, but it doesn't change anything. Perhaps her death wasn't an accident. One could assume that whilst Evan was spying on her, he witnessed her death or her murder. And now the poor soul is looking for justice and wants her killer exposed."

"No, too far-fetched, Evan has seen the coroner's report and it stated quite clearly accidental drowning. So any more bright ideas, Sherlock?"

David pulled off the Autobahn in to the services. "None at all, Holmes. We should get a drink and something to eat. I need to have a nap and then if we get a push on we should be there by the morning."


True to his word, David parked the motor home in the shade of a cluster of olive trees a few minutes before midday.

The nearer they had drawn to Spain the sicker Evan had become and now that they were here, he was feeling frightful.

"Evan, you look green my friend. Perhaps you need some air, why don't you get out and stretch your legs. I will make some tea," David said, climbing out and stretching his tight chest muscles. "I must say this is a glorious spot, the views are fantastic. Do you intend to build here?"

Evan watched Benita run off across the stony earth, arms outstretched like a bird flying free from its cage. He sensed her euphoria for he had felt that too, first time back.

"To be honest, David, I don't have a clue what I am going to do."

David's eyes were fixed on Benita too. "That's a shame because you could build a great place out here. Benita was raving about this place all the way from England. Looks like she isn't disappointed."

"Was she really?"

David gave a soft throaty laugh. "Oh, she wouldn't shut up. She has really missed Spain. To quote, she said it felt like she was coming home."

Evan was thoughtful for a moment, his aching muscles and nausea forgotten. "I never knew she felt like that."

"Ah, well I think there is a lot you don't know about Benita. For starters she isn't as tough as she makes out to be."

Perturbed, Evan cut in, "I always knew that. Benita is a very different person on the inside. She is very sensitive and caring and nowhere near as confident as she makes out."

David gave an agreeable grunt. "So very true, she is a beautiful fragile creature and one that is heartbreakingly in love with you." He put on his cap, shot Evan a knowing smile and climbed back into the van to make tea.

Evan felt a warm rush flood his limbs. Slipping a miniature bottle of scotch from his pocket, he took a large swig, eyes firmly fixed on Benita. He needed her so badly, he wanted to be reminded how good it felt to be inside her, feel her fingertips run along his skin, feel the bumps of anticipation rise on his flesh. How could he make a pass at her in this state, he thought sadly? She would most probably laugh in his face.

Things would never progress until he had dealt with Alexis - the other woman. The woman who consumed him. He was divorced but he may as well not been. She had come between him and Caroline and now she would come between him and Benita. At once, he was filled with rage! Goddamn her, she would not rule his life. This woman could not keep him from the things he desired. He strode away from the camper, his footfall heavy on the hard-baked ground. He wanted to rip her away from his body. She resembled a cobweb that had tangled itself around him, round and round until he was cocooned like a helpless fly waiting to be devoured. He felt in his pocket for the stone but it was empty. He cursed aloud, as he pushed on toward the foot of the mountain. There was no calming him. All he could think was to be free.

Benita and David sat sipping their tea; they watched him walking off in a silent brood until he was out of their view. David slipped his hand across the table and gave Benita's a comforting squeeze. "Don't worry, sweetie. He is so angry, he will be back later. I feel he needs to walk it off, he will feel heaps better later. You'll see." He winked at her.

"Let's hope you're right, David. I mean I don't have a clue. We're here now and so what? Do we wait for inspiration or is something going to happen? It's all bizarre, I am beginning to regret coming."

David hurried round the table to throw his arms around her shoulders. "Oh, kitten, no," he soothed. "You don't mean that. Granted it's all very strange but it's the right thing to do. Don't ask me how, I just know so."

He kissed her lightly on the cheek. "Don't give up, not yet! Tomorrow we will have a look around the village, ask about, and see if there is something to be learned. We don't have to be totally useless."

Benita squeezed his hand. "You're right of course, we should go and look at Alexis' old house and maybe I can show you where I used to live. As for Evan I hope he finds some sort of peace." She signalled to the impending darkness. "He will need to get a move on, his not familiar

144

with this terrain and if he has gone up into the mountains he will never make it down before nightfall."

Evan had carried on in a blind rage. Deciding against climbing the mountain with its craggy rock and narrow path, he had skirted round it and dropped down toward the river, which had dried up some weeks before. He followed its course along to the east, where, on the horizon, rising up into fine wispy cloud he could see the peaks of the Sierra Nevada. The route he followed angled this way and that, between slabs of broken rock and spiky cacti. He passed no one and as the anger began to subside, he slowed pace. The riverbed had progressed now into a canyon. The silvery rock was smoother here, raised either side of the river. The sun had disappeared, allowing a welcome cool to envelop his body. He took off his shirt, laid it down on the ground and knelt on it, looking around. This spot reminded him of the rocks they had climbed to the secret house. He knew it couldn't possibly be, but for a moment, he was filled with excitement. They must go tomorrow and see if it was still there, just him and Benita. If he planned it right, they could give David the slip and go together. Perhaps once they were there he could try to kiss her, make his move. Let her know just how he felt.

The welcoming cool intensified and with sickening dread he realised it was Alexis, she had returned once more.

He would not cower this time. He would fight her! It was about time she knew the truth. She could not force herself onto him like this uninvited. If not for him, he would do it for Benita.

Alexis appeared ahead of him, in the middle of the riverbed, as clear as any living person. Her smile told him that she welcomed the challenge, and although she beckoned, he made no move to follow her.

"Come to me if that's what you want!" he whispered under his breath. "If you must do this, then come to me." He felt his heart pounding in his chest. The sickening smell of her scent poisoned the air. "Tell me what you want, and then leave me alone. Go back to hell," he yelled.

# CHAPTER 15

Benita found it difficult to relax. It had grown late and David's casual response, "He is a grown man! He will be fine. Don't fret so," only made her feel worse.

Benita couldn't help fretting. After all, it had been their idea to come here and maybe that had been a stupid mistake, perhaps they were close to pushing Evan over the edge.

Evan hadn't seemed keen to return to Spain, resigning himself to the fact that Alexis may haunt him forever. He had hinted that maybe he was a little bit mad and that Barbara and Fiona were fakes. That maybe they hadn't a clue what they were dealing with. For a time, she had had her doubts too, when she recalled the past and the Evan she had first encountered, mixed up, confused, a little irrational too.

Of course, with the sort of parents he had, that was to be expected. She had grown close to him though and she had witnessed the change in the short time she had known him. If he was mad, she would have suspected then, surely?

Mind you, she was hardly a good judge of character, for had she been, would she really be here in Spain now? She wasn't married and didn't have a family, come to that; she hadn't much of a life. How could her opinion account for anything?

David's snoring was the most annoying sound in the stillness of the night as she lay wide awake, frantically trying to rationalise her thoughts. For a moment, she felt angry with David. How could he sleep when Evan was somewhere out there, cold and alone?

No, that was unfair, she thought. She rolled over onto her side with a restless sigh and remembered that David had been nothing short of an angel from the moment she had first met him.

Of course, this was a bit of adventure for him and a welcome change from the monotony of his everyday existence.

She wasn't stupid; she had read the signs, overheard his telephone conversations with Craig and sensed his inner despair. David was playing the part of the poor cheated wife.

Benita had instantly disliked Craig, if only from the picture that David had shown her in the study. A thickset man with cold calculating eyes and thinning blond hair. In the picture he stood with arms crossed, looking menacingly at the camera. In comparison David was a deeply sensitive man, who she believed was desperate to muster the strength to leave Craig and change his dull lonely existence.

Benita pitied him and if they ever got this mess sorted out, she would have words with him. He didn't deserve a man like Craig, who clearly bullied him.

Evan eyed Alexis with contempt. He would not cave in this time; she would not take his soul. From a distance, he surveyed her, their eyes held a steady gaze. He saw no malice there, only pain, and when the anger subsided, he began to feel her sorrow. How could she hope to express what she was feeling? Suddenly he understood that she needed to show him in order for him to understand. He needed so badly to understand and so he relaxed and in his mind's eye pictures began to unfold.

The rush of adrenaline he felt as he climbed back through the window and collected his bag from beneath the geraniums was euphoric.

Benita had pissed him off. She had made him so angry and in a way coming here had calmed him, eased his tattered nerves.

In the same way spying on Alexis had given him an enormous boost, going through her things and nosing around her house had helped him deal with this sexual frustration and the pain and hurt he felt at Benita's rejection.

He slung the bag easily over his shoulder and headed across the terrace toward the gate, looking down at the pool. At first, he ignored the dark shadow beneath the surface, until the moment it burst from the depths where it had been lurking in a wave of water.

Evan gasped, shocked and surprised, stepping back and losing his balance, to topple backwards onto his bottom. The gurgling choking sound was the worst; for a moment he was unable to move, he hadn't expected this! His heart hammered so hard he thought it would burst from his chest. He tried to rationalise what he was going to do.

Somebody was drowning; he must save them and quickly.

It was odd in that moment; his body seemed to shut down. The sun, which had been so bright and warm, was gone in a moment. Now it was dark and cold. He shivered, chewing nervously on his bottom lip, desperate to comfort himself. The terracotta tiles which he had crashed upon just moments before were no longer there. Beneath his cold and shivering body, there was only damp patchy grass.

The sky, grey and heavy with rain, felt lifeless overhead.

What was that sound? It rushed and crashed around him, it made his ears buzz. He had no idea where he was and what was happening. The terror and desperation he felt inside churned his stomach, tears springing to his eyes. He needed to escape this terror. Shakily he rose to his feet. Then he saw it, the angry bubbling water cascading over the worn rocks as the swollen river rushed past him. The sound of the hissing water blocked out all other sounds. It was a moment or two before he noticed the helpless child clinging to the rocks on the opposite bank. Her hair strewn across the ruthless waters, she looked at him, her eyes pleading desperation, her face somehow familiar.

"Daddy, please help me!" Her voice was barely audible, but he heard it just the same. For a second he felt compelled to dive into the river but something stopped him and with a sickening dread, he realised that no one could save her now.

The pain was sharp and angry in his right side, it caused him to groan. Evan opened his eyes, blinking furiously against the intense sunlight. The little old man looked down with concern before giving him another sharp prod with his walking stick.

"Ouch," Evan yelped, looking up at the man with an impertinent glare.

"Ah, so you're English. I should have guessed as much!" he rasped. "Whatever are you doing rolling about on the ground down here?" he asked, peering down at Evan, his eyes twinkling. "Did you lose your way or something, son?"

Evan sat up to take in his surroundings and then he remembered. "What time is it?"

The man looked at his watch. "A little after seven, I'm out for my early morning stroll and find you strewn across the river bed. Have you been out here all night?"

Evan stood up and brushed himself off. "Looks that way," He looked up at the clear sky and then back to the man. "I'm not a drunk, if that's what you're thinking. To be honest, I have no idea why I am still here. I guess I must have fallen asleep."

The man shook his head and seated himself on the stump of an upturned olive tree.

"No need to explain. Are you on holiday? Staying local are you?" he questioned.

Evan eyed the man suspiciously. Thoughtful for a moment; he seemed somehow familiar. Grey beard, merry eyes, but he dismissed it.

"Sort of, look I hate to be rude but I'd better get back. My friends will be worried." He gave the old man a pat on the shoulder. "Perhaps I will see you again sometime." Then, turning, he retraced his steps back along the riverbed.

"David, look, its Evan! I can see him," Benita screeched, leaping up from the chair which she had been planted in since sunrise, scanning the horizon from left to right and back again, awaiting Evan's return.

David's lathered face peered out of the van, razor in his hand. He looked to where Benita pointed and saw their friend ambling back across the stony ground.

"Thank goodness, I was starting to worry."

"Starting to!" Benita shot him a steely glare. "I have been awake half the night."

David came round to her. "Well you can relax now, he is back. I wonder if he has come up with anything on his travels."

Benita slipped on her shoes she headed across the field. "I don't care; he is one piece," she called over her shoulder, gathering pace as she made her way to welcome Evan back.

Looking down at the breakfast that David placed in front of him Evan groaned as a wave of nausea clutched his belly. Benita, noticing his look of anguish, leapt across to remove the offending plate. "You look a bit squiffy, if you don't mind my saying. Perhaps it would be better to skip breakfast. How about a shot of brandy in that coffee instead?" she asked.

Evan nodded. "Yes please. I'm sorry, David. I appreciate the thought but I just can't face it at the moment."

David nodded his head in agreement. "I'm not offended, don't worry. I am, however, intrigued to hear what happened, just one more time if you don't mind. I think it has some significance. Especially the drowning bit."

"Well not really, David. I mean that is how Alexis died and so I suppose that is what she is showing me."

David poured himself a glass of the brandy that Benita had put on the table in front of Evan and interrupted, "Yes, that seems obvious, but your visions or dream or whatever it was, well that was set in another place, another time. It reminded me of something Barbara said. Do you remember, she said about you having spent another lifetime together?"

Evan was thoughtful. "So what are you suggesting?"

"I'm not really sure but perhaps we could focus on the possibility that Alexis and whatever message she needs to get to you isn't just about her drowning here in Spain twenty years ago. That perhaps, as far-fetched as it appears, there is some link from another time!"

Benita, who sat idly looking out across the fields, turned to David. "So we would all have to admit to believing in reincarnation, if we are to go along with your suggestion."

"Maybe so! I mean it's not that unbelievable considering what is happening to Evan at the moment, is it?"

Evan stood up and paced the length of the motor home. "I don't think we can rule anything out. It is easy for me, you two only have my word for any of this, don't you!"

Both turned to look at him. "So what if, in another lifetime, we were together. What on earth can I be expected to do about that now?"

David came to his side and placed a placating hand on his shoulder. "Try to relax as much as possible and if you can, I know it's not what you really want, but if you can try to reach out to her in your mind. Ask her to help you. Tell her that you are willing to listen."

David gulped back the last drop of brandy in his glass. "I suggest we go into the village and take a look around. Benita can give us a tour and then I will treat us all to lunch."

Evan looked across at Benita.

"Come on, let's go and take our minds off this for a while," she said, trying to lighten his mood.

Evan shrugged. "I guess you're both right. Maybe we could run by father's old place. I would like to see it."

David cleared the table. "Of course we can. Come on, Benita, let's put this lot away. We have places to go and people to see and a mystery to solve."

Nothing much had changed in the village. It was hard to believe that twenty years had passed.

David, dressed in a short-sleeved shirt and cotton shorts, looking every bit the tourist with his camera slung around his neck and a pair of expensive shades, strolled along the pavement.

Evan hurried ahead, keen to go into the bar. He wasn't expecting to find Esmeralda but he wanted to see how it looked.

He stepped through the front door and stopped. Benita caught up with him and brushed past him into the dingy bar.

"Why, it is exactly the same in here. Nothing has changed." She turned to look at Evan. "Just as boring. Well, I think we should stay for a coffee at least."

Evan went over to a table by the window that looked out on the street. David joined him.

"Benita is getting the coffees. Are you ok Evan? You have gone awfully pale."

Evan fidgeted nervously. "I don't really know," he said, looking across at David. "It's Alexis, she is here. She has decided to join us. How fitting."

"Where!" David shrilled, launching backwards, nearly knocking the tray that Benita was carrying right out of her hands.

"Quick, sit down, Benita," David hissed. "Alexis is here." He looked nervously around. "Can you see her Evan, where is she?"

"No, but I can feel her she is so close. In fact I think she is talking to me in my mind."

"How do you know?" Benita asked, passing them their coffees and sitting down next to David. David took a quick gulp of coffee.

"Shush, let the man concentrate or he will lose her." He hurriedly pulled a pen and notepad from his bum bag. "Go on, Evan, describe what you're feeling."

Evan had gone deathly pale; Benita noticed the goose bumps on his flesh. It appeared he was staring into thin air.

"Evan," she said softly with an encouraging nod.

Evan was still for several moments and then he cleared his throat. "She wants us to go to her house, I think. At least that is what she is showing me. I just keeping seeing a picture of her house in my mind." He sat upright and rubbed at his eyes. "It's ridiculous, all I could see was her house coupled with a feeling of urgency."

David pulled his chair in closer to the table. "No, it is not ridiculous. It is a start, if anything. Do you think that is where we should head when we have drunk these?"

Benita looked across at Evan. "Are you ok? You look terrible."

"Cheers, I love you too," he replied playfully. "I am fine. It is weird in a way, I don't feel afraid anymore. I am beginning to understand that if I help her she will leave me. David is right, I have to encourage her, speak to her, if we are to sort this fiasco out. I think we should head over to her house. Obviously it will be difficult, I mean somebody must live there but we could have a drive by and see what happens."

David stood up. "Let's strike while the iron's hot!" He strode across to the bar to settle up.

Benita watched him, then she turned to Evan. "Are you sure that you're ok with this? David is lovely but he can be annoyingly bossy at times."

"Absolutely fine, don't worry Benita; I was being truthful when I said that I am not as freaked out about this anymore. Come on," he said, taking her arm and guiding her out into the street. "Soon this will be settled and we can all get on with our lives. Thank you, Benita. This means an awful lot to me, I know it all seems so…"

Benita held a silencing fingertip to his lips. "Don't say anything. It was mainly David's idea. I am just glad I can be of help. Besides, I didn't exactly have a lot on." She grinned. "You know, if we hadn't had believed in this, then neither myself nor David would be here. We need to sort out what Alexis wants from you and then perhaps you can get back to normal. As a good friend it is the very least I can do."

David was waiting in the sunshine; he stood on the other side of the street gazing in the window of the estate agents. He turned to smile at them as they approached.

"I can't believe how the price of property has rocketed over here. Gone are the days when you could find a bargain."

Benita looked in the window and gave a low whistle. "Jesus, I should have stayed out here and bought somewhere. I would have made a fortune."

Evan laughed. "Hindsight is a wonderful thing. However, it won't last forever. I believe the market will level out soon. All the Europeans buying property have really pushed the prices up but it's fair to say we have missed the boom and prices are on the slide now. Another couple of years and there will be something within your reach." He smiled at Benita. "If you decided you wanted to come back of course."

David gave a throaty cough. "Well that's a shame. Evan, If that is what you believe, I suggest you flog that bit of land

Foggy left you." He pointed in the shop window. "Look there is a plot there not dissimilar to yours and there asking over a hundred and fifty thousand Euros for it."

There was a piercing squeal from Benita's direction and both turned in alarm to look at her; she bounced excitedly up and down on the pavement.

"Oh my, Evan, look at that!" she pointed at one of the properties in the window. "If I am not mistaken, isn't that your father's old house, look that one for sale there."

Evan scanned the properties before him. "Where, show me?" Then he stopped in recognition of the house on the mountainside, with the small porch draped in jasmine. "My, oh my," he breathed. "So it is, how very strange."

David clapped both hands together in delight. "Looks like the Gods are with us today." He strode to the door. "I will pretend that I am interested in buying it and we shall make an appointment to view. Just perfect!" he declared, winking at them both.

"Well it would be interesting, David, but it hardly helps our cause, does it?"

"More than you realise, Benita darling." He raised a knowing brow and then looked across at Evan. "Let's not forget that one can see an awful lot from the terrace of that house. Especially with a pair of binoculars," he added, grinning from ear to ear.

"But we don't have any, David," Benita wailed, stating the obvious.

David pushed open the door and turned back to face both of them. "Who says that we don't!" He gave a boyish chuckle.

# CHAPTER 16

The agent was keen. "The property is currently empty and has been for some time," he informed them, eagerly handing over the keys.

"It needs lots of work and the pool needs rebuilding," he warned. "But the views are spectacular and it will make a great holiday home with a little TLC."

Pulling up at the front of the rusty gates, Evan felt a lump in his throat. He never believed he would be back here again. He found himself momentarily lost in the emotions of his father and those lost years.

As he climbed out of the car, Benita linked her arm through his. "A lot of memories, huh."

"Yes there is, but I'm ok." Straightening his shoulders he looked across at the property, now desolate and sad. "The place looks ever so run down, doesn't it?"

Benita nodded in agreement. The years had taken their toll.

David stood at the end of the terrace where he stretched his arms up toward the sky. "It is glorious. You didn't exaggerate, the views are marvellous. What a fantastic little place," he enthused, turning back to smile at Evan.

Benita walked across to the edge of the terrace, hugging her arms around herself as she looked out across the valley. Everything seemed pretty much the same. Some new properties littered the mountainside on the other side of the valley but it didn't distract from the beauty of the place.

Evan plonked himself down at the edge of the empty pool, which was now a muddy pit with several large cracks in the side. Feeling more relaxed beneath the warming sun, he closed his eyes, listening to Benita, who was explaining to

David what had changed since her last visit and in which direction the plot of land was. At David's insistence, she pointed out where Alexis' house was. Evan could hear the scratching of David's pen as he hastily jotted notes down in his note pad.

Evan opened his eyes at the mention of her name. "Alexis, Alexis." The word whispered through his mind. She was back. He could feel her energy cocooning him.

"What do you want?" he asked, closing his eyes again and tuning into her energy.

He felt a stirring in his loins and a pleasurable ripple of heat coursed his body.

Her energy felt softer, much gentler today. Benita's voice faded into the distance as he submerged into the energies that swirled around him.

The pool was shimmering beneath the Mediterranean sun. He had to get into the water, the heat was unbearable today. He looked across at Benita draped on the adjacent sun bed; she was naked, lying very still, relishing the heat. He made his way across to her, knelt down at her side where his fingertips hovered above her nipples. Evan watched them rise in anticipation of his touch. He felt his manhood struggle beneath the cotton material. Benita gave a low murmur and stretched her body out before him. Lowering his mouth to her breast, he flicked his tongue across her burning skin, savouring the sweet taste he encountered as he gently nipped at her.

Benita, opening her eyes, looked down at him, a smile crossing her lips. She pushed his head gently downward where he traced her flesh with the tip of his tongue, exploring each crease and contour.

He could contain himself no longer. Taking off his shorts, his manhood pulsed in his guiding hand. He looked down at her stretched before him, only to recoil in horror as his eyes met with Alexis' satisfied gaze.

Evan opened his eyes against the blinding sun. David peered down at him.

"Did you drop off for a bit?" he asked, scratching his head, looking down on Evan as if he were a small child in need of assistance. "Thought we would leave you be for a while, just in case Alexis was trying to make contact. We didn't want to disturb you."

Evan swallowed hard and looked guiltily up at Benita with a flicker of shame in his eyes. He couldn't exactly tell them about his little fantasy, the one which Alexis had so rudely gate crashed.

"No I was just dozing. It must be my night under the stars, it is finally catching up on me."

David handed him a beer. "Well, we are set up over there." He pointed across the terrace where they had assembled a table and some chairs. Evan noticed with horror the binoculars lying on the table. Taking a swig of beer, David signalled that they should join Benita who, seated at the table, was waiting expectantly for him.

"We have already sussed Alexis' house out. Benita reckons it looks empty but we figure you should take a look." He handed him the binoculars. "If it is, then I agree we should go and have a snoop around."

Evan grew cold at the prospect, he gave an inward groan. This was becoming too uncomfortable for his liking but David stood waiting, and so with a sickening dread, he knew he had no other option.

With shaking hands, he took the binoculars from David, who smiled encouragingly, then adjusting them to his eyes he peered down into the valley.

Alexis' house stood just as he remembered it. He took a couple of deep breaths, reminding himself that this time it was totally innocent; there was no Alexis there nude sunbathing on the terrace.

"So what do you think?" David pressed, eager to find out if there would be any chance of them nosing around.

Evan panned in on the house; he looked around the pool area then across beneath the carob tree. He had to admit the place seemed deserted.

"I agree, it looks like it is empty but you can't be sure. Perhaps we should forget it. We don't want to be arrested for trespassing. Don't think I would fancy being holed up in a Spanish jail really."

David more or less wrestled the binoculars from him. "Here, let me take another look. I mean it's silly if we don't. The odds are we won't get another chance after today."

Benita came to Evan's rescue. "Don't force it, David. Evan has had enough today."

"Oh, don't be so ridiculous. He is not a child. Of course he is up for it." He banged the binoculars down on the table. "It didn't stop him a few years back, did it?"

"David! How could you be so..."

Evan stepped forward and placed a hand on her shoulder. "It's ok, Benita. He is right. I came here to face my demons and that is exactly what I am going to do. Today is as good as any. Just one thing though, you should stay here and keep watch. If anybody comes along the track then call my mobile, ok?"

David gave him a swift pat on the back. "That's the spirit. Come on, let us not waste any more time." He looked across at Benita. "You really shouldn't worry so much, kitten."

Benita would have liked to take a swing at David, but she smiled despite herself. She just couldn't help being protective of Evan and as she watched him climb in the wagon with David she thought how stupid that seemed. He was a big powerful man yet all this stuff with Alexis had made her lose sight of the fact that he really was rather handsome and capable.

She scolded herself. She could not think that way. He was her friend and romance would only complicate matters. Besides, she thought as she watched them leave, it would be the kiss of death; romance and Benita were not a good mix by any measure.

Evan and David parked at the end of the new track where it formed a junction with the old.

The heat was unbearable. David cursed softly, the adrenaline coursing through his veins the only thing to spur him on.

"So much for that lunch you promised, David," Evan grumbled, as they climbed the steep track, the rising dust stinging their eye balls.

"Oh, don't moan. We will have dinner tonight instead. It really is best to make the most of this opportunity. We only need to have a quick look around. I figured that if Alexis has anything to show you she will make contact quite quickly. Don't you agree?"

"Perhaps, you can never tell with Alexis." For a moment, he pondered telling David about what had happened earlier by the pool but then he thought better of it. Maybe it would be better to keep some things to himself. Besides, he didn't want to run the risk of David telling Benita all.

He looked across to the north, to the mountain and picked out several houses. When they turned the next bend, they should be in Benita's sight. He thought of her sitting alone on the terrace watching them and for a moment, he wondered if she would zoom in on his profile; take the opportunity to examine him more closely, just as he had done to Alexis all those years ago.

The thought excited him. Benita could be so close and yet so far but as they rounded the bend, the thought was forgotten. Alexis' house on the horizon beckoned and a raw fear gripped Evan's insides. He turned to look across at David; beads of perspiration peppered his brow. He looked down at the rising hairs on the back of his own hand and shivered. This was exactly what she wanted, him here on her territory. In that moment he felt like a puppet, Alexis controlling the strings.

David broke the silence. "A nice little place really, although I must say a bit of a jaunt to get to."

"You wanted to come," Evan said flatly.

David stopped to pull a handkerchief from his pocket and mopped fiercely at his brow. Evan carried on. The sooner he could get this over with the better. The iron hate was ajar. With a shiver he stepped through and for a brief moment, he thought of Benita somewhere on the mountain keeping watch. The thought comforted him as he strode across the terrace. he was surprised to see that the pool was scrupulously clean, implying that the place wasn't as deserted as they had first thought.

David emerged beneath the archway panting. "Holy Moses, I think I am going to have a heart attack!" He made his way delicately across to the low rise wall, bordered by pastel pink geraniums, and plonked himself down on it. "Guess I am not as fit as I used to be," he said, dropping his chin to his chest and taking a moment to regain his breath.

Evan turned away, his body beginning to twitch. To admit he was feeling uncomfortable would be a vast understatement. He looked around, purposefully avoiding looking down at the pool.

There was no sound at all. It was quiet here, the birds they had heard earlier up on the mountain seemed to have disappeared; there wasn't even the whispering sound of the wildlife that lurked ever present in the wild grasses.

Evan had expected to experience Alexis but there was nothing. He felt suddenly emotionless, as he walked toward the carob tree and sat down on the tiled floor beneath its shady branches. There was a gurgling sound from the terrace and he looked back to see David sound asleep on the wall.

Evan grinned. David was a great assistant to have by his side. He wondered if Benita could see them, she would have a few things to say to David on their return.

Evan was here now so he supposed that he should at least take a look around. He stood up, brushing the dust from his shorts. A short raspy cough from somewhere behind made him jump. He turned in alarm, surprised to see a little old man sitting on the doorstep of the house. After the initial shock he cleared his throat to speak but the old man beat him to it.

"So, we meet again. What are you up to this time?" he asked, a look of amusement crossing his wrinkled face.

Evan recognised with a start the old man from the riverbed; sheepishly he took a step toward him.

"I know this looks really bad but I used to know someone that lived here," Evan croaked nervously.

"Did you now!" He eyed Evan suspiciously, "You're a bit of a bad penny aren't you?" He scratched his balding head and chuckled. Lifting his fragile body up onto rickety legs and using his stick for support, he glanced across at David. "And what about him, did he come to hold your hand?"

Evan cursed David under his breath. He knew from experience that Benita would not see him here, either. How could he explain to this man what he was doing? There really was no feasible explanation, so he changed tactics.

"Is this your place?" he asked, offering his arm to the man as he stepped shakily toward him. He took it gratefully, winding his bony fingers around Evan's wrist. Evan looked down at the veined and leathery hand with distaste and suddenly his blood ran cold. Every hair on his body spiked in terror. His chest tightened, restricting the flow of air to his lungs. He felt queasy and very afraid.

The hand gripped tighter and he looked back down, horrified at the long elegant fingers with crimson nails that dug into his flesh.

"Please don't fight me Evan, we don't have much time!"

Evan tried to yank his arm away but her grip was much too tight. "This isn't happening," he whispered through gritted teeth. "This isn't happening, I'm dreaming, I must be." As her nails dug deeper, he knew that it wasn't a dream. He looked up at her face, his body frozen with fear.

Their eyes met. For a moment, he lost focus, mesmerized by the jade green eyes and the empty space they inhabited, but now he could see beyond them, see the sorrow and pain and reluctantly he relaxed his arm; it was he realised of no use to fight her.

I'm sorry," he sobbed, dropping his gaze down to the floor, "I should have helped you, I know I could have saved you. Forgive me, Alexis, please forgive me."

"It is not that easy, you must forgive yourself first. Look at me, Evan."

He felt her fingertips on his skin, her touch cold and scratchy, not of this world. He looked back at her through the tears.

"How can I forgive myself? Only a coward would leave a drowning woman. Only a coward," he repeated through trembling lips.

"And who would drown their own child?" she asked, her eyes searching his.

Evan's body shook beneath violent sobs, tears streamed down his cheeks. "Somebody evil," he croaked. "A despicable person who doesn't deserve to live."

Alexis' tone softened, a smile touching her lips. "Evan, you gave up. Life is a test, understand that."

The sobs subsided, the fear decreased and he looked back at Alexis, puzzled.

"What do you want, Alexis? Tell me and it is yours."

"Dearest Evan, I need a second chance too, but I cannot complete my task without you. You must forgive the past, what's done, is done. Now you can offer a new life, another chance to connect with your soul. We can do it this time. Please help me, Evan, I seek eternal peace." She released her hold, her eyes pleading with his. "But it must be together this time."

Dropping his head to his hands and pressing his eyes into his palms he was thoughtful. He didn't understand; how could he? He rubbed at his eyes before having the courage to face her again, fearing it with all his heart.

Evan looked up, steeling himself for her questioning gaze, but was startled to find David in her place whom peered closely at him, brow creased in concern. Then David smiled.

"That's good, Evan. Well done!" He congratulated him, thrusting his notebook forward. "I think I got most of that down."

"Got what down, where is Alexis?" He rubbed his temples. "David, I am confused, she was right here."

David slipped his arm around Evan's shoulders. "No she wasn't, just us. So sorry to disappoint you. We are at her house though. Do you remember, we came to take a look around and..." he trailed off.

Evan shrugged off the comfort of David's arm. "I know, I remember all that. We came here and you fell asleep on the wall and then I..."

"No, you fell asleep on the wall, Evan. It was you old chap, not me," David said, keen to get the facts straight. "I tried to wake you, but you were so deep and then you started sleepwalking. It was quite scary at first, your eyes were open and you were pacing up and down. Muttering under your breath, then your voice became clearer more tangible and so I grabbed these." he held up his pen and book and grinned. "I mean after all, this is what we came for and it's brilliant, one sided of course but I think we can call it a day. We can discuss this over dinner tonight and you…"

He caught Evan by the arm just before he crashed to the floor, breaking his fall. "Oh dear," he muttered, holding on to him tightly. "I think we may have overdone it again."

Benita was furious at David.

"I can't believe you didn't call me. Had it not occurred to you that it could be dangerous, letting Evan be taken over by spirit!"

David blushed, his tone defiant. "Oh Benita, don't you think you are overreacting a little?" He looked over to Evan, who was polishing off a second can of beer. "There is no harm done. See, your boyfriend looks well enough to me."

Benita sat staring across the valley with her arms folded, avoiding David's eyes. "It was foolish, and in future I won't trust you alone with him. In addition, Evan is not my boyfriend."

"But you would like him to be, wouldn't you?" David replied in childish tone.

Benita couldn't tolerate any more. "We have been here over three hours. I suggest we pack up and get these keys back to the agent," she said, tossing them at David. Turning on her heel, she strode over to Evan. "We're leaving. I am tired and hungry and I think we have had more than enough ghost hunting for one day, don't you?"

David raised a brow at Evan. "Ignore her, it's the heat," he whispered, gathering his things up from the table.

David returned from the bar with a bottle of Rioja and three glasses. "A peace offering," he declared, looking pointedly at Benita.

"Come on, let's enjoy this evening." Evan nudged her

arm. "It's a great choice of restaurant and a fantastic menu," he encouraged, waving it beneath Benita's nose.

Reluctantly, Benita took it from him. "Good, it better be, I am bloody well starving," Then looking up at David, she said, "make mine a large glass, I deserve it."

As David speared the pork fillet in wild mushroom sauce on his fork, he decided that maybe it would be best not to mention this afternoon. Benita was only just beginning to thaw out about the whole episode. Evan, draining his second glass of wine, seemed unfazed by the day's events. They hadn't had a chance to discuss it fully but David was certain he was right in his assumption of the situation. They had to shift their focus onto the past, the distant past and, as absurd as it seemed, another lifetime. Benita was going to prove the difficulty in getting any further forward with the whole case. She was so damn protective of Evan. It would be a start if she loosened up and could admit she was in love with the guy.

Perhaps they needed some gentle guidance, he wondered. Tomorrow he needed to make some calls, there was a little research he needed to do and he needed to escape them in order to complete his detective work.

"I thought we could all take a day off tomorrow," he eyed his companions agreeably across a plate of mixed salad. "I need to make a few calls for Craig and check on a few things back home. I thought maybe you two could take a trip down memory lane."

Evan jumped at the chance. "Sounds like a good idea," he said, topping up their wine glasses. "If you don't mind working from one of the bars in the village, Benita and I could take the van for a drive. What do you think?" he asked, turning to her.

"If you want to." Her tone was flat and nonchalant, much to Evan's disappointment.

"That would suit me just fine, to tell the truth I could do with a day out of the sun," David said smiling, adding extra vinegar to his share of the salad.

"Would that really be ok with you, Benita?" Evan asked hesitantly.

Benita, looking a little flushed from the wine, smiled.

164

"Yes, anything but ghost hunting and I'm happy. Let's have another bottle of wine." She signalled for the waiter.

David woke first to a marbled grey sky. "Looks like we may have a drop of rain on the way," he said, handing them both a mug of tea.

Benita took it shakily from him. "I think I've got a hangover," she wailed.

David chuckled, making himself more comfortable on the sofa, "You and me both, darling. That wine was delicious but bloody strong. How about you Evan, how are you feeling today?"

"Not too bad to tell the truth." Evan never got a hangover anymore. He wondered if the alcohol ever left his body. It couldn't continue. When this mess was sorted out and after yesterday's events at the house, there was the faintest glimmer of hope it might be. Then he was going to quit the booze.

Later on, he would have to have a chat with David and go over exactly what did happen, he was desperate to understand it.

They dropped David at the bar on the hill, which looked out across the lake.

"Can we drive past my old house? I'd like to see what the place is like now," Benita asked, glad of a break from David and pleased to have some time alone with Evan.

She had been so cross with David but she had to admit that since the episode at Alexis' house, there had been quite a dramatic change in Evan. His mood had lifted and he seemed far brighter in himself. She observed him discreetly from behind her shades as he manoeuvred the camper van along the winding mountain road. He had caught the sun, sporting a healthy glow and he hadn't shaved since their arrival. The dark shadow crossing his jaw line only added to the appeal.

Benita felt an inner longing. He was, after all, quite a rarity. Not only good looking, he actually had a heart as well. She had to admit there was something going on, David was right, but she could never admit how she felt to Evan.

Tearing her eyes away from him she focused on the road.

"If you take the next left, it should be just on our right," she said confidently, excited to get a glimpse of the home she grew up in.

As they turned the corner, she felt her heart sink. The small casita with the gnarled vine hanging heavily over its veranda, which was nearly always laden with grapes, had vanished. In its place stood several crates of bricks awaiting the arrival of the builders.

Evan pulled up on the side of the road, her disappointment washing over him too.

"I am so sorry, Benita." He leant across to stroke her cheek.

Benita took a deep breath. "Oh well, that's life. The place was half falling down anyway." She shrugged.

"But it was your home, it must be sad for you." Evan gave a half smile, uncertain how she really felt.

Benita slid off her sunglasses. "It's just a house, Evan. Nothing more," she snapped.

They drove back down the mountain in silence, Benita silently brooding as she looked out across the view below them. Evan left her to it. He knew better than to force the issue with Benita; she would only despise him for it.

As they drove in to the village, she finally spoke. "Do you fancy going to the old house?" she asked, looking across at him, her eyes hidden behind the black lenses.

"I would love to if you're ok with that?" Evan couldn't help smiling.

"I just asked didn't I! I mean why would I suggest it if I wasn't prepared to go?" She took off her glasses and placed them on her head before scowling across at him.

"Tell you what, Benita. Why don't you just lighten up? You're so fucking up your own arse all the time, it makes me sick!"

Benita's eyes blazed as she swung round to defend herself. "I'm up my own arse. What about you! Poor Evan this and poor Evan that. Let me remind you this whole Goddamn trip is about you."

"No one forced you to come along. You came because

your life is so shit back home and it's a chance to escape, a free get away!" He ground the gears down for the long trawl up hill. "You have always been so bloody minded. I should have known better than to get involved with you again. You broke this heart once and you will do it again, for sure. You haven't changed, Benita, and you sure as hell haven't grown up either." Adrenaline flooded his body as he waited with bated breath for her defence but to his surprise, she fell silent. After several seconds, he sneaked a glance across at her. She sat rigid, staring out of the window, her jaw set. They drove a few miles further, he hadn't a clue where he was going as he had only ever walked to the house before and he didn't even know if the place had a proper entrance. He pulled off the road onto a dirt track and stopped. Switching off the engine, he crossed his arms and looked across at Benita.

"So are we going to the house or not? Because if we are I will need a little input from you. Like which direction for starters?"

Benita was struggling to come to terms with what had just happened. She had never seen Evan like that. At first she had felt angry but since leaving the village she had thought about it and realised that perhaps he had a point. It took every ounce of courage she had to look across and smile at him, now that her pride was bruised.

"Yes, I would like to go. Straight up this road about two miles, then we turn off on to a track, I will tell you when. Is that ok?"

"Definitely!" he replied, restarting the engine, careful to conceal the smug smile that threatened to saturate his face. For once Benita had given in and it felt fantastic.

"Turn left here." She pointed to a dusty track a hundred yards ahead of them. "Can't promise that we will get anywhere near it of course, but it's worth a look."

Evan drove up to the dilapidated gates held together by a rusty padlock.

"Now this place is certainly deserted." He walked toward the gates and peered in, Benita hot on his heels.

"Look, we can squeeze through here." She signalled to a

small gap where the bars were bent. "Let's head around the side, I don't think we should try and get in, do you?"

"No I agree, let's take a look around the back."

As they surfaced on the rear terrace, Evan felt saddened at the sight of the place. It was rundown and deserted, the pool empty. The only thing that remained intact were the cypress trees, and twice as tall as he remembered them.

Benita stood with hands on hips surveying the sorry sight. "What a pity. A grand old place like this in such distress. I never thought it would be like this. I had visions of it being somehow grander. That perhaps some wealthy businessman from Madrid had brought it. A country retreat in which to entertain his friends and that we would not be able to get anywhere near the place."

Evan kicked at the dry earth. "Sure is a shame, but you know what," he took her hand and guided her to sit down with him on the hard baked ground. "If you close your eyes and are still, just for a moment, then you can remember the way it was."

She giggled. "Let me try," she said, closing her eyes.

It was true, the sun hot on her skin and the fragrant smell of jasmine and she was back in time. The shimmering pool stretched before her and there was Evan laughing as he plunged into its cooling waters.

She opened her eyes, her mouth crinkling into a smile as she met Evan's heady gaze.

"It could be even more realistic," he whispered, moving in closer and letting his lips brush the side of her neck. She didn't pull away as he had anticipated she might but softened toward him. Surprised and excited he sought her lips until the soft gentle strokes became a passionate kiss.

Evan tasted good and fresh. A hungry shiver coursed down her spine. She remained softly pliable as he circled her body with his arms. His strong hands stroked her bare flesh. She returned Evan's kiss feverishly, and was suddenly painfully aware just how much she had missed a man's touch. It felt good, she didn't want it to end, but the sound of tyres on the gravel at the front of the house caused them both to break apart in alarm.

"I think we have company." Evan scrambled to his feet, pulling her up at the same time.

Benita, a little bedazzled, straightened the glasses hanging lopsided on her head. "Shit, let's just say we got lost," she hissed.

"Oh yeah, that's a good one. And we just happened to climb through the locked gates and nose around uninvited."

A smart couple appeared on the terrace and smiled welcomingly as they headed across the jaded terracotta towards them.

Extending a friendly hand the man lunged toward them. "Mr and Mrs Hall, so nice to meet at last."

# CHAPTER 17

David, still laughing, clutched at his aching sides. "I can't believe you both went along with it. I mean what if the real Mr and Mrs Hall had shown up?"

Benita swirled the aged brandy around her glass.

"I guess we would have been in the mire, to put it bluntly. As it happens we had a free tour of the house and Evan appeared to be so interested that they took us to the local bar and brought us a drink."

"Absolutely classic!" David said, rubbing his hands together in delight.

Evan smiled across at Benita and winked. "It was fun though wasn't it?

She giggled. "It certainly was. After all the *'Alexis business'* it was most refreshing."

David summoned the waiter to order another round of drinks, then, straightening up in his seat, he cleared his throat. "Which brings me to another matter. Whilst you two have been having fun I haven't been sat on my thumbs. In fact I have been doing a bit of investigating and if it is alright with you, Benita, I think Evan and I are in need of a serious chat?"

"So I take it that I am to be excluded from whatever you have discovered?"

David looked sheepish. "No, I don't want to exclude you from anything, it just seems you get a bit upset about all this and perhaps it would be easier."

"It's ok. I need the ladies anyway but make it quick." Standing up, she smiled across at Evan, "Keep an open mind on whatever he has to say, I think David is enjoying all this ghost hunting a bit too much." She peered at David. "Don't worry, I'm going."

David waited until she was out of sight before he spoke. "Quite frankly, Evan, we are running out of time. Apart from your experience at the house, we haven't learnt very much. I feel we require a helping hand, and so I took the liberty of seeking the help of a local psychic."

Evan nearly choked. "Oh, Benita is going to love that!"

"I don't care," David retorted, hotly. "It really isn't up to Benita is it, or me, this is about you and the reason we came," he said pointedly, trying to gauge Evan's reaction.

Evan raked his fingers through his hair, a look of amusement about him. "I see, so tell me what is this psychic like and more importantly does she speak any English?"

"Well of course she speaks English, you fool. Lydia comes highly recommended and so she should, she charges a hundred Euros an hour."

Evan took a sip of brandy. "My, you must want to get to the bottom of this. Strange really, I mean what's in it for you?"

David shifted uneasily in his chair. "Nothing, except I like to get to the bottom of things and, well, I guess in a way it would be rather comforting to know that death isn't the end. That it may, in fact, be only the beginning."

"And what if there is nothing, no proof to satisfy your hungry mind? That after this whole charade you may find that maybe I am mad and the whole Alexis drama is a load of cobblers. What then?"

"Let's say I am confident that it is not." He paused while the waiter served their drinks. "Besides, I'm paying so don't moan and just agree that you will see Lydia."

"That really depends."

David gave a restless sigh, "On what exactly?"

"When and where is this little spectacle to take place?"

"Is that important?" David asked, avoiding looking at Evan but gazing vacantly around the bar instead.

"Yes, very!" he snapped.

"Ok, it seems Alexis' house is up for rent. So, yes you guessed. I have rented it for a month. I mean after all, the motor home is getting a bit cramped and we really need to be at the hub of all this psychic activity, don't we?"

Evan drained his glass, grimacing at the strong brandy which seemed instantly stronger.

"Hey steady on, that's twenty Euros a glass!" David reminded him.

"No way, David. I'm not staying there at that house."

"Oh don't be daft, it will be fine," he said, leaning back to get the waiter's attention and signalling for him to refill Evan's glass.

"It's not you that has to contend with Alexis," Evan wailed.

"No, and you're right of course. Perhaps you could think of it another way. After all, it is obvious by the change of mood around the table here tonight that something happened between you and Benita out there at the old house earlier, the admiring glances between you have not gone unnoticed. That, of course, is none of my business," he said hurriedly, "However, renting Alexis' old place would mean far more privacy for us all and the bedrooms are divine. You know we never got to look inside but the place has had some renovation to the interior apparently and it is in good shape. I have instructed that the gardens be tidied." He stopped and, raising his glass to his lips, he peered over its rim at Evan to be sure that he had his attention. "We should be in residence by the end of the week."

Abruptly he sat up. "Ah, now here comes Benita. The only thing you have to do, Evan, is convince her and I will take care of the finances."

"Benita darling, we thought you had deserted us." David rose to pull out her chair. "I took the liberty of ordering you another brandy," he said, glancing across at Evan with a knowing grin.


Evan waited until he could hear the satisfied grunts of David asleep.

"Benita, are you awake?" he whispered into the darkness.

"Yes, I'm finding it difficult to sleep, it's so hot."

"Me too, shall we go out for some air?"

Silently they emerged from the camper into the sultry night, lit by the glowing moon.

It was cooler outside, the gentle breeze a welcome relief from the stuffy air inside.

"What a beautiful night," Benita breathed, looking up at the stars. Evan gazed across at her, illuminated in the silvery light of the moon; her flimsy cotton pyjamas hugged tightly to her body, showing every luscious curve.

"Shall we take a walk?" He slipped his hand around hers, feeling a deep sense of comfort in her touch.

"We are going to stay at Alexis' house as from Friday, for a few weeks. David thought it would be better that I told you." He felt her tighten her hold around his hand. "I am fine with it," he reassured her.

"Yes, but I'm not sure that I am." She pulled back.

"Really, and why is that?" he asked, stopping to face her.

"Too spooky there. After what happened to you the other day, well, I'm not sure I would feel comfortable."

"It isn't you she wants though, is it?"

"What does she want, Evan? I am not sure I really understand any of this anymore!" She turned away, hugging her arms around herself. "I know this has all gone to David's head. I don't have to ask if this was his idea, he is becoming obsessive about the whole thing."

"I know he is, but what's the harm? From a personal point of view, I wouldn't mind solving the riddle, if only to be free of Alexis."

Benita began to walk, "How do you know that you're not?"

"I still feel her. I haven't seen her for a few days, just the fact that I sense her. After what happened, things seemed to have calmed down somewhat. I'm not sure if you believe me, Benita, and I wouldn't blame you if you didn't but I need to find the underlying cause of this, however bizarre it seems. Something inside tells me that it is the right decision to go and stay there. I know David instigated this but in a way…"

"Go on," she said softly.

"I think she is pulling David's strings as well."

Benita shivered as she turned to face Evan. "This is crazy, I know. I think we all have our part in this. I'm frightened about going there but somehow I know I must."

Evan stepped forward, pulling her closer toward him. He bent to kiss the top of her head. "It is going to be ok. Trust me, Benita; I won't let anything happen to you."

David looked out of the window and saw Benita busy washing the breakfast dishes.

He turned to Evan. "Have you told her yet?"

"Yes. Benita is fine with it."

"I am surprised." David raised a brow. "I thought she would freak out."

"Well she hasn't and we are in your hands, David," he said, smoothing gel through his hair. "As you well know, of course."

"It will mean you two can have some time alone."

"How is that then?" Evan paused to look across at David.

"Let's say I met an interesting man yesterday."

"Oh yes, is this the same man who recommended Lydia?"

David looked mysterious. "No, not at all, dinner in fact. I may have other fish to fry, leaving you free to romance Miss Frosty."

Evan pulled on his trainers. "Oh I see, and what would Craig have to say about that?"

"It is only dinner, Evan!" David blushed. Who was he trying to kid? Karl had introduced himself in the bar yesterday and the man was bloody gorgeous, he couldn't wait to connect.

Evan found himself down by the riverbed; his aimless amble had brought him to the rocky pathway alongside it. Benita and David had gone to Malaga for essentials but he had opted to stay behind. In truth he had wanted Benita to have a bit of breathing space, he didn't want to stifle her and he couldn't risk screwing it up all over again.

Sitting on the gnarled rock he looked across to the adjacent almond grove. Vacantly he stared between the lines of trees, lost in thought. He remembered their kiss. He had so wanted to kiss her again last night but she had seemed vulnerable and he had feared that she would be offended. She was softening though, at last, she was lowering her defences and now there was a chance of her allowing him in.

"Evan." The voice was soft and gentle, yet still the hairs on the back of his neck rose in fear. He sat still for a moment, hardly daring to breathe.

"Evan." She spoke again, now her tone urgent.

Evan went to move, but as she spoke again, he found himself paralysed with fear.

"Please don't turn around, Evan, just listen. It makes it easier for me then."

He took a deep breath; her voice was alarmingly clear. Human, in fact. He felt sure if he looked, she would be standing behind him as clear as any other living person. As if reading his mind she continued.

"Sometimes things we have never witnessed and don't understand can seem alarming. To materialise, as you would recognise me, is very draining. By remaining in spirit, I can communicate more clearly with you. Look toward the trees, Evan, and speak with me."

The temptation to face Alexis was unbearable but her voice was so clear and there were so many questions going round in his head that he daren't risk it.

"I blocked it out, didn't I? It was as if it never happened," he asked in alarm.

"That is a very earthly thing to do but you were there, Evan, and I know you remembered when I showed you what had happened."

Evan felt tears spring to his eyes and wiped fiercely at them. "I was just a young lad, I was terrified and I shouldn't have even been there."

"I know and that's how it was arranged by the powers that you don't comprehend. It was thought you would save me then and redeem yourself."

"What do you mean redeem? Are you saying that I am a bad person?" He felt the air grow ever colder behind him despite the sun. It crept across his skin. He shivered, each nerve ending twitched restlessly, her being there in whatever form was uncomfortable.

"No, not bad at all, just learning as we all do in our times. You didn't complete what you started." Her tone was patient.

"What did I start, I don't see it." Forgetting her warning, he turned to face her; the brilliant ball of light hurt his eyes, momentarily blinding him. There was a piercing sound followed by a strange feeling of emptiness and once again, he knew he was alone.

For a moment he felt angry and cheated, everything was a riddle, but his anger was lessened by the comforting sound of his mobile phone ringing in his pocket, returning him to normality.

David, sounding cheerful, asked, "Are you out on a jaunt? We are back now and Benita is threatening to make lunch. Hurry along, I have just opened a very chilled bottle of cava."

After lunch, David retired to the hammock in the shady area beneath the trees and Benita went for a siesta so Evan sat alone finishing off the wine. He hadn't mentioned Alexis' most recent visit to the others. It was becoming more manageable and somehow more believable now; he didn't need their endless questions. He didn't, he decided, really need the help of Lydia; he was capable of communicating with Alexis on his own, he just didn't understand her.

David on the other hand couldn't wait, convinced that Lydia could be the missing link of the puzzle.

Surprised, Evan realised that he was looking forward to moving into the house, if only for the sake of having a swimming pool. Then, in a moment of horror, he realised he couldn't possibly swim in that pool. The one he had witnessed someone drown in.

The though made him quite nauseous and, slipping on his sunglasses and pulling down his cap, he lay back on the firm earth with its wispy covering of dry grass, closing his eyes, keen to sleep and wanting to escape the memory of that day.

Benita, stripped to her underwear, slept fitfully under the fine cotton sheet. Evan weighed heavily on her mind. Her subconscious knew the truth, she was in love with him and only as she slept could she dare to let her mind wander.

David stirred he stared up at the branches above, comforted by the sound of the crickets that occupied them. He was glad he had organised this trip, everything was going to plan and the unexpected offer of dinner had been most welcome. Earlier, while Benita had been pacing the supermarket looking for nail varnish remover, he had slipped off and found a trendy clothes store at the other end of the shopping centre, where he had bought something special for his date with Karl.

After all, that's what it was; a date. He had been surprised at the feelings that had surfaced as he had sat opposite Karl, drinking shots of strong coffee laced with aniseed.

The attraction had been instant and most definitely mutual. Craig would be livid but he would never know; besides he was always away and if David's suspicions were correct, he was a bit of a player and probably not very loyal. David had sensed this on numerous occasions; he just hadn't wanted to admit it.

Whenever Craig had returned from one of his business trips, David had an inner knowing that he had been with other guys, although of course Craig always denied it.

David swung his legs lazily over the side of the hammock. That was one of the reasons why he liked Evan and Benita so much, they didn't judge him. He only hoped he could get them together by the end of the trip, four and a half weeks and counting; he prayed time would be on their side. For he knew once they returned home the spell would be broken and possibly lost forever.

# CHAPTER 18

Benita doubted David's decision to move to the house. Now, however, sitting by the pool sipping her second sangria she looked across at Evan, who lay sprawled across a sunbed sound asleep. In that moment, she was thankful that they had given in to David's insistent whingeing.

David had graced them with his presence long enough to help unpack the van, after which he had showered, done himself up to the nines and disappeared. He had said he was attending a meeting. Whatever, he had been acting most mysterious and Evan confessed to knowing nothing. He had simply said that he didn't have a clue where David was going and that he didn't much care. Maybe she should do the same; it was no concern of theirs what David did.

She had only been curious but now as she watched Evan sleeping she turned her full attention to him, it was far more interesting.

It had been over three days since their kiss. Secretly she longed for more but how could she orchestrate it? Evan seemed more concerned about being here at Alexis' house and if she were in his shoes, she guessed she would feel exactly the same. It didn't ease her longing though; sadly, she realised that all those years ago she had bypassed her biggest chance of happiness.

Running her gaze across his tanned torso, she shivered. It had been quite something then, all those years ago. How it would be now, she thought, goose bumps rising on her skin, despite the dying rays of the warm, Mediterranean sun.

Benita's love life had been pretty miserable and sex a terrible disappointment. The day they had shared at the old Cortijo, when they had made love, she had thought of often. Sometimes, she could still feel Evan's soft exploratory touch and smell the warm apricot brandy on his breath as he kissed her tenderly, his lips a whisper against her skin.

Evan stirred as the sun slid down behind the mountains in the west. With a start she realised she had been lost in her daydreams, horrified to find it was nearly nine when she checked her watch.

"Oh, I needed that siesta." Evan sat up, stretching his arms above his head. "It's grown chilly though," he commented, smiling across at her.

Benita threw his sweatshirt across to him. "It is quite beautiful here, don't you think?" she asked, rising and sauntering past him to the pool where she dived in.

He waited for her to surface and when she did, she turned to face him. "Come on in, the temperatures great, it's warmer in here now that the sun has gone down."

"No, I think I'm ok here. Can I get you another drink?" He stepped back from the pool, shuddering as he did so.

"Please, Evan, I want you to come in the pool?" Her eyes pleaded with his. He felt a deep stirring, Goddamn it she was beautiful but inner fear tipped the balance.

"No, I want a drink," he snapped, turning abruptly away from her and going inside.

Benita tried not to take it personally. It was hard, she understood that, but she wasn't used to the word no and it was the second time he had said it to her in the last week. She tried to shake it off. Pouting furiously, she found her towel and dried off.

Within the hour, Benita emerged from the shower to hear a soft tap at the door. Grabbing her robe, she went across to open it and found Evan standing in the hallway. He was dressed and smelt extremely appetising. He looked sheepish. "Sorry about earlier." He shrugged his shoulders. "Well you know how it is." He paused, aware that she wasn't dressed yet. "Sorry, I didn't mean to rush you but it's nearly ten, shall we slip out and get a bite to eat, otherwise we shall go hungry."

Benita's rumbling stomach appeared to answer the question, to which they both laughed.

179

"That's a yes then. Get dressed and we'll leave." He turned to smile at her once more before leaving.

Evan drove on a hunch, he wanted to take Benita somewhere different and he certainly didn't want to run into David and his date.

They came across a small whitewashed village on the other side of the mountain range and spotted a bar with its front veranda tilting beneath the weight of the laden vines that grew over it and where a few candlelit tables nestled beneath the ripe fruit. At once Evan knew that this was the place he had hoped to find, and turning in he pulled up at the front.

Squealing in delight, Benita touched his arm. "What a fantastic little place, I love it." Her eyes were glassy, excited

The proprietor, Pedro, spoke only a little English, but welcomed them like old friends.

"Que pasa amigos." With arms outstretched and obligatory kiss on each cheek he ushered them in.

Immediately they were seated, and a young girl, who they later found out to be Pedro's daughter, appeared with tapas and a glass of red wine. A welcome drink from Pedro, who harvested his own grapes and was obviously very proud of the rich flamboyant vino he had produced.

Pedro arrived with a chalkboard and, placing it against the back of a vacant chair, he rattled through the special dishes of the night in broken English.

Benita followed Evan in his choice of the salt cod served with potatoes bravos and salad. As Pedro left she looked across to smile at Evan.

"I don't want to sound nasty but it is nice to have an evening to ourselves. David means well but sometimes he can be a bit overbearing, don't you think?"

Evan gave a knowing smile. "I know, bless him, and yes he would think you rather horrid if he heard you say that about him," he teased.

Benita giggled then asked, "Is that horrid really?"

"I'm only kidding. I agree with you and yes, he does mean well. In fact I haven't told you before, as I haven't had the chance, but he has arranged for a psychic to visit the house tomorrow."

"Crikey, we have only just moved in! What is he hoping to achieve?" Benita asked in alarm.

Evan paused as Pedro appeared with more of his wine; the first glass had gone down so well, it seemed rude to order anything else.

"David wants to solve the riddle, but you know what, Benita? I think I have done that already." Evan looked at her.

"Really," lowering her tone, Benita leant further across the table. "So why is Alexis following you and what are the dreams and visits all about?"

"In truth I don't know that I actually have," he admitted. "The other day when you were in Malaga, I took a stroll down by the river. Alexis and I had a conversation. Not in the way that you or I would have one but well, it was a conversation compared to how things have been." He stopped to pour the wine.

"Did you see her?" Benita probed.

"No I didn't, it was just a conversation. I have analysed it since. You see the thing is when I went to her house that day all those years ago I thought she was out, when in fact she was actually drowning in the swimming pool. I could have saved her."

"But you don't know that!" Benita objected.

"Alexis said that, not me. It was an opportunity to redeem myself, she informed me." He looked questioningly at Benita, who shrugged her shoulders in confusion.

"Exactly, redeem myself for what? I may not be perfect but apart from that day, to the best of my knowledge I haven't done anything wrong. Well, except..."

Benita took a large gulp of wine; she looked across at him, her pupils dilated.

"Except for...?"

"Be an absolute idiot and let you go," he said, looking deeply into her eyes, "that is my only mistake."

Benita felt herself blush. "We were never an item."

"I know, but we should have been."

"It would never have worked, Evan."

He shrugged. "Who says so?"

Benita, feeling out of her depth, looked away. Tearing her bread roll in two she sighed.

"So, what about Alexis?" she asked.

"I could have saved her, but I didn't. Nothing else that I can hold my hands up to and say I didn't do. So, what else can it be?" He looked puzzled and took a moment before continuing, "I think, and I hate to admit it, but David may be right. That vision, if that is what we should call it. The one that I had when the young girl was drowning in the river, maybe there was another life and that's what I was experiencing at that time. I don't for one second recall any of it, but if it is true then this drowning thing, it seems to be vying for my attention."

"But I still don't see why that would involve Alexis? Where is the link?"

"Perhaps, and this is a long shot, she was there too. I mean it could fit, couldn't it?"

Benita opened her mouth to speak and stopped as Pedro appeared with their meal. Picking up her fork she embedded it into the fleshy cod then, perplexed, she glanced at Evan.

"Yes, I believe it could fit but only if we accept the belief of reincarnation. If the young girl that drowned in another lifetime was, let us say Alexis, then she died before you did, so therefore it could be possible to be born again before you, we know for fact she was…"

"Yeah, by about twenty years," he interrupted her.

"So it is feasible in a sense, far-fetched and not really provable, unless of course this psychic can help us by filling in the missing pieces."

"Do you think she could?" Evan looked hopeful.

Benita looked smug. "You already seem on the right track. If you are right we could ask her to take you back to that previous lifetime."

"What, like time travel?"

Benita threw her head back and laughed. "In a way I guess it would be. I have seen it on TV. We can ask her to regress you. Basically she will hypnotise you and take you back in time."

Rubbing his jaw between finger and thumb, Evan smiled. "Is this a joke?"

"No, it is possible, as I said I have seen it on TV. What time is she coming?"

"David said sometime in the evening, she couldn't be more specific apparently."

"Whatever, before she does we will take a trip down to the coast, to the English bookstore. I'm sure that they will stock something about regression."

Evan topped up their wine glasses and gave a broad grin. "You know what Benita, you're beginning to sound just like David."

Benita grimaced. "Oh please don't say that."

"Don't worry, you are far more beautiful." He noticed her uneasy fidget at his compliment. "More than you realise," he added, sipping his wine, not taking his eyes off her for a moment.

"I have said it before and I wasn't joking but that was the worst thing that ever happened to me, when I lost you. You know what, I have to thank David for a lot. He kept you there in Devon while I was away and he brought us back together again here in Spain. If I never get to the bottom of any of this, it has been worth it just to spend some time alone with you."

Benita opened her mouth to speak but he held up a silencing hand; unusually she remained quiet.

"I don't expect you to reply to any of what I have just said. I just wanted you to know how I felt. Now let's raise a glass to Alexis and the secrets of the past, which hopefully, God willing, are soon to be revealed."

David moaned for the entire drive to the bookstore.

"I'm not even sure if she does this regression thing. Can't we just have an open mind and see what she comes up with?"

"No," they chorused in unison.

David, still grumbling, looked out of the window. He was tired and hungover, the previous night had gone on into the early hours of this morning and he had had very little sleep. Karl had been insatiable; sex had taken on an entirely new meaning. They had arranged to meet Monday but already he was feeling incredibly guilty and in fear of being caught out. He had switched off his mobile phone just in case Craig cared to call. Craig would notice the edge in his voice and would suss he had been up to no good.

"I forgot to ask how your evening was. I didn't hear you come in?"

Benita asked keen to distract him from his whingeing.

Managing an awkward smile he croaked, "It was very nice, thank you. What did you guys do?"

Evan eased back from the accelerator. "We found a great restaurant, perhaps you could join us there sometime?" He looked across at David and winked, "If you can squeeze us in to your busy schedule?"

David blushed as he looked back out of the window. "I'm sure I can accommodate you both," he replied sourly.

Benita emerged from the shop triumphantly, holding a book aloft. She crossed the street and joined them at the bar opposite.

"Well done you," Evan enthused, pressing a large glass of wine into her hand. Seated just across from the beach on the dusty pavement she looked out to the ocean then back to both men.

"Let's wait until we get back to look at this." She tapped the book before her. "I don't know about anyone else but I am starving. Does anyone fancy a pizza?" she asked, browsing the tabletop menu.

David, feeling too green, declined. He sat very still, saying little as he watched them devour a twelve-inch Hawaiian between them.

The downpour was sudden; without warning, the heavens opened. Hurriedly collecting up their things they dashed inside to shelter.

David, flushed from the sudden exertion, wiped the rain drops from his bare head.

"That was a rude awakening." He looked out at the sky. "More than a passing shower I fear."

Evan pointed to the TV. "Looks like we are expecting

storms for the rest of the day." He looked across at Benita.

"To tell the truth I am not that bothered. Looks like a cosy afternoon indoors with a good book." She wiped the book's cover and smiled across at David."You look in dire need of a siesta, shall we head back?"

The mountains didn't hold the same appeal in the unseasonal weather. Putting the book down Benita went across to the window. Opening the shutters she looked out at the clouds gathered low around the house, creating a heavy mist that descended across the terrace. The wind picked up and the shutters rattled on their hinges. The arrival of the storm had brought a marked change in the atmosphere within the walls of the house too.

David and Evan were both sleeping. Benita wished she could too, as she headed to the bathroom. Making her way along the unlit passage, she shivered as a feeling of unease engulfed her. Reminding herself that she wasn't alone and there was nothing to fear, she closed the bathroom door behind her, pausing to take a few deep breaths.

Despite the rain the air was humid. Turning on the tap, she plunged her wrists under the jet of cold water, looking at her tired reflection in the mirror and stiffening as she met with Alexis' cold eyes staring back. The scream that left her lips echoed around the house.

David and Evan were on their feet and hammering on the door within seconds.

"Are you alright?" Evan called anxiously.

With trembling fingers, she unlocked the door and fell into David's arms.

"Whatever is the matter, Benita? You look like you have seen a ghost!"

Shocked, she began to sob, clinging to David more tightly.

"Oh my God, you have, haven't you? It was her, it was Alexis," he breathed, hardly daring to believe it himself, as he fumbled in the pocket of his chino shorts for a tissue.

"I knew this was a bad idea." Frustrated, Evan smashed his fist into the bathroom door. David, busy ushering Benita towards the sitting room, scowled back over his shoulder at him.

"Evan, why don't you go and make a pot of coffee, perhaps put a shot of the strong stuff in it as well. Poor darling kitten has had a bit of a fright."

Evan, rigid with anger, supposed he was better out of the way for a while. As the kettle chortled into life, its sound bringing normality back to the quietness of the house, he cursed himself for losing control.

Finally, with a laden tray he joined the others in the sitting room. Benita, now composed, smiled up at him.

"I'm sorry guys; I didn't mean to panic you. It was a bit of a shock, that's all."

"Goodness, I'll say." David took the role of mum, pouring the coffee and handing them each a cup. "Tell us what happened, lovely." He looked at Benita and smiled reassuringly. "Biscuits, Evan," he signalled to the kitchen, "We need sugar for the shock."

Benita looked over to Evan, who sat with his shoulders to his ears staring into his untouched coffee cup, face expressionless.

"Evan, I'm fine, please don't be mad at David."

"Believe me, I am trying not to be. I don't want you upset, Benita, and I think this nonsense should stop." He peered at David, who grinned sheepishly back.

"I didn't think Benita would see her, I thought her interest was with you, Evan." He turned back to Benita, "If you are upset and you want to leave, Benita, then I will understand," he said, patting the back of her hand sympathetically.

Evan sensed his inner smugness; things couldn't have turned out better for David. He was getting what he wanted, even more proof. For if Benita had really seen Alexis, then it was the clarity he hoped for.

Benita poured herself another coffee. "That's better," she declared, standing up and rolling her shoulders gently back to dislodge any remaining tension.

"I think it was the shock really." She turned to face both men, whose eyes followed her keenly. "I only went to freshen up and when I looked in the mirror, she was there, staring back at me."

"Did she speak, say anything at all?" Evan asked, running his hands through his hair.

"If she wanted to she didn't have the chance. I freaked out and like a total idiot screamed. With hindsight I wish I hadn't but you know, at the time..."

"We forgive you." David made a light-hearted attempt to clear the air, aware of Evan's scornful gaze burning a hole in the side of his head.

"Well, I don't think I can go back to sleep now, so anyone for a game of rummy?" David asked cheerfully.

With Benita safely out of earshot, having retired to her room for a nap, Evan cornered David in the kitchen.

"Cancel the psychic," he demanded, offering his mobile to David.

David, despite what had happened earlier, had been looking forward to tonight's spectacle and shrunk away from Evan with a look of horror.

"Why? Benita has assured me she is happy for the appointment to go ahead."

"That may be so but I'm not. I don't want Benita any more involved than she already is and if you go ahead with this, God only knows what we will unleash."

"Or put to rest!" David replied hotly.

"Nothing is to be cancelled." They both looked up to see Benita standing in the doorway, hands on hips, surveying their heated exchange. "David is right, this all needs to be laid to rest and I am of the opinion that we have gone as far as we can with this ourselves. We need the help of this psychic, my only hope is that she is as good as David claims."

David, relieved, skirted around Evan toward her. "Oh she is good, one of the very best I am told. I promise that you won't be disappointed."

Evan, outnumbered, flopped down in the adjacent chair. "I have had enough, I miss my place, I want to go home. I am tired of ghost chasing and quite frankly I don't give a damn."

187

"We all are, silly, but what good is it going back just to continue the torment of Alexis? Wouldn't it be far better to leave her here in Spain and go home to a fresh start? Who knows what the future holds," David said, smiling and looking across toward Benita for support.

Evan didn't have the energy to argue. In truth tonight couldn't come soon enough. A new start was the only thing on his mind but it was no use and totally worthless if he didn't have Benita by his side. Kicking off his shoes, he managed a lopsided grin in their direction.

"Ok David, you win - again! Open a bottle of vino and I will forgive you." He looked across at Benita. "And I suggest you stay away from mirrors for the rest of the evening. In fact …." he paused, pulling the chair out next to him, "you can come and sit here where I can keep my eye on you, and help me drink this exquisite bottle of red that David is just about to open. Comprende?" he asked, winking and sinking back into the chair, glad to surrender.

"Si," depositing herself into the opposite chair she kicked off her shoes, then tasted the wine, "Muy bien, David."

# CHAPTER 19

David swept into the sitting room closely followed by Lydia Martenez, the renowned psychic. Benita was unable to conceal her surprise at the elegant creature. Lydia could have easily dropped by fresh from a glossy photo shoot. She shifted uneasily in her chair.

"Good evening." Lydia offered a slender hand in her direction. Her English was crisp, although her sexy Spanish roots were evident.

Benita gave an inward groan, wishing she hadn't opted for baggy jeans and faded t-shirt. She had visualised Lydia to be older, maybe dressed in a robe with a cross hanging from her neck. She was quick to notice the look of delight on Evan's face as keenly he made his way across the room to greet Lydia. Clasping his arms around her narrow waist he planted a lingering kiss on her cheek.

"Lydia, tell me, are all the psychics in Spain as glamorous as you?" His eyes swept appreciatively across her body.

Lydia gave a soft throaty laugh. "You are too kind Evan, too kind."

"It's the truth; you are not what we were expecting at all," David crooned, taking her jacket. "Now, perhaps I can offer you a glass of wine?"

"Oh, no thank you, I never drink when I am working with the spirits. The two do not go well and that is not what we require. A glass of water would be most welcome."

David hurried off at her request and then, to Benita's horror, Lydia strode across to Evan and took his face between her hands.

"This is not good," she declared looking at him with concern. "You look tired and drawn. We must rid you of your unwelcome visitor and soon as we can!" she said, with

189

her voice rising to a pitch. At that moment, the room was lit by a flash of lightning, followed by the heavy rumbling of distant thunder, and then there was complete darkness. It took a moment for Benita's eyes to adjust to the faint light surfacing from the candle on the table, which was nearing the end of its days and flickered precariously.

Lydia broke the silence. "Well this is not a very auspicious start to the evening. Do we have more candles we can light?"

David sprang into action, whilst Evan, who appeared to be quite mesmerised by Lydia, sat on the sofa, rendered useless of any kind of movement at all. Benita watched with distaste and made no offer of assistance as David pottered around the room lighting candles, which bathed the room in a soft muted glow. When he had finished he looked across to Lydia, who nodded her head in approval. Benita looked on, feigning a smile.

Evan appeared to break his stupor. Rolling the stem of his glass between his palms for several seconds he looked across to Lydia. "Would it be possible for you to regress me, Lydia? For I feel we need to look at the past?"

"Indeed it would," she said, surprised at his request. "How far do you want to go back?"

"As far as it takes!" Evan declared, draining the last of his wine.

Lydia decided it would be best if she took Evan through to one of the bedrooms where it would be quiet and he could lie down and relax. As they disappeared down the hallway, David leant forward, waving a hand in front of Benita's vacant gaze.

"Damn, we are going to miss all the action," he hissed.

Benita shrugged. "Good, I am getting rather tired of watching Evan fawning over Lydia."

"Oh, do I detect a hint of jealousy?" David's eyes twinkled teasingly, "I think it is plainly obvious that Lydia isn't Evan's type at all."

"Really, and what makes you so sure?" she asked with interest.

David stretched back on the sofa and placing his hands

behind his head, smiled. "Because Evan is hopelessly in love with you my dear, that's why."

Benita looked doubtful. Once she would have believed that, but something had changed; despite their kiss she feared that Evan was losing interest and watching him tonight with Lydia, she had definitely witnessed a spark between them.

David sat up. "Stop looking so pensive, you are making me depressed. Forget about Evan for five minutes. How about a game of Scrabble? That usually takes an age and I think it is going to be a long night."

The sound of Lydia's soothing voice, coupled with the low rumbling of thunder, made it very easy for Evan to relax. Compelled to close his eyes, upon Lydia's instruction he turned his focus to the rhythm of his breathing only to find himself submerged in a cyclone of brilliant colour, shades of purple and blue dancing before him.

"Where are you, Evan?" Lydia asked softly.

In truth he didn't know, a silver haze marred his view and for a moment, he panicked. Nevertheless, as the mist rolled back he found himself with a clear uninterrupted view of a beautiful meadow and felt a great sense of calm.

"It is amazing here," he breathed as he looked around in wonder.

Lydia was speaking but her voice was fading into the background, the sound of tranquil birdsong filling his ears. Peacefully he made his way across the soft grass amongst the brightly coloured flowers to the brow of the hill and gasped in wonder at the sight that met his eyes.

Below him was a crescent shaped expanse of white sand, the aquamarine ocean beyond. The lapping waves licked gently at the edge of the bay, their sound soothing. He looked with awe at this beautiful place to which he had arrived and in his heart there was a sense of recognition. He stood motionless, his eyes sweeping across the landscape below and then he noticed the gentle sloping path carved into the hillside. Instinctively he knew the path would lead him closer to the ocean and so he turned towards it.

Stepping from the pine forest he was surprised yet

delighted to find that his feet were quite bare. Sinking his toes into the powdery sand, he became aware of the warming sun on his chest and for the first time noticed that he was naked apart from a thin cotton wrap tied at the waist.

Dropping down onto the shore, he marvelled at the view, then he became aware of someone standing behind him. He turned to acknowledge their presence with a smile, for instinctively he knew this to be a friend.

Benita was edgy. As she reached across to top up her glass she sent the Scrabble board flying across the terracotta tiles.

"Oh, that's done it." David sat back in his chair, arms folded, and glared at her. "Just because I was winning, you didn't have to sabotage the game!"

"Sorry," she mumbled, slipping across to the window to look out into the darkness.

David observed the way she stood, arms protectively wrapped around herself, and shook his head. To his mind, it was so simple. Neither of them wanted to be the first to declare their true feelings. Things would never move forward at this rate, he feared.

"They have been a long time," he commented wistfully, wondering what on earth was happening in there and jealous that he wasn't able to witness the regression in progress.

Benita remained silent, looking out into the dark. It was obvious her mind was elsewhere. Reluctantly he got up and taking her gently by the shoulder asked," What is it, Benita?"

Her voice was steady, she didn't flinch. "I can see her out there in the mists."

"See who?" he asked, surprised by her statement.

"Alexis, she is out there and she is pleased with herself."

David, scratching his head, made his way across the room to retrieve his notebook. He didn't want to miss an opportunity. There was a faraway look in Benita's eyes and something told him that she wasn't actually present in the room with him at this time.

"Alexis adores Evan, she loves him more than I. Do you know that?"

David grunted, not sure how to react, "I wasn't aware of that," he said finally.

"She wants him back; she needs things to return to how they once were." Benita shivered and turned to look at David.

"Go on," he urged.

Benita looked at him in surprise. "Did I say something?"

"Mmm, you must remember, you were listening to Alexis. You said that she wants Evan back."

Benita, turning on her heel, raised her eyes upwards. "Just quit it, David. I did no such thing. You are obsessed with this whole Alexis thing. I on the other hand am becoming completely bored with it. I am going to bed now." She looked down the hallway. "Goodness knows how long they will be. I am sure you can tell me all about it in the morning." She smiled. "Night, David."

David watched her leave then turned to look out of the window. There was nothing except darkness, not even the pale light of the moon. Benita had seen something, he was sure of it, and she knew she had. That was why she had left so abruptly. He could only imagine that the lure of Alexis was strengthening and surely that must mean things were coming to a head at last.

The water swirled furiously at his waist. The icy cold numbed his limbs and with horror he realised he would never make it across to the other side. He hadn't meant to let her go; he had been crazy to think of ever bringing her here.

He missed his darling wife Francine so much. The fever had taken her and he had watched in horror as she had died in his arms, succumbing to the overwhelming pain.

What sort of a world would it be for her without her mother? Who would look after the child when he too left this earth? For he knew that would be soon; without Francine life was meaningless and empty.

There was great unrest in the southern part of the country, as the soldiers fled the north they left disarray in the wake of their presence. The villagers had prepared for this invasion; their defences had proven useless. The Druid priest had predicted this long ago, the lands were changing and greed was driving the armies down to their sacred grounds. How could he leave Clara, his beloved daughter, to such a fate? The child was just beginning to blossom; she would be a handsome find to one of the young boisterous scavengers when they invaded. The child was special, she deserved more than that. The Druid had said she was *Gifted*, she was that for sure, she had inherited the sight and the old wise ones were keen to whisk her away into hiding. They had said there was an isle to the west, were she could be mastered in her unusual ways but alas, he couldn't bear the pain of their parting.

Now he held grimly onto the swollen bank as his nails raked through the damp earth, losing his grip. He looked helplessly toward the spot in the angry rushing waters where he had last seen her.

She had cried out, fought the savage current of water, her small body twisting and rising above the foamy spray until she could fight no more.

Apart from the angry hiss of raging waters, it had been silent for some time now and with heavy heart he knew it was too late, she had been swept away and he could only hope that Francine would be there to welcome her to the after world.

Mustering all of his strength, he hauled himself up onto the muddy bank and curling into a ball he threw himself against the sodden earth. Whatever had he been thinking?

He had drunk too much mead, had this caused his irrational behaviour? No, for in truth he would do it again, this very same thing.

As the child had lain sleeping, he had lifted her from the straw bed, pausing to draw her blanket up around her, and carried her down to the river with a purpose.

Kneeling at the edge of the swollen river, he had dropped her down into the cold murky water. Briefly, her eyes had flickered open, her angelic face pale against the dark woollen mantle.

"Father." the word was a mere whisper on her lips. He acted swiftly before she had time to realise what he was to do. With one swift push, he held her beneath the water. She was too fragile to fight him, it had been surprisingly easy. After a few minutes, he released his hold and watched as her lifeless body drifted across the river.

He should have fled then, left and never looked back, but he had underestimated her spirit. The child coughed and spluttered back to life, her limbs desperate against the strong current as they thrashed in the icy water. His heart cried out to his head, how he could see her suffering and he leapt into the water, if only to finish the job.

The cry of an owl poignant in the distance foretold what he already knew. He stood helpless as she disappeared from view.


"What are you doing now, tell me where you are?" Lydia probed, despite the tears rolling down her cheeks.

Evan's skin was translucent, his eyes remained closed but the eyeballs fidgeted restlessly beneath their lids. "I have taken the hemlock. I lie here and wait for death to take me to my girls. I am aware I have been a coward but for Clara I truly believe I have done the best thing."

Lydia looked at Evan with admiration, the terrible tragedy he believed to be right. He considered this an act of love, that his beloved daughter should not suffer was of utmost importance to him.

"Let us leave this time, and move forward. Where does this lead us to, Evan, tell me what you see?" Lydia was gently coaxing, keen that Evan should leave the past. The trauma of reliving it had etched lines at his brow, and tiny lines of worry around the corners of his mouth.

"So Evan, what do you see?" she asked brightly, then puzzled that the horror and worry had returned once again to his face, which contorted in pain and anguish.


Benita decided she would leave in the morning; restlessly she climbed into bed, still seething with David. What gave him the right to play God? How foolish she had been to participate in this game. Evan was being shamelessly manipulated by David to find answers that didn't exist. What made them so special that they should uncover the answers to one of the greatest mysteries of time! You were born and you died, that was it, there was no afterlife or second chances and how she had managed to be sucked into this completely pointless exercise was beyond her.

She needed to go home and get on with life. Find somewhere new to live and get a new career. Evan really was history and to think that she could rekindle what she had when she was sixteen years old was foolish and naive.

Angry at herself she twisted and turned, wondering if she would ever learn how to be normal. If Connie had any idea what she had been up to over the last few weeks, she would have her certified.

She heard David outside the door; he gave a gentle tap which she chose to ignore. She didn't care anymore and planned to get up before everyone else and call for a taxi to the airport, where she would get on the next plane out of here.


Alexis held him in her arms for several seconds, reluctant to release her hold. When she did she stood and looked hard at him for some time.

"Is it so wrong to want this?" she asked unsure, looking at him with hope.

Taking a deep breath, he reflected on his newfound knowledge. *If everybody were to be offered this same opportunity, would they need to be asked twice? He didn't doubt for one moment that this was a great honour and that Alexis had wanted this for him, for the two of them!*

Alexis took a step back, perplexed. She asked, "Did I not do the right thing?"

He was puzzled, then relaxing his jaw he smiled. "When do you leave?"

Alexis looked out across the ocean, her eyes twinkling mischievously, "As of now. My work is done. The rest is up to you, until we meet again of course."

Evan reached out to touch her face, where he traced a line with his index finger across the bridge of her nose. "And when will that be?" he asked curiously.

Alexis grinned, her face alive. "Now, that really is up to you, hopefully not long though."

Smiling, she waved in recognition as her spirit guide Timarn joined them on the shore. He placed an arm around her shoulder. "Come now, you have been away too long and once again your stay is too short."

Evan watched as arm in arm they walked across the sands, to the shade of the pines. Smiling, he turned back to the ocean, distracted by a white feather that fell from above and danced on the breeze before him until gently falling at his feet.

Benita hauled the heavy case from the bed and struggled along the hallway with it, cursing as the wheels caught the edge of the wall with a low thud. Stopping for a moment she waited but nobody stirred. With a last look around, she let herself out onto the terrace. Sitting on her upturned case in the early morning sun she waited for the taxi. She had mixed emotions; the decisions made last night didn't seem quite so appealing this morning. Goddamn she was stubborn and she hated that trait more than any other but if it was the last thing she ever did, she would make that flight.

# CHAPTER 20

Evan watched from beneath the shade of the parasol as David appeared with a jug of freshly squeezed juice and a pot of steaming coffee. Placing them on the table David sat down to join him.

"So, I am dying to know how it went. Come on, spill the beans. What happened?" he asked, rubbing his hands together in anticipation.

Evan poured a glass of juice. He shrugged. "There really isn't that much to tell," he lied, looking across the valley, ignoring the heavy sigh of disappointment from the other side of the table.

"There has to be something to tell, you were in there ages with Lydia!" David objected, his eyes pleading with Evan's. Any snippet of information would do for now, he could not survive without something to go on, however insignificant.

Evan knew he would have to feed him a line, something he could sink his teeth into, if only to keep him off his back for the rest of the day. Deliberating for a moment what this might be, he paused, then looking David square in the eye, announced, "I was right, she haunts me because I could have saved her and now that Lydia has helped me, with her spiritual mediation, she has gone."

David eyed him suspiciously. "Gone!"

Evan, growing restless, fidgeted in his seat. "That's what I said, gone. End of chapter old chap, so you see, you were right. All it took was a gifted psychic and I am released from the torture and torment of the last twenty years."

David spooned sugar into his coffee and shook his head. "I don't believe you. I mean all that you have been through, Evan. She just leaves, disappears into oblivion. It doesn't stack up?"

"Well, I wouldn't say it was quite as simple as that." Evan looked out across the valley then turning back to David, he sighed. "It was all very traumatic. She appeared in the room in a swirling mist and only when I had begged her forgiveness…"

David pulled his chair round closer to Evan's. "A swirling mist you say?"

Evan nodded. "Yes, I was afraid but of course but Lydia was there to reassure me and then…" he stopped short, looking down at his watch. "Where on earth is Benita? She never sleeps in this late!" He looked accusingly at David, who gave a nonchalant shrug.

"Expect she is tired, a lot has happened."

Evan stood up, much to David's annoyance, who didn't want the story to end here! In fact this just wasn't satisfying enough.

"I expect she is still sulking," he mumbled, looking up at Evan and signalling for him to sit back down. "Leave her alone, she will come out when she is ready. She is attention seeking and if…"

"Sulking, what about?" Evan demanded, bearing down on David.

David felt the colour rise in his cheeks. It was all about Benita. He had paid for this wretched trip and he deserved a bloody good explanation. Sod Benita for five minutes, but as Evan leaned menacingly in, pushing his face right in front of his, he caved in.

"She thinks you fancy Lydia. She was as arsey as hell last night. I tried to reassure her of course, but you know what they are like." He shrugged. "Now back to the other troublesome female, Alexis. What happened?"

Evan was already walking away; he strode across the terrace and disappeared inside. David didn't bother to follow him. Hitching his shorts higher, he reclined his chair and settled down to face the warm sun.

Evan, looking hot and flustered, appeared five minutes later.

"She has gone!"

David sat up. He watched in exasperation as Evan, tight-lipped and with visibly throbbing temples, paced before him.

"Gone for a walk I expect. Calm down, this is exactly what she wants, you fool." He gave a soft tut and went back to his sunbathing.

"David, when I said she has gone, I mean she has gone. Packed all of her stuff and left us."

Spluttering in disbelief, David sat up. "Bloody hell, that's taking it a bit far. Selfish bitch, after all…"

"Keys," Evan interrupted, holding out his hand.

"Where are you going?" David asked, leaping up in alarm and fishing frantically in his pockets.

"Jesus, hurry up," Evan exploded. "We need to get to the airport before she leaves." He snatched the keys from David, who had begun to tremble despite the temperature being in the eighties. With a shake of his head, Evan headed to the van.

The airport was busy. Benita sat on the bench, bewildered, watching the activity in the departure hall with mixed emotions. She had overreacted again. Why did she have to be so mulish? she wondered, drumming her fingers against the tarnished paint of the steel framed bench.

Angel Rogers stood behind the counter of Sandways Air surveying her. Wobbling on her three-inch stilettos she managed a half-hearted wave along with a tight-lipped, half smile to reassure Benita she hadn't forgotten her and was doing the utmost to get her on the next available flight.

Benita raised her hand in acknowledgement but she wasn't holding out much hope.

David pulled up outside the main doors. Evan was exiting the vehicle before it ground to a halt.

"You better go and park up, David." Evan signalled to the no waiting sign.

"I just hope we are not too late," he said slamming the door with such force that it made David jump.

With shaking hands, David slipped the gears into reverse. He was feeling quite unnecessary and thanked the Lord that he had convinced Evan to pull over half way along the

Autopista and let him drive the rest of the way. Had he not, then he feared they would have never arrived in one piece.

This was so selfish of Benita. She had caused a terrible commotion. Clutching his hand to his chest, he tried to calm his racing heart.

'*I will bloody well have to kill her for this,*' he vowed, trawling the underground car park looking for a vacant space in the crushing heat.

Benita yawned. It seemed an endless wait. Pulling the battered case behind her she left the main doors of the terminal, glad to step out into the warm sunshine. Leaning against the wall she fished in her pocket for some gum and set about watching the goings on.

The exasperated cry of an elderly lady as her husband dragged his case into the back of her legs caught her attention. Bemused, she watched the couple's angry exchange.

The man, in his early seventies looked hot and bothered, beads of perspiration peppered his balding head and his two front teeth resembled those of a rabbit.

"Come on, Janet, we're already late!" he grumbled. He glanced in Benita's direction and, seeing that he had an audience, raised his eyebrows with a look of endless suffering.

Janet had stopped and was clutching her right calf. She seemed to be in a lot of pain and was ignoring her husband, who huffed and puffed impatiently.

Benita went over to her. "Are you ok, I couldn't help noticing what just happened?"

Janet had a kindly face and she smiled apologetically. Benita instantly felt sorry for her and helped her across to a vacant bench.

Her husband trudged back. "What's wrong?" he demanded, looking down accusingly at his wife.

Benita took over. "You nearly took your wife off her feet ramming that case around and you have caught her leg with your careless attitude."

"Who are you?" he asked, disgruntled, "and who asked

201

for you to poke your nose in? We are running late, that's if we haven't missed our blessed plane already. Come on, woman, pull yourself together or we will never make it back!" He turned his back on Benita and offered his wife his arm. Janet nodded to Benita and obligingly followed her husband into the terminal.

Benita watched them leave and shook her head, some men were so pig-headed. Then she thought of Evan and suddenly she wished she was with him. He would never treat her like that, not now and not in years to come.

Benita went back into the terminal and saw the lady from Sandways Air waving frantically.

"I've found you a flight, but you will have to be quick, the gate closes in five minutes."

Evan scanned the departures hallway; he peered anxiously along the lines waiting to check in. There was no sign of her. His heart sank; she had gone, he was too late.

When David appeared, he found a desolate Evan slumped across a bench.

"No luck, then?" he asked, silently cursing Benita for being a nuisance.

Evan looked up. "I have searched everywhere and there is no sign of her. Perhaps you could ask over at the agent's desk. See if she bought a flight, I don't think I can face it." He looked pleadingly into David's eyes, reminding David just how vulnerable Evan could be.

David felt guilty; he hated seeing Evan so down. "Of course I will, wait here, I will see what I can find out."

Benita looked wistfully out of the window of the plane as they circled across the sea and back in towards the land. She looked down on the white farms and cottages nestled in the hills below her, many with sparkling pools. Somewhere down below, David and Evan would be wondering why she had left.

It was too late now, no time for regrets. She looked up to see a familiar face peering at her between the headrests of the seat in front.

"I never got the chance to say thank you earlier." Janet smiled. "Perhaps we could buy you a drink?"

Her husband twisted his neck and peered around her. "Oh it's you," he grunted with a look of distaste but a sharp dig in the ribs from Janet made him catch his breath and he managed a tight-lipped smile of sorts.

"Manners, Frankie, "Janet chortled.

Benita smiled back; she would accept the drink most gratefully, in her haste to leave Spain she hadn't thought to get any cash out of the machine. God only knew what she would do when she arrived at Bristol.


David tried his best to calm the situation as Evan raised his voice several octaves. Passers-by had started to take an interest in what was happening and David warned him for the umpteenth time that shouting at the poor woman wouldn't get him on a flight to England.

Exasperated, David finally pushed Evan back into the van, although he continually protested.

"Look," said David, climbing in beside him. "If you are serious that you want to return to England then we may as well drive back."

"But that will take over three days and goodness knows where Benita will be by then," Evan protested.

"So, you will find her. As they say, true love conquers all. Besides, our work here is done, disappointing but completed nonetheless, so we may as well head back."

David stopped to pay the parking fee then turned out onto the carriageway that led to the Autopista and the mountains beyond.

"We should head back to the house pack up and in the morning we can hand the keys back to the agent. If we take it in turns to drive we will probably make it back by Sunday."

He looked across at Evan and winced at the pained expression etched on his face. "On second thought perhaps I will do all the driving, I do actually want to make it back to England in one piece, despite what you think."


Benita had to admit it, she appeared to have a knack of

falling on her feet and meeting Frankie and Janet had been a blessing in disguise.

It appeared that Frankie's bark was far worse than his bite and as the trip unfolded she found she warmed to him.

Frankie in particular was nosey but she had nothing to hide and on learning her plight, they were most insistent on driving her back to Connie's house.

"It's only twenty or so miles further for us and I would never leave a damsel in distress," he said, patting the back of her hand.

Janet looked on proudly. Despite Benita's first dismal impression of them, this was in fact a couple that, despite what the years had thrown at them, were still deeply in love with each other; maybe they just didn't like each other. Right now she could have hugged them both for they would ensure her safe return to normality.

Benita thought of Connie and Ben, the new family member and their cosy cottage. She was already there, sitting in the conservatory with a glass of wine telling them all about the madness of Spain, and for a while it took her mind off Evan, the man whose love, try as she might, she could not deny.

# CHAPTER 21

Connie crept down the stairs to the living room. "He is sleeping, finally," she whispered. "Did you open the wine?" She plonked herself down next to Benita, who duly handed her a glass.

"So where did we get to?" Connie smiled, unfazed by the story so far.

Benita looked at her friend. "You haven't once questioned my sanity. Don't you find everything that has happened just a little weird?"

"Not at all! Had you asked my advice, which you could have done at any time, I could have put you onto several good mediums. I am a great believer in reincarnation and to be honest I am rather surprised you left when you did. Don't you wonder what Evan discovered and if indeed he will be free of Alexis at last?"

Benita shook her head wearily. "And I foolishly thought you would be on my side."

"I certainly am on your side, as you like to put it." Connie looked thoughtful for a moment, "but you did overreact and it is blatantly obvious that Evan is in love with you. No, that's too mild, it is more than that. He is simply crazy about you!"

Benita, pouting as she topped up their glasses, exclaimed, "You haven't met the guy. Rather a bold statement, don't you think?"

Connie threw her head back and laughed. "You don't have to be a genius to work that one out. I can't wait to meet him. I suggest you get over your fit of envy and get on the phone and sort out what happens next!"

Benita shrunk back against the sofa with a look of horror. "I couldn't possibly," she hissed.

"I don't expect you to do it right this moment, by lunchtime tomorrow will do." Connie looked mischievously across and winked.

Just south of Caen in France, Evan entered a petrol station to pay for diesel. Whilst he was in there his mobile rang on the dash of the camper van. David snatched it up and looked at the display. He shook his head; it was Benita calling. He shut it off and then switched off the power. It would only upset Evan and the petulant woman had caused them twenty-four hours of non-stop grief. No, he decided, it could wait at least until they were on British soil. Then she could whinge as much as she liked, he would be back at the Hall and not have to suffer their childish little disagreements anymore. Good job too, he thought, watching Evan stride back toward the camper, his chin set determinedly that he had intercepted.

"Not too long now, eh," he said sliding back behind the wheel. As they rolled out of the forecourt he began to whistle.

Connie watched her friend from the kitchen. Baby Thomas was fast asleep on her lap and she noticed how Benita watched him sleeping, squeezing one of his toes affectionately every now and then.

Connie came into the room. "It suits you," she said, smiling.

Benita looked up at her. "Does it? I never really thought about having a family before but all of a sudden I am painfully aware that time is running out."

"Nonsense, these days lots of mothers wait until their early forties to have children. Besides, it helps if you can meet the right fella first."

"Well, there you go then." Benita gave a weary sigh and handed her towelling swathed, milky scented son back to her. "I guess I will be over the hill by then."

Connie accepted her son with a maternal grin as she traced the child's lips with her forefinger and the outline of his delicate little features.

"True love never dies, Benita. Whatever you think he is

coming for you and this time you should rush in and embrace the best chance of happiness you will ever have. Oh, and to remind you, they were your words, not mine!" She nodded at her friend firmly.

Benita grimaced. "Ok smart arse, but that's if he comes, maybe he is sick of chasing me. Perhaps Lydia has lured him away, she could offer him so much more and he obviously has no intention of ever contacting me again. Maybe he has decided to stay in Spain after all. I mean there isn't really anything here for him." Connie chose to ignore her, the proof would be in the pudding so to speak and only then would she take any notice.

"I am going to bath Thomas. Perhaps you could make lunch?" Connie stood up and headed to the stairs. "I'm afraid you will have to go into the village, we could really do with some more supplies. I made a list earlier, you will find it on the side in the kitchen and why don't we be naughty and treat ourselves to something nice from the bakers too?"

Evan was disappointed to discover that Benita wasn't at the Hall. David wasn't too pleased either to find Craig in residence. Evan left them to it; there was no way he was going to get caught up in their domestic dispute and one look at Craig revealed he was spoiling for a fight and to be fair to the man they had been in Spain for over two months, he had every right. Then, of course, there was David's little indiscretion.

Evan had tried Benita's phone several times but it was always switched off and so he had to make a decision. There were only two places he could imagine she would be and that's was either with her friends in Somerset or back at her flat in Scotland.

Evan opted for the first choice. He had come to know Benita well, she couldn't stand to be alone for too long and there would be far more activity in Somerset what with the new baby. Just the welcome distraction she needed, anything but face up to her true emotions, he thought ruefully.

Benita had just finished washing the lunch things and was

boiling the kettle for a pot of tea to go with their iced Belgian buns when there was a loud hammering at the front door. She peered into the lounge at Connie, who was feeding Thomas. "Were you expecting somebody?" she asked frowning.

Connie shifted the infant to her shoulder and began winding him, "No, not me, but you most definitely are. I will finish this upstairs," she said, gathering the baby's things together then turned to face Benita. "He sounds perfect, be yourself, Benita. Don't be afraid to let yourself go." Squeezing her friend's cheek affectionately, she turned and left.


Evan stood on the doorstep, a wild urgency in his eyes, his tousled hair and coloured cheeks reminiscent of his boyish innocence.

He brushed past her into the hallway. "Where the hell did you go?" he demanded, turning angrily toward her, his eyes questioning.

Defensive, Benita's eyes flashed. "I had enough of your little spectacle and decided it was time to come home to the real world. I see you have come to your senses too!"

Evan caught her wrist and pulled her toward him. She tried to resist but he was too powerful as he spun her around to face him. He pressed his lips down against hers with such ferocity that for a moment she was totally disarmed. Nevertheless, as his mouth circled hers with an insatiable hunger she found herself melting in to his embrace and returning his kiss with a fiery passion. It was several moments before they parted.

"This is the real world," Evan said calmly, looking down into her eyes. "There are things we need to talk about, Benita, things that I have learnt. If there is ever to be an 'us', then you must listen and understand all the things I have to tell you."

Benita looked wary. "We have plenty of time, perhaps we should…"

Evan caught his arm around her waist. "Come with me now, we haven't much time. Let us go up to the Tor, for it seems the perfect place to explain the secrets of the past."

Evan didn't give her a chance to protest. Instead, he whisked her out in to the lane.

"Tell me what is so urgent," she hissed, trying to keep up with his long stride.

"I'm sorry to rush you, Benita." He stopped briefly to look down at her, and then lightly he brushed his lips against her forehead, causing her to shiver with excitement and a sense of longing.

For a moment she felt giddy then scolded herself for allowing herself to be so easily led. In a last ditch demonstration of defiance she jerked back her arm.

"Why did you come?" she demanded.

Evan looked deeply into her eyes. There was a childlike innocence within them, and a knowing smile crossed his lips, "Because I am hopelessly in love with you. You are my soul mate and I think you know that too," he said softly.

Benita was speechless for several seconds. She looked at him and knew she couldn't deny what he had just said.

"Come, we must hurry," he urged. Then, taking her hand, he started up the path that led to the Tor.

Evan looked out across the lands below them. As he spoke there was a strange air of detachment in his voice as if he were talking about somebody else entirely.

"Much of what we surmised was correct. It's true, I did leave Alexis to drown when I could have saved her, should have saved her and for that, I will always feel a terrible inner shame. I was young, naïve and very frightened. I should never have been at her house that day and that is why I left in such a hurry. If I had not been in such a blind panic to leave then maybe I would have realised what was actually happening."

Benita touched his arm. "Hindsight is a wonderful thing. You didn't know she was drowning."

Evan's eyes misted over and he took a deep breath. "That is one thing but that is not the reason why Alexis hounded me."

Benita looked surprised. "You used past tense. Does that mean…"

"Yes, she has gone but I am still in debt to her." He gave a heavy sigh as he turned to look at Benita. "The night that Lydia came to the house was a truly remarkable experience. I was honoured to visit another place, a place that exists in the same moment as this one but on a different vibrational level.

"Dear Benita, I know that this is going to sound so far-fetched and strange but you have to trust me one final time, for everything that I am going to tell you is true and I know because I have seen and experienced it with my own eyes." Taking her hand, he gave it a gentle squeeze. "This is the only time I will ever talk about this to anyone. Once we leave the Tor I will never speak of it again, the memories will stay here at this sacred site." He looked across at her. "Do you understand, Benita?" He searched her face, for he had to be sure.

Slowly she nodded. This was real, the sincerity in his eyes, she could tell.

"I promise this will go no further." She looked around. "The secrets stay here at Avalon with the goddess."

"Good, for life is an eternal circle and there are special people who always stay together through eternity."

Evan sat down on the grass and signalled for her to do the same. He stopped, thoughtful for a moment. Then taking her face in his hand he tilted her chin toward him.

"I love you so very much. Never ever doubt it for one second."

# CHAPTER 22

Ben returned from the van with the last box and placed it alongside the tightly packed cases on the living room table.

He stood back to admire the cottage. "It is a great place you have here. You were lucky to find it," he said wistfully.

Evan stepped forward, giving him a friendly pat on the back. "Thanks for helping us move in. We must take you and Connie for lunch at the weekend by way of thanks."

Ben chuckled. "That would be great. You know, it is going to be nice having you two here on our doorstep. Enjoy your first night in your new home," he said, pulling the door closed behind him.

Benita gave a squeal of delight, rushing through the kitchen and out of the back door onto the small terrace bordered by dwarf lavender and rosemary, looking beyond to the patch of lawn shaded by tall silver birch which created a patch of velveteen moss.

"It is divine," she cried, turning back to Evan who watched her in amusement.

"Just what Madam ordered?" he chuckled. For he had to agree it was the perfect place for them. A small eighteenth century cottage with a snug living area leading to a cosy kitchen complete with Aga and flagstone floor. The heavily beamed bedroom was just large enough to house their bed and an old oak wardrobe but boasted uninterrupted views to the Tor, which today stood shrouded in mist.

It wasn't their cottage but it was available to rent for as long as they wanted it and for now it had everything they required. Evan had rented his home out on a long term let as he wanted so much for the both of them to have a fresh start.

"How delightful this is." Benita leant to pull off a few

sprigs of rosemary. "Perfect to go with our lamb tonight." She turned to smile at Evan.

He nodded, words seemed inappropriate for he didn't think he had ever seen her look so happy and alive.

Benita took a deep breath. "I could sit out here all night but I guess I should get started?"

"Well, darling, I will leave you to your culinary delights while I go and check out the shower." He kissed her full on the lips. "And after that I will select a full bodied red to accompany our meal, if I can find the right box."

Benita laughed, "Ok you do that."

She watched him leave then sat down beneath the trellis trailing with honeysuckle. Twirling the rosemary between her fingertips, she felt reluctant to leave. The soft hum of bees busy amongst the lilac flowers was comforting. She gave a delighted gasp as a dragonfly, its body a shimmering blend of turquoise and mauve, alighted at the far end of the table. It was late September and the evenings were drawing in; it would not be light much longer, she thought, shivering. The air was becoming damp, and the rich amber sun was soon lost behind the birch as it dipped down in the west.

At first, she thought she had imagined the movement down between the pale trunks of the trees. Intrigued, her eyes searched the foot of the garden. She caught her breath as a shadow emerged and she recognised that face from the past, the one she hoped never to see again.

"Evan…" she tried to call out for his help but her voice fell silent.

Craig had deserted him again. How many times must he be treated like this? David wondered as he brushed the loose dirt from the carrots he had just unearthed. The Hall could be a lonely place, he thought, starting back up the garden, peering at its grey bleak walls and wishing he had the courage to up and leave.

Evan and Benita had texted earlier in the day inviting him up to see the new cottage. They had only just moved in, it would be rude to go now but perhaps next week he would visit. He would be glad of some stimulating company for it had been weeks since he had seem them last, there was bound to be a lot to catch up on.

Evan left early on Monday, off to an art exhibition in Cornwall. Benita dragged herself from their bed and sat by the window looking out at the Tor. Evan had said she didn't need to work, that he could provide for them both, but the day would seem endless with nothing to fill it. However, she had decided to put job hunting on hold until after their forthcoming trip to Spain, where Evan was due to complete the sale on the piece of land.

Evan had struggled with the decision to sell it but decided it was for the best, perhaps it was wise to move on. Secretly she feared that he was making a terrible mistake and that one day he would regret his decision. In truth, that little piece of Andalucía held a special place in her heart too.

There - she was doing it again, denying her own feelings and worst still not sharing her thoughts with Evan.

Benita hadn't revealed her experience that first evening in the garden, when Alexis had visited her. She didn't want to scare him. He seemed confident that Alexis had disappeared from their lives forever and it would appear that she had, save that one last call, a final message.

Benita wondered if she may have imagined it but in her heart she knew the woman had been with her and in the stillness of her own soul she knew her words to be true. If only she could cope with actually knowing. Briskly she brushed the memory of Alexis' visit aside. There was plenty of time and Evan was working so hard for their future. Slipping into a cotton dress, she looked out at the ancient Tor, a place that held their secret, a beautiful sacred place.

David cut himself another chunk of the homemade fruit cake.

"Excellent!" he declared through a mouthful of light sponge and brandy soaked currants.

Evan appeared with another bottle of Chablis. "So what do you think?" he asked.

213

"Of which are you asking, cake or the house?" David teased, smiling up at him.

"House, suits her, don't you think?" he said sliding his arm around Benita's waist. "As you can see she has become very domesticated since we moved in. I'm not complaining, absolutely loving it in fact."

"So I see." David pursed his lips and looked disapprovingly at Evan's protruding stomach. "Reckon she is trying to fatten you up so nobody else will find you attractive. It's what they do you know, part of their plan. Minxes, the lot of them."

Benita frowned. "Oh David, you have given the game away!" She burst into rapturous laughter.

Evan opened the wine. "A toast to the future," he said, pouring them each a glass.

"Ooh, we've done this a few times," David snorted.

"Which brings me to Spain," Evan said, spreading his hands across the table. "We have to go out next week to sign some papers. Call us raving lunatics, but we thought you may like to come too."

"You're not having a romantic trip for two then?"

"Would you like to or not?" Evan pressed.

David's face brightened considerably. "I would be delighted, if you're sure that I wouldn't be intruding?"

Benita returned with a dish of rich Cornish cream. "It wouldn't be the same without you, David."

"In which case, I most definitely accept."

"There is only one condition though," Benita said, spooning cream onto his slice of half-eaten cake. "There is to be no camper van or haunted houses."

David raised his glass in the air. "Agreed!"

Evan sat back and looked at his two companions. How things had changed; Benita now his lover and David his best friend. For the first time since he could remember he felt whole, part of a family again and at peace.

Connie had asked Benita to help out with the housework. It was her way of giving Benita a little pocket money until she sorted herself out with a job.

"Don't bother washing the floor today," she said, seeing her appear with the mop. "No point, Ben's mother is arriving later and she will have her darling little poodle with her! Muddy paws and all that malarkey, besides I expect you need to get home and pack a case. What time is your flight?"

Benita mindlessly filled the bucket at the kitchen sink, Oblivious of Connie standing with Thomas nestled to her chest at the far end of the kitchen.

Connie strode toward her and removed the mop from her hand.

"You are in a world of your own today! I said not to bother. Oh, never mind," she said, steering Benita toward the nearest chair with her spare hand.

Benita sat in it and frowned at her.

"Stay put while I go and put Thomas down and then I will put the kettle on. You look as though you could use a brew and a chat."

"Yuk, this coffee is sour!" Benita grimaced.

Connie drained her cup. "Actually I quite like it, Brazilian I think."

Standing up, Benita took hers over to the sink and threw it away. "You can keep it," she declared, reaching for the mop once again.

"Stop it!" Connie yelled exasperated, "No floor cleaning today, ok?"

Benita shrugged. "It's what you pay me for. If poodle doodle comes and makes it dirty, I will just do it again next week. It really isn't a big deal."

"You're scared, aren't you?" Connie gazed across the rim of her cup at Benita.

Benita scowled back. "Scared of what?"

"I have no idea, how about you tell me. It is so obvious that you have something on your mind. Come on, you know what they say, a problem shared…"

Benita took her coat down from the peg. "Well I guess I'm pretty well done here," she interrupted, flinging her scarf over one shoulder and heading for the back door.

Turning the handle, she paused to look back at Connie. "I am fine, really. Maybe a little tired. Thanks for your concern,

I know you mean well. See you Tuesday about nine. Oh, and don't forget to give baby T a big kiss from me." Then she let herself out, only pausing to wave as she passed by the window.

Connie drummed the side of her mug. There was something wrong. Benita could be difficult, at times, unintentionally rude with her abrupt manner, but this was something different, something more emotional. Things seemed perfect between Benita and Evan, they were head over heels about each other. Perhaps it was the visit to Spain; the last time had been fraught to say the least. That had to be I,Connie decided. Last minute nerves, apprehensive about the trip and whether David would behave himself. Connie still couldn't fathom why they had invited him along.

Evan threw the large holdall in to the boot of the car. Getting in, he turned to look at Benita sat beside him. "I know you're not keen on this trip but it will be another weight off our minds. Trust me," he said smiling, then leaning across scooped her toward him and placed a lingering kiss on her forehead.

David relished taking charge at Malaga airport, sorting out the hire car and loading the luggage, which he did with an air of confidence. He loved nothing better than to be in control.

Benita wondered why he stayed with Craig when he was so obviously capable of going it alone, then it occurred to her how much he must love him despite their differences and in that moment she thought what an extremely foolish man he must be.

The hotel was light and airy, the staff was welcoming; it promised to be a fantastic break, no hidden agendas. They left David in the bar and arranged to meet him later at dinner. Stepping into the elevator on the way to their room, Benita felt a little faint. Evan looked across at her and frowned. "Are you ok, you look rather pale darling?"

Benita shrugged. "Am I, I feel fine, honest."

Evan smiled, reassured. The elevator doors opened and he led the way down the hall.

216

The room had a great view and for a moment Benita fought aside the gnawing anxiety in her heart. Stepping across to the window, she looked out to the sea and took a deep testing breath. Evan circled her within his arms and bent to kiss her neck.

"The first time we ever made love was here in Spain." Tightening his grip, he spun her round to face him. "It is a special place for us. It makes me feel so horny just remembering," he whispered, nuzzling her neck.

Benita, disarmed by the familiar shiver that rippled through her body, melted against him, her breath low and easy. As Evan unbuttoned her blouse he felt the knot of excitement in his belly tighten, he could never resist her, nor did he ever wish to.

Flicking through his diary David found the number of the lawyer in Marbella, who had been highly recommended to him. If he could arrange a meeting for tomorrow, then he could leave the lovebirds in peace. The trip couldn't have come at a better time; there were things that needed sorting and major decisions that he had made would now have to be put into action. As soon as he had confirmed an appointment with the lawyer, he ordered up room service, a selection of pastries and a pot of coffee, which he blissfully consumed looking out across the ocean as he masterfully put the final touches to his master plan.

Fighting their way along the crowded street, Benita followed Evan down some steps to a tapas bar just along from the port.

Warily she took in Evan's thoughtful gaze, not sure whether to sympathise with him or feel blessed that the buyer of the land had pulled out. There was a stony silence until the waiter appeared to take their order. As Evan appeared not to acknowledge him, Benita ordered them both a beer.

"How disappointing," he said finally.

"Yes, it seems a bit of a wasted trip now." Benita hesitated before continuing, "Talk about leave it to the last moment and they have lost their deposit."

Evan accepted the beer gratefully from the waiter and took a long swig.

"Oh well, it can't be helped." His face brightened. "Besides, it hasn't been a wasted journey. At least I get to spend the next four days with you in the sun and we..." His mobile ringing interrupted him. As Benita listened intently, she saw the look of surprise on Evan's face and tried to surmise who was on the other end of the phone.

"Well, that's a surprise," he said, placing the phone down on the table in front of him and looking at it with a sense of disbelief. "That was the lawyer again. It appears there is a new buyer who has come forward, they have offered the full asking price, are paying cash and if I am in agreement the sale can be completed by next week. Isn't that amazing?"

"Extremely. Who is it?" she asked cautiously.

"Who cares? At the end of the day with the money from the sale, we could put an offer in on the cottage. Would you like that?" he asked, smiling.

"Well yes, it would be nice. We are both very happy there and it would mean we could decorate and make it our own."

"Exactly," Evan said, pleased with himself, "Our first home together." He ordered the best bottle of wine on the menu and a selection of tapas to accompany it. "Relax, let us enjoy ourselves while we have the chance. If this really comes off it looks like you will be spending the next couple of weeks with a paintbrush in your hand." He laughed.

"But we don't even know if they will sell it yet!" she said objectively.

"Oh they will. We will make them an offer they can't refuse. It will be ok, you'll see."


David sat patiently at the hotel bar waiting for Evan and Benita to join him. He was sure they had said seven.

At half past they appeared, most apologetic.

"Oh well, you're here now, " he said, looking pleased with himself as the bartender placed a bottle of champagne and three flutes before them.

"Please sit down. I have some very exciting news that I

wish to share with you both. You are the first to know and I am bursting at the seams."

Filling the glasses, which he passed to them with a broad grin, he stood up.

"I bought a house today. I am having it done up and then I am going to live in it."

"Where?" Benita asked, incredulous.

"Here in Spain. I'm so excited, it's not just any house. It's the house!" he declared, looking at them in turn trying to gauge their reaction.

Evan looked bewildered. "I had no idea you had seen any houses or were even thinking of moving over here. What house, David? I'm not sure I follow."

Benita took a sip of her champagne. "Why, you sly old dog! You have gone and brought Casa de Suenos, haven't you?" she exclaimed.

David started to giggle. "Indeed I have. The house has a story! And it is my job to see that it is told. From there I will write my book, the story of two lovers who met fell helplessly in love and then spent two decades apart, only to be brought back together by a restless spirit."

Evan nodded. "You are something else, David. And what of Craig, dare I ask?"

David looked thoughtful. "It was over a long time ago, it is about time I made a fresh start. Of course, you know you two are welcome any time and I will be most offended if you don't visit me often. I want you to witness the house being returned to its former splendour."

Benita wept, that house was so important. "That's beautiful, David. I hope you will be truly happy."

"Oh come here darling kitten," he soothed, pulling her toward his chest. "Now this is a time to be happy, not sad!"

"Yes, I know and I am so happy for you. It is so romantic and I couldn't imagine a more fitting owner. I know you will make it fabulous," she said amid a fresh wave of tears.

"Oh, here, I think she needs you," David ushered Benita into Evan's open arms. Embarrassed and not sure if she really approved of what he had done, he knocked back his champagne. "I hope you are not offended?" he asked.

Evan smiled as he smoothed Benita's hair as she sobbed against his shoulder. "We are delighted for you, David. Truly we are."

Evan climbed into bed and turned toward her. "What was all that about earlier, you seemed so upset? Poor David thinks that he has offended you by buying the Casa. Has he?"

Benita snuggled in beneath his arm, resting her head against his shoulder. "I know, I feel so foolish. It was surprise, more than anything. It is such a random thing to do."

"No, not really. I think he always fantasised about buying the place from the first time he ever set eyes on it. When you went to the ladies earlier, he was explaining how by chance he came across it in a classified section. He felt it was fate directing him and then we asked him to join us on this trip. Well, he felt it was a sign, serendipity. I must admit I'm really rather pleased; my greatest memories are there, as you well know. Despite that I must confess it was a bit of a shock that he actually went ahead and bought it."

Benita sat upright she turned to look at him. "I know, that is what I meant. Evan, I have something I have to tell you."

"Oops, you are looking serious. Suddenly I am worried," Evan said, alarm in his eyes. "Please don't tell me anything bad, darling. Life has been so good these last two months I don't want to change a single thing."

Benita turned away. This was what she had been afraid of. Evan took her in his arms. "Sorry darling, I didn't mean to sound negative, you must tell me whatever it is. How selfish of me, please forgive me and tell me."

Benita took a deep breath, she didn't want to start bawling but she didn't seem to have any control over it; she was, she feared, an emotional wreck.

"What is it?" Evan asked alarmed, reaching to comfort her. Abruptly she pulled away from him.

Evan sat for a moment deciding what he should do next. Benita had grown and flourished in recent weeks but now she was acting so strange.

He came round to sit on the bed beside her. "Whatever it is it can't be that bad. I will look after you no matter what."

"I'm sorry," she whispered, looking absently across the room, avoiding his questioning gaze. Sniffing hard she pulled her knees in to her chest and took a moment to compose herself. "We talked about children, do you remember that day at the Tor?"

"Of course, I told you it didn't matter; I loved you whatever and that so long as we had each other that was all that mattered. I know it must hurt but I meant what I said."

"A lot was said that day, things we swore we would never speak of again," she sniffed, turning to face him, misery deep within her eyes.

"Yes, many things. Why, is there something I should know?" Evan felt a rising panic; he didn't want to address the past when they had their whole future to look forward to.

"I am pregnant, Evan."

Evan sat very still, too shocked to reply.

"I know what you are thinking. I still can't believe it myself. The doctor confirmed it. He was stunned too after he read my medical history."

Evan began laughing. "My God, I don't know what to say. Am I dreaming? Are you sure, I mean one hundred percent?"

"You sound pleased, "she said hesitantly.

"Pleased, are you joking? I am ecstatic. Benita darling, come here." He pulled her into his arms and squeezed her hard. Tears filling his eyes, he was going to be a dad. "I love you so much darling. I will make sure you and the baby have the very best care, everything will be fine, you'll see and ..." he stopped, she was crying.

"You do want to keep it?" he asked warily, confused by her behaviour.

"I'm not sure what I think. I never thought this would happen and now it has and I should be so happy but..."

"But what, gorgeous? We should be celebrating and rejoicing." He looked into her eyes. "Benita, if you don't tell me how I can put your mind at rest."

Benita appeared edgy; her eyes darted to and fro around

the room then focusing into thin air she said shakily, "Because of her."

Evan ran his fingers through his hair. There was fear in her eyes, instinctively he knew but he had to ask the question anyway. "Are you referring to Alexis?"

"Who else? Evan, you know we will never be free of her." Benita stood up, crossed to the mirror and dragging a brush through her hair, stared at her reflection in the mirror. "Her prediction has materialised. We thought it was impossible that her words had empty meaning. I guess we should have known better." There was bitterness in her tone as she turned to look back at Evan. "I'm not sure if I can go through with this. Alexis is a part of your life, not mine. I was stupid to think it would ever change."

"You can't mean that." Evan crossed the room. He looked desperate, his eyes pleaded with hers. Benita turned away, the tears threatened to fall again; she held them back, turning away from him. A moment or two passed before she was aware that Evan was sobbing.

David missed them at breakfast and now he was certain that he had upset both of them. Yes, he loved the house but he had also considered it to be a nice gesture. A little bit of their past would always stay in their future and foolishly he believed that it would please them. No time to regret his decision, he thought as he emerged out of the hotel lobby into the warm sun. At last, his life had a purpose and as he wandered down towards the beach he wondered if Craig had been back and discovered that half of his art collection was missing. Well, it wasn't as if he got the time to look at it much anyway. David had always considered it quite disgraceful to have a painting hanging on the wall that cost as much as, if not more than, a very grand house. Craig would survive. David took his new Spanish bank statement out of his pocket and took another look. Oh yes, he would certainly survive quite nicely and for a very long time. Smugly he folded it up and slipped it into his back pocket. His attention was then drawn to a lithe fair haired guy on the other side of the street who was watching him closely. Aware that finally

David had noticed him, he smiled and hurried down toward the sea.

"Interesting, very interesting," David said aloud, deciding to give chase, keen not to lose sight of him. His mind had been working overtime these last few weeks and this looked like being a very welcome distraction.

# CHAPTER 23

## 12 MONTHS LATER, ANDALUCIA

David watched bemused as Jay went across to the house to fetch the drinks. David was mindful to conceal the deep stirring at the sight of Jay's neat behind in striped Versace shorts as he hurried across the terrace. They had company; he really must behave and keep his naughty little thoughts to himself.

"So how long have you two been an item?" Benita asked, watching the extremely handsome lad, young enough in reality to be David's son, returning with refreshments.

David gave an indulgent smile. "Nearly six months, just how irresistible is he?"

Evan stood up. "I'm sure he is if you are into that sort of thing." He lowered his daughter in to David's arms as Benita watched proudly. "There, say hello to Uncle David," he cooed.

David looked down at the infant and smiled. "She's beautiful," he breathed, taking in her angelic features. "Just like your mummy, a gorgeous girl," he sighed, looking up at them both. "Congratulations, you must be very proud."

"As must you," Evan said, straightening up and looking around. "This place is awesome, even more so than the very first time I set eyes on it. You have done a great job. You have brought this place back to life."

Benita rescued her daughter from David, who struggled to stand up. He smiled kindly as he passed the child into her arms, joining Evan by the side of the pool.

"I am glad you like it, I tried to picture how it was for you back then and add my own expressive interpretation to your past."

"Oh, you have certainly pulled it off, it is breathtaking."

Benita joined them. "I knew it would be paradise. You

have a good eye, David. You missed your vocation in life, you would have made a wonderful designer. Not to say you still couldn't, of course. Although I have to say you look like you've got your hands rather full." She signalled over toward Jay, stretched out by the pools edge lapping up the fierce sun rays. "We are really pleased for you; you deserve some real happiness at last."

"Likewise," he put an arm around each of them, pulling them in for a group hug. "My very dear friends, I am so glad you are both here and in true David style there is one more surprise yet!"

It was hard not to like Jay, he was so unassuming and it was obvious that he adored David. Benita noticed the rapport between pair of them. David had definitely mellowed. She much preferred the new David, the David who had nothing to prove now, and oh boy he had certainly had the last laugh. Craig had never forgiven him for selling one of his finest paintings for mere peanuts compared to its true value. That didn't seem to matter, she thought, gazing idly out toward the mountains; this scene was a far more appealing vista than any painting could be.

Evan appeared at her side. "Amazing isn't it? I could spend hours gazing out at this view. But David is waiting!" He winked. "Just like old times, eh?"

Benita smiled. It was all so strange. She could never have imagined she would return here, older, wiser and now a mother herself. She looked across at her daughter strapped into her pushchair, a floppy sunhat shielding her porcelain skin from the morning sun. "Are you sure it will be ok to leave her with Jay? What if she gets upset and won't settle?"

Evan steered her towards the jeep, where David sat impatiently revving the engine.

"Come on you two, stop dragging your heels. This is supposed to be a surprise. You should be champing at the bit to clamber in and see what old uncle David has in store for you this time." He gave a deep throaty growl. "Hop in, let us be off!"

Evan barely had chance to put his seat belt on as David stuck his foot hard down on the accelerator and sped off through the iron gates, onto the rutted dirt track between the heavily laden olive trees and oleander bushes to the road which led to the village.

Jay gazed down at the infant in his arms. This was the only regret he had about the way he had chosen to live his life. He would never have a child, especially one as beautiful as this.

The little girl blinked hard and looked up into Jay's eyes. He gasped at that intensity in those deep green eyes.

The last time he had looked into these eyes he had been a Druid priest and she his favourite seer. She was destined for great things and even then he knew if she had lived they would have become lovers by the next fall, but her father took her life. This was the trouble with young inexperienced souls, they always thought they knew best. Jay was the seventh son of the seventh son. By some this was said to be lucky. Yes, he was special, but that was because of her. He looked down at the infant cradled in his arms. He had not protected her then as he should have done; this time he would guard her with his life, for it was ordained, his purpose for this lifetime. Jay remembered all of it, one day he would remind her too. Evan had been told of these things but did he really believe? How could he, Jay wondered. Clearly Benita had no recollection of her lifetime as Clara and maybe that was for the best. He looked down at the pool where the waters were still. He shuddered, she must be kept from water but he would personally see to it that she learned to swim like a fish.

Alexis was a great spiritual being and he her eternal guide and once this lifetime was through, he smiled indulgently, well, then when she died a natural death, one of old age, then their spirits would be free and they could stay in the spirit realms for eternity, where life was bliss. Evan was the danger, third time lucky and Jay hoped that he would see his responsibility through and never would they be forced to play the Drowning School again. Jay knew all of the past but he couldn't see the future. He looked down at the child. "I love you," he murmured.

Evan sat in the front alongside David, Benita in the back trying not to fret about leaving her daughter behind. Alexis wasn't used to being minded, she spent all of her time with Benita and now she was concerned for her daughter. Evan looked back over his shoulder at her and winked. "It is fine darling, she will be fine," he said, as if reading her mind.

David sped through the village, clearly on a mission. Evan, aware of David's anxious mood, smiled indulgently.

"You seem tense. Is everything ok?" he asked.

David chuckled. "I'm not tense, just excited. I have waited months to show you two this surprise." He forged on, turning left out of the village and heading uphill. Holding the steering wheel tightly between tense fists he negotiated the natural curve of the road as if he had driven it a hundred times before. As they reached the brow of the hill he pulled off the road and stopped.

Fishing inside the glove box, he pulled out two silk scarves.

"I am going to have to ask you both to cover your eyes," he said with an impish grin. "Trust me; otherwise it will spoil the surprise." He looked back at Benita. "It is only for another ten minutes and I promise it will be worth it."

Gingerly Benita took the scarf from him and placed it across her eyes and around her head then turned for Evan to secure it in place with a bow.

Evan did the same and when they were ready David continued, but this time at a much slower pace.

Evan couldn't imagine what was in store. David had always loved his games and still to this day he liked to keep them both guessing.

Finally, the jeep drew to a halt. Evan heard the click of the handbrake.

"No peeking now!" David warned, as he came around to open the doors and guide them out.

"Wait for the signal," he breathed, pulling them alongside each other.

He felt the knot in his stomach tighten, he had waited so long and now the moment was here. What would they both think? Shame Jay wasn't here, he knew how important this was.

"Go ahead and look," he squealed in delight, leaping back to watch the expressions on their faces as in unison they pulled off the scarves.

In took a moment for their eyes to focus after the dark confines of the blindfolds. Both stood speechless, taking in the scene before them.

A small rustic cottage stood ahead of them. Its wooden porch ran the length of the property, young vines entwined around the wooden frames. The vibrant red and pink of potted geraniums offered a splash of colour against the whitewashed walls and a heavy wooden door at the centre of the building stood slightly ajar.

"Wow," Benita exclaimed drawing in breath. "What a cute little place." There was no garden to speak of, in fact no boundaries surrounding the house at all. It sat in the middle of a vast meadow where dried yellow grasses licked the base of its walls and wild poppies grew around the steps that led to the porch.

Evan took in the neat little house and then looked beyond to the horizon. A glimmer of recognition showed on his face then he looked across at David, who smiled smugly back.

"I don't believe it," Evan exclaimed, scratching his head in disbelief. He took hold of Benita's hand. "Do you recognise it?" he asked gently.

Benita looked questioningly back. "Should I?" she asked, taking another more concentrated look at her surroundings.

"David, it's the land isn't it?" she gasped, squeezing Evan's hand more tightly.

David started laughing. "It most certainly is. Are you impressed?" he asked, eyes searching theirs, his joy evident.

Evan took a deep breath; He was trying to work out how he had missed the clues.

"It was you all along!" he gasped, looking accusingly across at David. "You were the mystery buyer. How come you never said a word to either of us?"

"Need you ask, and ruin the surprise?" David chuckled. "Oh trust me, it took a lot of planning. I have wanted to tell you so many times but believe me it has been worth it to see the look on your faces."

Benita let go of Evan's hand and flung her arms around David's neck. "You sly old fox. I can't believe you didn't tell us." She looked across to Evan and smiled. "I can't think of anyone better to own this. The house looks like it has been here forever, so fitting with the landscape. Can we go and look inside now? I know it is going to be divine!"

Evan strode across to David. "Mmm, got to hand it to you, you had me fooled and Benita is right, it looks like the house has been here for years."

"I can't take all the credit for this one. Jay was the brains behind this project. He was insistent that we keep it in character of the old Spain you remember and throw in a touch of glamour as well."

"It is amazing," Benita commented, running her hand along the wooden rail as she climbed the steps to the porch and turned to survey the almond groves in the distance.

"Of course, there is still a lot to do. We didn't put a pool in yet. We thought that perhaps you would like to design the gardens yourself and it is pretty basic inside the house. A blank canvas for you to work with, one on which you can put your own stamp." David turned to smile at them both.

Benita looked confused. "What exactly do you mean?" she asked, raising a quizzical brow in David's direction, then, perplexed, looked back to Evan.

"Exactly that, Benita darling." It dawned on David that neither was really up to speed with his suggestions, at which he roared with laughter. "I thought you understood. Perhaps I should make myself a little clearer. I bought this place for you two. This is a gift, your own special holiday home. Besides, now I am living out here I had to give you both a good excuse to come and visit me, didn't I?"

Evan was speechless. He stood motionless; Benita was crying. He took a minute or two "But why would you buy this land from me only to give it back ten months later?" he asked, bewildered.

"Oh come, don't be so precious!" David exclaimed. "You are my best friends. I made a killing out of Craig's art collection and I had a little nest egg of my own tucked away. Besides, I have everything a man needs. A great partner, a fantastic house and money in the bank, pots of it in fact. As I said, there is a lot to do here but I thought that would be part of the fun for the pair of you. The house is in trust for Alexis but of course it as good as yours and you may do with it whatever you wish. I only ask that you drop by and visit myself and Jay whenever you are here." He pressed the keys to the house in Benita's hand. "You best take care of those. You know what we men are like."

Benita threw her arms around him; she squeezed him so hard he winced. "David, you never cease to amaze me!"

Evan watched their warm exchange. Too choked to speak he looked out across a sea of wild grasses which ran down to the valley in the distance. Through the tears he didn't see the outline of the houses in the far village or the shepherd out for an afternoon stroll with his herd. Or hear the soft tinkle of goat bells as they darted amongst the wild asparagus and garlic that grew abundant in this area.

Instead, somewhere in the distance he heard the gentle strum of Foggy's guitar, the haunting tune that had played in his heart ever since the first time he had heard it. He felt the warmth of the fire, smelt sausages cooking. His mouth began to water at the memory of their moonlight suppers. With a fingertip he wiped away the tear that fell to his cheek.

Benita joined him; slipping her arm around his waist, she tucked her head in beneath his shoulder and snuggled close to him. Evan smelt her scent, a smile crept to his lips and he looked down at her. Their eyes met and she held his gaze. He trusted this woman with all his heart. He loved her as he had loved no other. For all of these years she had held the key to his heart and if he had never come to this land he would never have met her. The thought was unbearable.

Together they had released the past and brought new passion to the future. Their love would live on in their daughter for the whole world to see.

Slowly he brought his lips down to meet hers, grateful she was there at this moment.

Instinctively he knew that he would die for this woman and that if he had to he would do it over and over again. For the first time he understood dear Alexis' words and the karma they had shared.

He would love Alexis in her new form too, a precious child, their daughter, for eternity and this time he really would succeed. There would never be a pool here, he wouldn't risk it. Drowning was not an option.

Two women with whom to share this lifetime, two women he would never let go of, two women that tried to break him in order to make him quite simply the happiest man alive.


The End

Lightning Source UK Ltd.
Milton Keynes UK
UKOW03f1613120317
296424UK00001B/7/P